哈福

Talking about Banking in English QR Code版

銀行金融英語
看這本就夠了

- **Banking Online** 網路銀行
- **Deposits and Withdrawals** 存提款
- **Credit Cards and Loans** 信用卡和貸款
- **Transferring and Exchanging Money** 轉帳和匯兌

附QR碼線上音檔
行動學習 即刷即聽

克力斯‧安森
張瑪麗 ◎合著

哈福

快速成為百萬高薪族

● ● ● ● ● ─────────

　　世界各國金融體系已然形成一個共同體！不過，不論小到個人存提款，或大到跨國企業的銀行業務往來，英語仍是共同語言。因此，本公司因應趨勢來臨、商業人士及一般大眾的需求，特聘金融界專家編寫：「銀行金融英語　看這本就夠了」，以深入淺出的方式，介紹銀行的各項服務業務，讓您輕鬆學會銀行金融英語。

　　本書編寫主要特色：是會話情境，豐富實用。以會話的方式模擬真實的情境，期望能用簡單的英語會話，明白表達出你的需求，使你在接觸銀行業務時能無往不利，成功完成交易。

本書分二部份：**Part　1**銀行金融英語入門；**Part　2**銀行金融英語會話應用。

　　Part　1銀行金融英語入門：分八章，以不同的主題，呈現銀行事務的會話情境。從開戶、存提款，到使用自動提款機、信用卡、轉帳貸款等，各類銀行業務無所不包，讓你輕鬆了解銀行的各項服務，並學會正確的銀行英語。

　　Part　2銀行金融英語會話應用：以四名人物作為主軸，設計各種不同的對話情境來介紹銀行金融業務。主題包含開戶、使用提款卡、旅行支票等與生活息息相關的銀行業務，讓你了解銀行業務運作、學會銀行金融英語。

課後測驗練習：

在每篇對話後附有文末測驗，讓你在學習銀行金融英語會話的同時，訓練你的聽力及閱讀能力，加深你對文章的印象，也有助於增強英語實力。

精選常用單字片語：

收集與銀行往來，常用的英文單字及片語，讓您能精確地使用銀行金融英語，順利辦理各項業務。你知道什麼是 bank account、ATM、paycheck 嗎？它們是銀行帳戶、自動提款機和薪資支票，這些常見的銀行英語，在本書中都有。片語除了提供中譯之外，還附有活用範例，在學會新片語的同時，更能有效運用！

不論你是銀行從業人員或是一般民眾，本書中所設計的各種有趣的情節，都可以讓你輕鬆掌握銀行金融英語、了解銀行金融業務的內容，自然融入英語會話中。

要學會銀行金融英語並不難，只要熟悉各項專業用語，套用在生活會話中，就能快速、清楚表達，跟著本書精心設計的內容學習，對銀行金融各種業務將有完整概念，輕鬆溝通無障礙！

配合線上 MP3 效果倍增：

本書特聘美籍專業錄音員，模擬真實的對話情境，錄製各種對話內容，讓你恍如身在現場辦理各項事務；只要反覆練習，必能輕鬆處理銀行金融業務，脫口說出流利的銀行金融英語。

編者　謹識

Contents

Part 2 銀行金融英語會話應用

Chapter 3

First Steps 第一步

Part 1 銀行金融英語入門

Chapter 1

BANKING INFORMATION

帳戶資料

Unit 1

Banking Hours
銀行營業時間

MP3-2

Banks try to *cut down* on costs by being open very few hours. The less they are open, the less money they spend in staff wages. Banks aren't open on Sundays or holidays. They're closed the same days **government departments** are closed.

提示　銀行為了降低成本，營業時間並不長。營業時間越短，越能省下薪資成本。週日或假日不營業，政府部門也不開門。

Conversation 1

A: Where are you going?

B: I have to go to the bank. I need to take out some money.

A: The bank's not open today.

B: Sure it's open. It's Monday. The banks are open on Mondays.

A: It's the Monday of a long weekend. Banks aren't open on holidays.

B: Oh. That's right. I forgot. Everything else is open. Why can't the bank be?

中譯

A: 你要去哪裡？

B: 我要去銀行一趟，領一些錢出來。

A: 銀行今天沒開啦。

B: 當然有開，今天是禮拜一耶。禮拜一銀行都有開。

A: 今天是長假的禮拜一，銀行假日不營業。

B: 啊，對哦，我忘了。大家都沒有關店，為什麼銀行不營業？

Conversation 2

A: I have to get to the bank. Can you give me a ride?

B: But it's only 8:30 in the morning. You'll have to go later.

A: The bank should be open by now; don't you think? The post office opens at 8:30.

B: It doesn't matter. The banks won't be open until 9:30.

A: All the government offices are open by 8:30.

B: Yes, but not the banks. They are closed the same days but, banks are open fewer hours.

中譯

A: 我要去銀行一趟。可以載我一程嗎？

B: 才早上八點半耶，晚一點再去就好了。

A: 銀行現在就開了，你不知道嗎？郵局八點半就開始營業了。

B: 那不重要，銀行是九點半才開。

A: 所有的政府機關都是八點半開始上班。

B: 沒錯，不過銀行不是。它們放假的時間都一樣，但銀行比較晚營業。

Conversation 3

A: Do you think the bank's open on Saturdays?

B: I think so. What time is it?

A: I don't know. I don't have my watch on. It's after noon. I'm sure of that.

B: You might be out of luck. I think the bank's only open until noon on Saturdays.

A: But people are out on Saturdays. That's when most people can do their banking.

B: I know. I think they're trying to force us to use the bank machines.

中譯

A: 你想銀行禮拜六有開嗎？

B: 我想有吧。現在幾點了？

A: 我不知道，錶沒戴出來。不過我確定現在已經下午了。

B: 你運氣不太好，我想銀行週末只開到中午。

A: 可是大家週末都會出門耶，大部分的人那時候才去銀行。

B: 我知道。我想銀行想要強迫大家使用自動櫃員機吧。

Conversation 4

A: What time do you think the bank is open until to today?

B: It's a weekday so they probably close around 4:30 in the afternoon.

A: What? By the time I pick up my daughter from school and get there, it'll be closed.

B: I know.

A: What a pain.

B: There's nothing you can do about it. Can't you use the bank machine?

中譯

A: 你覺得銀行今天開到幾點？

B: 今天是平常日，大概下午四點半才關門。

A: 什麼？那等我去學校接完女兒再趕到那邊就來不及了。

B: 我知道。

A: 真討厭。

B: 你也沒什麼辦法。不能用自動櫃員機辦理嗎？

Conversation 5

A: I wonder if the bank is open.

B: Let's see. It's Tuesday and it's not a holiday. No other businesses are closed.

A: So it should be open, right?

B: What time is it?

A: It's noon. They don't close over lunch, do they?

B: No, but I bet they'd like to.

中譯

A: 不知道銀行關了沒。

B: 我看看。今天是禮拜二也不是假日，其他店也都沒有關。

A: 所以應該有開對吧？

B: 現在幾點了？

A: 中午了。午飯時間銀行不休息吧？

B: 不，不過他們一定想休息。

Conversation 6

A: I can't remember what time the bank is open until tonight.

B: Don't they always close at 4:30?

A: No. Different banks have different hours.

B: I wish they'd all keep the same hours. It'd be so much easier to remember.

A: They're open late at least one day a week. I can't remember if that's today.

B: I don't know what time they'd be open to even if

it was today.

中譯

A: 我不記得銀行今晚開到幾點。

B: 銀行不是四點半就關了嗎？

A: 不。每家銀行時間不一樣。

B: 真希望銀行營業時間都一樣，那就好記多了。

A: 銀行每週至少有一天營業較晚，可是我不記得是不是今天。

B: 就算是今天，我也不知道開到幾點。

Conversation 7

A: Good morning, North West Bank, how can I help you?

B: I don't know if I phoned the right number. Are you open?

A: Yes. We're open extended hours today.

B: What does that mean?

A: We're open until 8:00.

B: Wow. That's what they're calling extended hours? The stores are open until 9:00.

中譯

A: 早安，這裡是西北銀行，有什麼可以效勞的地方嗎？

B: 我不知道這支電話對不對，你們還沒關門嗎？

A: 還沒。我們今天會延長營業時間。

B: 什麼意思？

A: 今天營業到八點。

B: 哇。這就是所謂延長營業時間嗎？別家店都開到九點耶。

Conversation 8

A: Good morning. What can I do for you?

B: Explain to me why I had to stand and wait outside while someone unlocked the doors.

A: Sir, we don't open until 9:30. We unlock the doors at 9:30.

B: Well, by the time the doors were unlocked, my watch said it was 9:35.

A: We go by the clock on that wall over there.

B: That's funny. In my business, once customers are waiting for us, we open the doors.

中譯

A: 早安。需要什麼服務嗎？

B: 請你解釋一下，為什麼銀行開門時我還要站在外面等？

A: 先生，我們九點半才開始營業，所以九點半才開門。

B: 不對吧，等門開好時，我的錶已經是九點三十五了。

A: 我們是以牆上那面鐘為準。

B: 真是奇怪。我們公司如果有客戶在等，我們都會先開門。

Conversation 9

A: I can't believe it. Banks drive me crazy. They don't seem to care.

B: What's the matter?

A: They're closed already. The door's locked. Every other business in town is still open.

B: Are there people still inside?

A: Yes. I saw at least two bank tellers finishing up. I knocked and they just ignored me.

A: You'll have to wait until tomorrow. No wait. Tomorrow is Sunday.

中譯

A: 我真不敢相信，快被銀行氣死了。他們好像一點都不在

　　　乎。

B:　怎麼了？

A:　他們已經停止營業，門也關了。城裡其他店都還開著說。

B:　裡面還有人嗎？

A:　有啊。我看到至少有兩個櫃臺人員在收拾。我有敲門，他們就是不理我。

B:　你只好等到明天早上。不對，等一下，明天是禮拜天啦。

Conversation 10

A:　I have no idea if the bank is open today.

B:　I know. It's really confusing around Christmas time.

A:　Sometimes the post office is open and yet the banks aren't.

B:　And it can be the other way around too.

A:　I know. I better go to the bank and see.

B:　Good idea. They will have their holiday hours posted on the door.

中譯

A:　不知道銀行今天有沒有開。

B:　沒錯。聖誕期間真的會讓人搞不清楚。

A:　有時候只有郵局有開，銀行卻沒開。

B:　有時候也會反過來。

A:　對啊。我最好跑一趟銀行看看。

B:　好主意。他們會把假期營業時間貼在門上。

Useful phrases and idioms
有用的片語和慣用語

Cut down 減少

make less, bring down

例 Taking lunch to work will cut down on the number of times I eat out.

帶便當去上班的話，就不用常去外面吃了。

Give a ride 開車載（某人）

to drive someone else in your car to someplace

例 Do you want me to give you a ride to work?

你要我開車載你去上班嗎？

Out of luck 運氣不好

a situation that can't be helped; nothing can be done about it

例 I'm afraid you're out of luck because there's no more bread.

你運氣恐怕不太好，麵包已經沒了。

Pick up 開車接（某人）

to go get someone in your car

例 My girlfriend is going to pick me up after work.

我女友下班後會開車來接我。

What a pain 討人厭

causing unpleasantness; causing a problem

A： My brother is screaming!

B： What a pain.

A： 我弟弟正在尖叫！
B： 真討厭。

I bet 我肯定

I think

例 I bet she takes him on a trip to Europe when she gets her bonus.
我肯定她拿到獎金後就帶他去歐洲旅遊了。

Wow 哇

an exclamation of surprise

例 Wow! The cookies you baked are terrific.
哇！你烤的餅乾好好吃。

That's funny 真奇怪

that's strange or unusual

例 It's funny that her boyfriend didn't come to the fancy dinner.
這麼精緻的晚餐她男朋友居然沒來，真奇怪。

Drive me crazy 氣死人

to bother or irritate me

例 It drives me crazy when my boss calls me by the wrong name.
我老闆叫錯我名字時，真被他氣死了。

Finishing up （工作）快做完

finishing an almost-done task

例 I'm finishing up the dishes.
我菜快做好了。

Vocabulary 字彙

government departments		政府部門
long weekend		長假
holiday	*n.*	假日
post office	*n.*	郵局
force	*v.*	強迫
extend	*v.*	延長
explain	*v.*	解釋
ignore	*v.*	不理會
confuse	*v.*	使困惑
post	*v.*	貼

Unit 2

Types of Accounts
帳戶種類

MP3-3

There are savings accounts, joint accounts, and checking accounts. Checking accounts are more commonly used because checks can be written from them and used like money at stores. They also can be used just like a saving account. Savings accounts are often used by young people who don't need to write checks. Some married couples will have a joint account that they share. Fewer and fewer stores will take checks, but it makes other business transactions like paying rent or setting up direct deposit easier if you have them.

提示　包括存款帳戶、聯名帳戶和支票帳戶等。支票帳戶比較常用到，因為和在店裡付現金一樣，有支票帳戶便可以開支票；另外它也有存款帳戶的功能。不需要開支票的年輕人，往往會開立存款帳戶；有些夫妻則會開立共同擁有的聯名帳戶。雖然接受支票的商店已越來越少，但如果有支票帳戶的話，像付房租或薪資轉帳等其他交易往來，都會方便許多。

Conversation 1

A: The landlord needs a postdated check for the last month's rent.

B: Then go ahead and give him one. I really like this apartment and I'm sick of looking.

A: I don't have a checking account. You'll have to give him a check.

B: But I don't have that kind of money. Can't we rent the apartment without it?

A: If we don't give him the last month's rent, he'll give the apartment to someone else.

B: Okay. You give me half the money and I'll write the check.

中譯

A: 房東要我開上個月房租的遠期支票給他。

B: 那就去開給他啊。我很喜歡這棟公寓，而且我已厭倦再找房子了。

A: 我沒有支票帳戶，要你開才行。

B: 可是我沒有準備這部分的錢，不開支票就不能租公寓嗎？

A: 如果我們不把上個月的租金支票給他，他就要把公寓租給別人。

B: 好吧。你先給我一半的錢，我來開支票給他。

Conversation 2

A: I need to get a bank account.

B: You already have a bank account.

A: I need another one. Mine's a checking account. I need a savings account.

B: What for? Why do you need two accounts?

A: I use the checking account as my every day account.

B: And what will the savings account be for?

A: The savings account will be for saving money to go on a trip.

中譯

A: 我需要去銀行開個戶。

B: 你已經有帳戶了啊。

A: 我需要再開一個，原來那個是支票帳戶，現在要開存款帳戶。

B: 做什麼用？為何需要兩個帳戶？

A: 我把支票帳戶當做日常帳戶在用。

B: 那存款帳戶要做什麼用？

A: 存款帳戶要存錢旅行用。

Conversation 3

A: Good morning. How can I help?

B: I need to know the difference between checking accounts and savings accounts.

A: No problem. With a checking account, you can write checks.

B: Is there any other difference?

A: Not really. Other than that, they're pretty much the same.

B: I guess now I just need to decide if I will have any need for checks.

中譯

A: 早安。需要幫忙嗎？

B: 我想知道支票帳戶和存款帳戶有什麼不同。

A: 沒問題。支票帳戶是用來開支票用的。

B: 還有其他不同的地方嗎？

A: 沒什麼不同。除了可以開支票外，其他的都差不多。

B: 那現在只要想想需不需要開支票就可以了，對吧？

Conversation 4

A: Having two different bank accounts is a good idea.

B: I can't think of any reason why anyone should have two accounts.

A: I need to keep my savings **separate** from my normal account.

B: Why?

A: That way, I don't spend my savings.

B: I see. If you don't use that account everyday, you have a better chance of saving.

中譯

A: 開兩個帳戶蠻不錯的。

B: 我想不出來為什麼一個人需要兩個不同帳戶。

A: 我必須把存款帳戶和平常在用的帳戶分開才行。

B: 為什麼？

A: 那樣的話，我才不會把存款花掉。

B: 我懂了。沒有天天在用的帳戶，才比較有可能把錢存下來。

Conversation 5

A: Can I get you to pay for the **groceries** this time?

B: Why? It's your turn. I thought you said you just got paid. You should have **enough**.

A: They won't take a check.

B: Then don't give them a check. Pay in cash.

A: I don't have any cash on me.

B: Then use your bank card.

中譯

A: 這回買的雜貨可以請你付帳嗎？

B: 為什麼？該你付了耶。我還以為你說你剛付過了。錢應該夠吧。

A: 他們不收支票。

B: 那就不要開支票啊，付現好了。

A: 我身上沒有現金。

B: 那用金融卡吧。

Conversation 6

A: I wanted the power company to automatically withdraw from my account each month.

B: I didn't know they could do that.

A: They can but I have to give them a voided check.

B: But you don't have a checking account.

A: I asked them if I could just tell them my banking information and they said no.

B: You'll have to see the bank about getting your savings account changed to checking.

中譯

A: 我希望電力公司每個月自動從我帳戶中扣款。

B: 我不知道有這項服務耶。

A: 有啊，不過我要先給他們一張作廢支票才行。

B: 可是你沒有支票帳戶耶。

A: 我有問他們可不可以只提供帳戶資料，他們說不可以。

B: 那你要去銀行問問看可不可以把存款帳戶變成支票帳戶。

Conversation 7

A: Should I get a chequing account or a savings account?

B: What did you have when you were married?

A: I didn't have my own account. We had a joint account.

B: That's when you have one account that is in both of your names right?

A: Yes. That's all we needed.

B: I can't believe you didn't have your own account. You should get a checking account because it has more options.

中譯

A: 我應該開立支票帳戶還是存款帳戶？

B: 你結婚時是用什麼帳戶？

A: 我沒有個人帳戶，我們是用聯名帳戶。

B: 就是用你們兩個人名字登記的共同帳戶，對吧？

A: 沒錯，就只有這個。

B: 真不敢相信你居然沒有個人帳戶。支票帳戶選擇較多，你應該去開一個。

Conversation 8

A: Once we are married, should I close my account? Should we open a joint account?

B: Joint accounts are fine but you should have your own personal account too.

A: So you think we should each keep our own accounts and have a joint one also?

B: Yes. I think that's best.

A: You're probably right. There will be fewer fights over money that way.

B: I heard that fighting over money is the number one leading cause of divorce.

A: 一旦我們結了婚，我應該把個人帳戶停掉嗎？還是該開一個聯名帳戶？

B: 可以開聯名帳戶，但最好也保留你的個人帳戶。

A: 所以你覺得我們應該個別擁有自己的帳戶，同時也擁有聯名帳戶囉？

B: 沒錯，我覺得那樣最好。

A: 或許你說的沒錯。那樣比較不會為錢爭吵。

B: 聽說為錢爭吵是導致離婚最主要的原因。

Conversation 9

A: I'm off to the bank. See you later.

B: You're going to the bank? Great. Could you deposit this for me?

A: Why don't you come?

B: I haven't showered yet. Will you wait for me?

A: You take forever to get ready. I've never seen a man who takes as long as you.

B: Just take this money and put it in my savings account. Here's my bank card.

A: 我要去銀行了，再見。

B: 你要去銀行？太好了，可以幫我存一下錢嗎？

A: 為什麼不跟我一起去？

B: 我還沒洗澡啦，可以等我一下嗎？

A: 等你弄好不知民國幾年了。沒看過哪個男生像你那麼會摸的。

B: 只要把這些錢存進我戶頭就好了。這是我的金融卡，拿去吧。

Useful phrases and idioms
有用的片語和慣用語

Go ahead 去吧

just do it; to tell another person they may begin

例　Go ahead and help yourself to more bread.

麵包多拿一點，不用客氣。

Sick of 夠了

had enough of; don't want anymore of

例　I'm sick of hearing about how good a bank teller he is.

他是個很棒的銀行櫃臺人員這件事，我已經聽夠了。

Pretty much 差不多

almost entirely

例　They are pretty much ready to quit their jobs.

他們差不多準備好要辭職了。

Take forever 真久

take such a long time; an exaggeration to express a long time

例　Doesn't it seem to take forever for the Manager to return her phone calls?

等經理回她電話要等到民國幾年啊？

Vocabulary 字彙

savings account		存款帳戶
joint account		聯名帳戶
checking account		支票帳戶
commonly	*adv.*	通常地
transactions	*n.*	交易
direct deposit		薪資轉帳
landlord	*n.*	房東
postdated check		遠期支票
separate	*adj.*	分開的
normal	*adj.*	平常的
groceries	*n.*	雜貨
enough	*n.*	足夠
power company		電力公司
automatically	*adv.*	自動地
voided check		作廢支票
option	*n.*	選擇
leading cause		主要的原因
divorce	*n.*	離婚

Unit 3

Opening an Account
開戶

MP3-4

Opening a bank account is a banking transaction that can't be done through the bank machine. The bank teller will be able to open a new account for a customer. The customer must remember to bring identification. Picture ID like a driver's license is the best. Be sure to shop around to different banks for the best interest rates and lowest bank charges. Different branches of the same bank will have the same rates and fees. Be clear on what this bank account will be used for. There are many different bank plan options. If you aren't going to use an option, make sure you won't be paying for it through your bank plan fee.

提示　開戶不能用自動櫃員機，要親自去銀行辦理才行。銀行櫃臺人員會幫客戶開戶。客戶要記得帶身份證明，最好是像駕駛執照這類有貼照片的證明。記得多問幾家銀行，看看哪家利率和手續費最低。同一家銀行各個分行利率和費用都一樣。另外也要弄清楚所開的戶頭是做什麼用的。銀行提供的功能有很多種選擇，如果某些功能你用不到，記得不要白白多付一筆使用費用。

Conversation 1

A: I'd like to open an account please.

B: I can help you with that. Can you please fill out

29

this application form?

A: Yes. Do you have a pen I could use?

B: Here you go. Can I see three pieces of ID? I need to **photocopy** them.

A: I brought lots of ID with me. What do you need?

B: I need some photo ID, a **major credit card**, and one other piece of ID please.

中譯

A: 我想要開戶。

B: 歡迎辦理。麻煩先填一下申請表格。

A: 好。請問有筆嗎？

B: 在這裡。請給我三張身份證明，我要影印一下。

A: 我帶了很多張證明過來，你要哪一張？

B: 請給我一張有貼照片的證明，一張信用卡正卡，一張其

他證明。

Conversation 2

A: Good afternoon. What can I do for you today?

B: I want to open a bank account.

A: Okay. You'll need to fill out this application form.

B: Oh, I'm not ready to open an account today. I need to find out some information first.

A: Of course. I can help you with that. What do you need to know?

B: What's the interest rate on a checking account? How does it **compare** to other banks?

A: 午安。請問需要什麼服務嗎？

B: 我想要開戶。

A: 好的。請先填好申請表格。

B: 哦，我今天還不要開戶，我想先知道一些相關資訊。

A: 當然沒問題。您需要哪方面資訊呢？

B: 支票帳戶利率如何？和其他家銀行比起來怎麼樣？

Conversation 3

A: Hello. How are you today?

B: I'm good. I want to know about the options I can get on my checking account.

A: I have a brochure that lists all that information. What did you want to know?

B: I think I'm paying way too much in bank charges. I write a lot of checks.

A: Can I have your bank card please? I'll see what kind of plan you have in place.

B: I didn't bring it with me. I know my account number by heart though.

中譯

A: 您好，歡迎光臨。

B: 謝謝。我想知道支票帳戶有哪些功能可用？

A: 這裡有一本小冊子上有各種資料。您想要瞭解哪方面的訊息？

B: 因為我常常在開支票，覺得銀行手續費付太多了。

A: 金融卡給我一下好嗎？我看看你有哪些功能。

B: 我沒帶在身上，不過我記得帳號。

Conversation 4

A: I've moved out of my parents' house and now I need a checking account.

B: That's no problem. Do you want to keep your savings account?

A: I don't think so. I can use my checking account the same way.

B: That's right. It has a bank card. You can pay by debit with it just like you're used to.

A: No. I'll close that account. I don't want to pay two sets of bank fees.

B: Okay. We'll open the new account first and then we'll do the closure on the other.

中譯

A: 我搬出爸媽家了，現在要開個支票帳戶。

B: 沒問題。那還要保留存款帳戶嗎？

A: 我想不用。支票帳戶也有相同的功能。

B: 沒錯。支票帳戶也有金融卡，你還是可以像以前那樣簽帳。

A: 不，我要關閉那個帳戶，我不想付兩種不同費用。

B: 好的。我先幫你開新帳戶，然後再把另一個帳戶停掉。

Conversation 5

A: Can I open an account here?

B: Of course you can. Do you have a bank account already?

A: But it's at a different bank. I just moved here so that's why I need a new account.

B: What bank is the account you have right now with?

A: The same bank as this one. North West Bank. It's over on River Street across town.

Your account's at a different branch but it's the same bank. Keep your account as is.

中譯

A: 這裡可以開戶嗎？

當然可以。你已經有銀行帳戶了嗎？

A: 有，不過是別家銀行的。我剛搬來這裡，所以需要新開個帳戶。

你原本的帳戶是哪家銀行的？

A: 和這家一樣都是西北銀行，在城裡大河路那邊。

你的帳戶總行是一樣的，只不過分行不同而已。原來的帳戶還是可以繼續使用。

Conversation 6

A: I've reviewed your bank fees and the transactions on your account in a typical month.

What did you find out? Am I paying too much?

A: Yes. You write a lot of checks. With your plan, you're getting charged for each.

So what should I do? Do I need to change accounts?

A: No. We will change your bank plan. Your account will stay the same.

As long as what I'm paying in charges each month goes down.

中譯

A: 我已經檢查過你特定月份的銀行費用和交易了。

你發現什麼了嗎？我是不是付太多錢了？

A: 沒錯。你常開支票，而根據你選擇的功能，每一張都要付手續費。

那我該怎麼辦？需要去換帳戶嗎？

A: 不用。只要變更功能即可，帳戶還是一樣。

只要我每個月付的費用變少就可以了。

Conversation 7

A: How can I help you?

B: My wife and I want to open a joint account. We just got married.

A: Congratulations. Here is an application form that both of you will need to sign.

B: You need both of our signatures? My wife is at work.

A: You can take the form home with you and fill it out, but we need both signatures.

B: It says here you want ID from each of us. I'll bring her with me when I come back.

中譯

A: 需要什麼服務嗎?

B: 我太太和我要開個聯名帳戶,我們剛結婚。

A: 恭喜。這是雙方都要簽名的申請表格。

B: 兩個人的簽名都要?可是我太太還在上班耶。

A: 一定要兩份簽名才行,你可以把表格帶回去填。

B: 上面說需要我們兩個的身份證明。下回我會帶她一起過來。

Useful phrases and idioms
有用的片語和慣用語

By heart 記得

memorized

例 I know every song on that CD by heart.

Vocabulary 字彙

identification	n.	身份証明

Picture ID		有貼照片的証明
license	*n.*	執照
interest rate		利率
bank charge		手續費
branch	*n.*	分行
fees	*n.*	費用
application form		申請表格
photocopy	*v.*	影印
major credit card		信用卡正卡
compare	*v.*	比較
brochure	*n.*	小冊子
debit	*n.*	簽帳
closure	*n.*	終止
review	*v.*	再檢查
typical	*adj.*	特定的
signature	*n.*	簽名

Chapter 2

DEPOSITS AND WITHDRAWALS

存提款

Unit 1

Making Deposits
存款

MP3-5

Deposits can be done two different ways. They can be done through the automated bank machine or through the teller. When a check is deposited through the bank machine, it's necessary to sign the back of it. The teller will ask the customer to sign the back of the check when a deposit is made in person. Businesses have a special bag that they put their money and checks into. At the end of the work day, this bag goes into a pull out drawer that is reserved for businesses. The bag falls directly into the bank where it will be safe until the bank reopens the next day.

提示　　存款有兩種不同的方式，利用自動櫃員機或親自找櫃臺人員辦理都可以。如果用自動櫃員機存支票，必須在支票背面簽字才行。如果親自到銀行存支票，櫃臺人員也會要求客戶在支票後面背書。公司行號有一個專門放錢和支票的特別袋子。當天結束營業後，這個袋子會進入銀行提供給公司行號專用的可拉式抽屜裡；直接由銀行安全的保管著，一直到隔天銀行打開袋子。

Conversation 1

A:　It's almost closing time. I'd better do the deposit. Where did I put the deposit bag?

B: Isn't it in the top drawer where you always leave it?

A: No. I wonder if I didn't get it back from the bank.

B: You usually go to the bank first thing in the morning after you've made the deposit.

A: I didn't today. I had no coffee at home so I went through the drive through for coffee.

B: It's too late to get it now. You'd better wait and do the deposit tomorrow.

中譯

A: 銀行快要關了，我最好趕快存款。存款袋放哪裡去了？

B: 你不是一直都放在最上面的抽屜嗎？

A: 沒有。我想大概放在銀行忘了拿回來。

B: 你存款後早上第一件事不是都會先去銀行一趟嗎？

A: 今天沒有。家裡沒咖啡了，所以我開車去得來速買咖啡。

B: 現在存款太晚了。你最好等到明天早上再去。

Conversation 2

A: What took you so long? It feels like you've been gone for hours.

B: I had to make a deposit through the bank machine. It was out of envelopes.

A: Out of envelopes? I've never seen it out of envelopes. What did you do?

B: I asked one of the tellers if they had any more envelopes.

A: Did you do your deposit through the teller?

B: No. I waited until she found some envelopes and then I did it at the ATM.

A: 你怎麼去那麼久？好像去好幾個小時了耶。

B: 我要用自動櫃員機存款，結果信封沒了。

A: 信封沒了？我沒遇過信封沒了的情況，結果呢？

B: 我問一位櫃臺人員信封還有沒有。

A: 你沒讓櫃臺人員幫你存嗎？

B: 沒有。我等到她找到信封後再用自動櫃員機存款。

Conversation 3

A: Good afternoon, Mrs. Miller. Happy New Year.

B: Thank you, Glenn. Happy New Year to you as well.

A: What can I do for you today?

B: I need to deposit this check, Glenn. Here's my bank card.

A: I see that you've already signed the back of the cheque. That's good. Which account?

B: Deposit that to my savings account. I don't want to touch it. I'm saving for a trip.

A: 米勒小姐午安。新年快樂。

B: 謝謝你，葛蘭。也祝你新年快樂。

A: 今天有什麼地方需要效勞嗎？

B: 我要存這張支票，葛蘭。金融卡在這裡。

A: 你都不會忘記在支票後面背書，真不錯。要存進哪個帳戶呢？

B: 存進我的存款帳戶，因為要當旅遊基金，所以不想再動這筆錢。

Conversation 4

A: Will you come with me to the bank? I have to drop off a deposit and it's a big one.

B: I'll come with you. Did you win the lottery or something?

A: No. It's for work. The manager is away so it's my job to drop off the deposit.

B: Oh. You have to put it in the pull out drawer. That's what you mean, right?

A: That's right. I'm not used to carrying around so much money.

B: Better safe than sorry. I'll grab my coat. Are you driving or am I?

中譯

A: 你要和我去銀行嗎？我要存一大筆錢。

B: 好，我和你去。你中了樂透還是什麼嗎？

A: 不是啦，是公司的錢。經理不在，所以我要負責存款。

B: 哦。你的意思是要把錢放進可拉式抽屜，對嗎？

A: 沒錯。我不習慣身上帶那麼多錢。

B: 小心駛得萬年船。我去拿外套。你開車還是我開車？

Conversation 5

A: What are you doing? Aren't you ready to go home yet?

B I'm just writing up the deposit slip. It'll just take a second. Then I'll be ready to go.

A: How come it takes so long to write up a deposit slip?

B: You write down how many of dollar bills to deposit and the number of each check.

A: I see. That does take a bit of time, doesn't it?

B: If you have a lot of bills and a lot of check to deposit, then yes, it does.

A: 你在幹嘛？還不準備回家嗎？

B: 我還在填存款單，要一下子，然後就要回家了。

A: 填存款單怎麼會那麼久？

B: 要存多少錢，還有每張支票的號碼都要填才行。

A: 原來如此。那的確要花點時間。

B: 如果你要存很多錢和支票，那的確需要一點時間才行。

Conversation 6

A: I hate making a deposit through the bank machine.

B: Why? What's the big deal?

A: It makes that loud beeping sound when you put your envelope in.

B: So? What's the problem with that?

A: It annoys me. It's so loud. I feel like everyone's looking at me.

B: It beeps for everyone else too, you know.

中譯

A: 我討厭用自動櫃員機存款。

B: 為什麼？有什麼大不了的嗎？

A: 信封放進去時都會發出很大的嗶嗶聲。

B: 那又如何？有什麼問題嗎？

A: 我覺得很煩。聲音好大，覺得每個人好像都盯著我看一樣。

B: 你又不是不知道不管誰存款，它都會嗶。

Conversation 7

A: Good afternoon. How can I help you?

B: Hi there. I need to make a deposit. Here's my bank card and the check.

A: Thank you. I'll just fill out the deposit slip for you

and get you to initial here.

B: It's funny that I have to sign to do a withdrawal but I only have to initial to deposit.

A: That's because you are putting money into this account.

B: I see. It's only if I'm taking money out that you need to see my signature.

中譯

A: 午安。需要什麼服務嗎？

B: 你好，我想要存款。這是我的金融卡和支票。

A: 謝謝你。我幫你把存款單填好，然後你在這裡簽姓名首字母即可。

B: 提款時要簽全名，但存款時只要簽首字母，蠻奇怪的。

A: 那是因為你要把錢存進帳戶的關係。

B: 我懂了。只有提款時才需要看到本人簽名。

Useful phrases and idioms
有用的片語和慣用語

Drive through 得來速

where you can get food or drink and pay for it without leaving your car, common at fast-food restaurants

例 Let's just get something to eat at a drive through.

我們去得來速買點東西吃吧。

It feels like 好像

it seems like, it's as though

例 It feels like I've been working at this job for too long.

這個工作我好像待太久了。

Touch it　動用

get at it, access it

例　I don't want him to touch his trust fund until he turns 21.

我不希望他在 21 歲以前動用到他的信託基金。

Better safe than sorry 小心駛得萬年船

It's better to be safe and cautious than to possibly face bad consequences

A :Do you think I should phone and see if they got my resume?

B :Better safe than sorry.

A　:　你覺得我應該打電話去問問看他們有沒有收到我的履歷表嗎？

B　:　小心駛得萬年船。

What's the big deal 有什麼大不了的

I don't understand what the problem is

例　So I used her pen. What's the big deal?

我是拿她的筆去用，有什麼大不了的？

Vocabulary 字彙

automated bank machine		自動櫃員機
reserve	v.	專用
envelope	n.	信封
lottery	n.	樂透
deposit slip		存款單
beep	v.	作嗶嗶聲
annoy	v.	使煩惱
initial	v.	簽姓名首的字母

Unit 2

Making Withdrawals
提款

MP3-6

Withdrawals can be made through the bank machine or by a teller. When a teller makes a withdrawal, cash is given to the customer. If it is a big amount and the customer is not confident carrying a lot of cash, they can ask for a cashier's check or a money order instead of cash.

提示 提款可以利用自動櫃員機或親洽櫃臺人員。若在櫃臺提款，現金會直接交到客戶手上。如果是一大筆錢，客戶沒有信心帶那麼多錢在身上，可以向銀行要求本票或匯票。

Conversation 1

A: I need to get some cash. Take me to the ATM machine.

B: Why do you need cash? Why don't you just use your debit card? The bar takes debit.

A: I don't like that. It means I have to go up to the bar every time I want to buy a drink.

B: I guess it's easier to have cash. That way you can order from the waitress.

A: That's right. It'll just take a second. My bank is on the way.

B: I think I'll get some cash out too. I'm coming with you.

A: 我要提一些現金出來，帶我去自動提款機提款。

B: 要現金幹嘛？用簽帳卡就好了啊？酒吧都可以用簽帳卡。

A: 我不喜歡那樣。意思好像每次想喝一杯時都要去吧台那裡才行。

B: 我想也是，帶現金比較輕鬆，可以直接向女服務生點東西。

A: 沒錯。又不花多少時間，而且去銀行又順路。

B: 我也想提一些錢出來。我和你去。

Conversation 2

A: Good morning. Can I help you?

B: Good morning and yes you can. I need to make a withdrawal please.

A: How much would you like to take out today sir?

B: Six hundred dollars please.

A: Mr. Gleason, it's only showing a balance of five hundred and seventy-nine dollars.

B: Oh. Better make it five hundred then.

中譯

A: 早安。需要什麼服務嗎？

B: 早安。是的，我想要提款。

A: 先生，你今天要提多少錢？

B: 六百塊。

A: 葛利森先生，帳戶餘額只剩五百七十九塊。

B: 喔。那提五百塊好了。

Conversation 3

A: I wish they'd let you take out less than a twenty from the ATM.

B: They used to let you withdraw as little as five dollars.

A: The smallest bill that they stock in the bank machine is a twenty now.

B: Why would you want to take out less than twenty bucks anyway?

A: I only need ten to go to the movie. Besides, if I have it, I spend it.

B: I always take out more so I don't get charged for as many transactions.

中譯

A: 希望提款機可以讓你提二十元以下的金額。

B: 以前連五塊都可以領。

A: 現在機器裡儲存的最小面額鈔票是二十塊。

B: 為什麼你一定要提二十塊以下？

A: 看電影只要十塊而已，再說，如果我提太多錢就會把它花掉。

B: 我都會領多一點，才不用被扣那麼多次手續費。

Conversation 4

A: Hi. I'd like to withdraw some money please. Here is my bank card.

B: I'm sorry. This is the North West Bank. This card is from the South Rivers Bank.

A: But they told me that I could take out money from a different bank.

B: What they probably meant is that you don't have to use your branch.

A: Branch? What does that mean? Can't I use my bank card here?

B: I'm sorry. There is a South Rivers Bank two blocks south of here. They can help you.

中譯

A: 嗨。我想要提款，這是我的金融卡。

很抱歉，我們這裡是西北銀行，但是你這張卡是南河銀行發的。

A: 可是他們跟我說我可以在別家銀行提款。

他們的意思可能是說，你不一定要在你原來那家分行提款。

A: 分行？什麼意思？我的金融卡不能在這裡用嗎？

很抱歉。往南過兩個街區有一家南河銀行，可以去那裡看看。

Conversation 5

A: I'm going to the bank. I'll be right back.

B: Listen can you do me a favor? Take out fifty bucks for me.

A: Why don't you just come with me and do it yourself?

B: But my favorite show is on and I missed it last week. Please? Here's my card.

A: Well what's your PIN number? And which account do you want me to take it out of?

A: I'll write it down for you. Just don't lose it or show it to anyone.

中譯

A: 我要去銀行一下，很快回來。

B: 喂，那你可以幫個忙嗎？幫我提個五十塊。

A: 幹嘛不跟我去自己領？

B: 我最愛看的節目開始了，上個禮拜漏掉沒看到。拜託一下好嗎？這是我的金融卡。

A: 好吧，那個人密碼是什麼？要提哪個帳戶的錢？

B: 我寫一下。不要弄丟了，也不要給別人看到哦。

Conversation 6

A: That's forty dollars for the groceries please.

B: If I use my debit card, can you give me some cash back?

A: Yes. How much do you want?

B: Forty dollars. I can never remember which stores let you do that and which ones don't.

A: Yes. Your new total comes to eighty dollars. It's a good way to avoid bank charges.

B: Yes. You're getting money out of your account, but as a purchase not a withdrawal.

中譯

A: 全部的東西一共四十塊。

B: 用簽帳卡的話，可以拿些現金回來嗎？

A: 可以。你要多少？

B: 四十塊。我老是記不得哪些店可以這樣，哪些店不可以。

A: 是啊。新的總額一共是八十塊。這個辦法不錯，可以不用被銀行扣手續費。

B: 沒錯。你還是一樣從帳戶中領錢，只不過是用來買東西而不是提款。

Conversation 7

A: What are you doing?

B: I'm taking out money. What does it look like?

A: No it's just that I know your account isn't with this bank.

B: I can still use their ATM machine. You can use any bank card in any bank machine.

A: Yes, but you get charged way more money. Your bank is less than half a block alway.

B: I didn't know about the charges. It's a short walk. You're right.　Let's go over there.

中譯

A:　你在幹嘛？

B:　我在把錢領出來，你難道看不出來嗎？

A:　不是啦，我只是想說你的帳戶不是這家銀行的。

B:　我還是可以用他們的自動提款機。你可以在任何一家銀行的提款機上用任何金融卡。

A:　是沒錯，不過你會被扣比較多手續費。你的銀行離這裡半條街都不到。

B:　我沒注意到手續費的事。的確很近，你說得沒錯，我們去那裡吧。

Useful phrases and idioms
有用的片語和慣用語

Bar 酒吧

a place that sells and serves alcoholic beverages

例 Tammy said you should meet her at the bar for a drink.

泰咪說你可以和她約在酒吧喝一杯。

Bucks 元

dollars

例 I need to ask my friend if he can lend me twenty bucks.

我要問問我朋友，看他可不可以借我二十元。

Show 電影

movie

例 Susan and Tom are going to go see a show tonight.
蘇珊和湯姆今晚要去看電影。

What does it look like 你難道看不出來嗎

a sarcastic way of saying that something should be obvious.

A :What are you doing with that apple and that knife?

B :What does it look like?

　　A :你拿那個蘋果和那把刀在幹嘛？

　　B :你難道看不出來嗎？

Vocabulary 字彙

confident	*adj.*	有信心的
cashier's check		本票
money order		匯票
waitress	*n.*	女服務生
balance	*n.*	餘額
bill	*n.*	鈔票
stock	*v.*	儲存
block	*n.*	街區
favor	*n.*	善意的行為
PIN	*n.*	個人密碼
debit card		簽帳卡
purchase	*v.*	買東西

Unit 3

Overdraft and Interest
透支和利息

MP3-7

An overdraft option is available on checking accounts. It allows the account holder to spend some money that is not actually in the account. This is to prevent bounced checking. Some people make the mistake of running into their overdraft every month. This is very costly because the bank charges and interest on the amount borrowed from the bank are very high. It is better financially to get rid of a checking account than to constantly go into overdraft.

提示　支票帳戶有透支的功能。這樣的話，帳戶持有者便可花一些帳戶裡實際上沒有的錢，這是為了避免跳票而設。有些人每個月都用到透支，這是一種錯誤；因為向銀行借錢的手續費和利息都很貴。從財務角度來看，經常透支的話還不如把支票帳戶停掉來得划算。

Conversation 1

A: I have been bouncing a lot of checks. I just can't seem to live within my means.

B: I was the same way. Now I have an overdraft on my checking account.

A: So you don't bounce checks anymore?

B: No. Let me think about that for a moment. Well

actually I still do.

A: So now you not only have zero money in your account, you also owe the bank money.

B: I guess so. It doesn't sound as good when you describe it like that.

中譯

A: 我跳票太多次了，好像做不到量入為出，快不行了。

B: 我也差不多。我現在的支票帳戶也透支了。

A: 所以你不會再跳票了？

B: 不會。我想一下，嗯，其實還是會跳票。

A: 所以你現在不但帳戶餘額是零，還欠銀行錢。

B: 我想是吧。那樣形容聽起來真不太好受。

Conversation 2

A: I'll use my credit card to pay for that.

B: Don't you have any money?

A: Yes. I have money in my bank account.

B: Why don't you pay by debit then? Just use your bank card.

A: But if I pay by credit card I get reward points. I won't get those if I pay by debit.

B: But you won't get dinged with high interest rates either.

中譯

A: 我要用信用卡付帳。

B: 你都沒有錢嗎？

A: 有啊，銀行帳戶裡有。

B: 幹嘛不用簽帳的？用金融卡就好了。

A: 可是用信用卡有紅利點數啊。用簽帳的就沒有了。

B: 但你也不用負擔銀行的高利率啊。

Conversation 3

A: I can help whoever's next over here, please.

B: Hi. How are you today?

A: I'm good. How are you?

B: Good. I want to get rid of the overdraft on my checking account.

A: Okay. Are you not using the overdraft protection?

B: No. The bank sent me a letter saying they'd just added it on for me. I don't want it.

中譯

A: 請問再來是哪位需要服務？

嗨，今天好嗎？

A: 很好啊，你呢？

不錯。我想把支票帳戶的透支停掉。

A: 好的。你不會再用到透支保障了嗎？

不會。銀行寄信給我說會自動把透支保障加進去，但我並不需要。

Conversation 4

A: Good afternoon. How can I help you?

B: I'm not sure about the interest rates on my credit card. It's through this bank.

A: The interest rate on this credit card is around 18%. Is there anything else?

B: Yes. What interest rate is the bank giving me on my savings account?

A: The savings account you have gives you 1.2% interest. Is there anything else today?

A: Yes. I need to pay my credit card in full. Please pay it off from my savings account.

中譯

A: 午安。需要什麼服務嗎？

B: 我想知道我這張信用卡利率是多少，是你們這家銀行發的卡。

A: 這張信用卡利率是 18%。還想知道什麼呢？

B: 那銀行給我存款帳戶的利率是多少？

A: 存款帳戶的利率是 1.2%。還需要什麼服務嗎？

B: 是的。我要把信用卡清償掉，請從我的存款帳戶中扣款。

Conversation 5

A: Hello. Can you please tell me how to go about applying for overdraft protection?

B: Yes. Do you have an account with us?

A: Yes. Here's my bank card.

B: Thank you. Miss, the computer is showing me that you have a savings account.

A: That's right. Why? Is there a problem?

B: Overdraft protection is to protect you from bouncing checks in a checking account.

中譯

A: 你好。可以告訴我如何申請透支保障嗎？

B: 好的。你有我們銀行的帳戶嗎？

A: 有。金融卡在這裡。

B: 謝謝。小姐，電腦顯示你的是存款帳戶。

A: 對啊，怎麼了？有什麼問題嗎？

B: 透支保障是用來避免支票帳戶跳票的。

Conversation 6

A: So we both have a day off. It's the first time in a long time. What do you want to do?

B: If it's all right with you I'd like to go to all the

banks in town.

A: Why? Are you a bank robber?

No. Don't be silly. I want to find out how the interest rates compare.

A: Oh. You want to shop around for the best interest rate on a credit card?

Not just that. I want to shop around for the highest interest rate in a savings account.

中譯

A: 我們兩個都放假耶，那麼久以來這是第一次。你想幹嘛呢？

如果可以的話，我想到城裡每家銀行走一趟。

A: 為什麼？你想當銀行搶匪嗎？

不是啦，別傻了。我想去比較一下各家的利率。

A: 喔。你要去找最好的信用卡利率？

不光是那樣。我還要找到最高的存款帳戶利率。

Conversation 7

A: This overdraft protection thing sucks. I'm going to get rid of it.

Why do you say that?

A: I'm not supposed to bounce checks, so the bank gives me some leeway in my account.

That's right. So what's the problem?

A: The problem is I'm still bouncing checks. Now I'm spending above my overdraft.

And you owe the bank money. You have to pay that overdraft down and get rid of it.

中譯

A: 這個什麼透支保障爛死了，我要把它停掉。

B: 為什麼那麼說？
A: 銀行有給我帳戶一些寬限額度，我不應該跳票的。
B: 沒錯啊，所以是什麼問題呢？
A: 問題是我還是跳票了。現在已經超過透支額度了。
B: 那你已經欠銀行錢了。你必須清償透支，然後把它停掉。

Conversation 8

A: Have you heard about this new internet banking?

B: Internet banking is not new. I think every bank has a website now.

A: No. There's a bank now that's only available online. There is no actual building.

B: I don't know if I like the sounds of that.

A: They have no costs so they give much better interest rates on their savings accounts.

B: Really? Let's go online and check out their rates.

中譯

A: 你有聽過這家新的網路銀行嗎？
B: 網路銀行已經不是新鮮事了，我想現在每家銀行都有網站。
A: 不是這樣，現在有一家只做線上服務而沒有實體建築的銀行。
B: 我也不知道自己喜不喜歡那樣。
A: 他們不用營運成本，所以存款帳戶的利率好很多。
B: 真的嗎？那我們上線看看利率多少。

Useful phrases and idioms
有用的片語和慣用語

Bounced checks 跳票

a cheque for which there is not sufficient funds to

cover it

例 I need to transfer some money into my checking
account or else I'll bounce a check.
我必須把錢轉到支票帳戶裡去，不然我會跳票。

Within my means 量入為出

*under the amount of money I make not above it;
affordable*

例 I have to learn to live within my means. I'm tired
of being broke.
我必須學著量入為出，實在不想再破產了。

Dinged 罰款，不利

penalized

例 He got dinged by the bank for not paying his credit
card bill on time.
他因為沒有準時繳交信用卡款項，被銀行罰款。

Get rid of 丟掉，停止

do away with; throw out

例 You need to get rid of that pen because it doesn't
work.
那支筆寫不出來，不要用了。

Silly 愚笨的

goofy or foolish

例 Bill looks silly when he pulls his hat down to hide his eyes.

比爾把帽子拉下來蓋住眼睛時，看起來蠻呆的。

Sucks 很爛，不好玩，不公平

is no fun; bothers me; an unfair situation

例 Having to work late and not getting paid for it really sucks.

要加班又不給錢，真爛。

Some leeway 寬限

some flexibility

例 I need some leeway on this deadline.

我需要一些寬限，才趕得上期限。

Vocabulary 字彙

overdraft option		透支的功能
account holder		帳戶持有者
actually	*adv.*	實際上
mistake	*n.*	錯誤
run into		用到
costly	*adj.*	昂貴的
amount	*n.*	總額（錢）
financially	*adv.*	財務上
constantly	*adv.*	不斷地；時常地
zero	*n.*	零

describe	*v.*	形容
reward points		紅利點數
either	*adv.*	也
overdraft protection		透支保障
show	*v.*	顯示
robber	*n.*	搶匪
shop around		貨比三家
available	*adj.*	可用的；可利用的
building	*n.*	建築物

Chapter 3

USING THE BANK MACHINE

使用自動櫃員機

Unit 1

Starting Out

開始使用

MP3-8

When a bank customer first starts using the bank machine, it's best if they learn from a teller. Lots of friends and family members will already know how and will want to help, but the bank teller knows more. He or she will explain better because it's what they do for a living. The back of the bank card should be signed. The customer should always shield the key pad and screen with his or her body. This is so other people standing behind can't see important things like PIN numbers and account balances.

提示　銀行客戶第一次使用自動櫃員機時，最好先向櫃臺人員問個清楚。雖然也可以問很多會操作的朋友和家人，但櫃臺人員總是知道得比較多。他們以此維生，會說明得更加詳細。金融卡背後記得簽名。客戶操作機器時，永遠不要忘記用身體擋住鍵盤和螢幕，這樣才不會讓身後的人看到像密碼和帳戶餘額等重要資料。

Conversation 1

A: Excuse me. I'm a bank teller. You look like you might need some assistance.

B: Yes I do. This is my first time using the bank machine. I'm confused.

A: It looks like you're trying to put your card in the wrong way. Do you see this picture?

B: Yes. It looks like a bank card. Is that the way I'm supposed to put my card in?

A: Yes. The black strip that's on the back of your card goes up and to the right.

B: That helps. I won't forget anymore now that I can always look at that little picture.

中譯

A: 抱歉，我是銀行櫃臺人員。看來您需要幫忙。

B: 沒錯。我第一次操作自動櫃員機，有點弄不清楚。

A: 看來你把卡片插錯了，有看到這個圖嗎？

B: 有。看起來像是金融卡。是不是應該把金融卡放進那裡？

A: 沒錯。卡片背後的黑色磁條靠右朝上插入即可。

B: 果然沒錯。既然有小圖可以看，我就不會再忘記了。

Conversation 2

A: Hey. You sure are taking a long time. Do you need some help?

B: Sorry to hold you up. No I'm fine. I'm not used to these bank machines.

A: Do you want me to give you a hand?

B: No thanks. I'll figure it out. I just need a moment.

A: Come on. You look like you need a hand. Let me help you.

B: Why don't you just go ahead of me? Go ahead and I'll go through the teller.

中譯

A: 嘿，你弄好久哦，需要幫忙嗎？

B: 抱歉造成你的不便。不過我沒事，只是不習慣這些自動櫃員機而已。

A: 你要我幫你嗎？

B: 不用了，謝謝。我會搞定的，只是要一下子。

A: 別這樣嘛，你看起來需要有人幫忙，我來幫你吧。

B: 不如你先用好了。你先用，我去找櫃臺人員辦理。

Conversation 3

A: First you put in your card like this. Then you punch in your PIN and hit "okay".

B: Okay? Oh the button that says "okay" on it. I see what you mean. Go on.

A: Then read the screen. It lists several different transactions that you can do.

B: So if I want to deposit I hit that button. If I want to pay a bill I hit that button.

A: Right. All you ever have to do is put in your card and PIN and then read the screen.

B: This is going to be easy. Thanks so much for your help. How useful.

中譯

A: 卡片像這樣先插進去，然後輸入你的密碼再按「確定」。

B: 確定？喔，是那個上面寫著「確定」的按鈕啊，我看到了。繼續。

A: 接下來看著螢幕操作。螢幕上會列出幾個你可以操作不同交易的選項。

B: 所以，如果我想存款就按那個按鈕，如果要繳款就按那個按鈕。

A: 對。你只要把卡插進去、輸入密碼，然後看著螢幕操作即可。

B: 這樣很容易，太感謝你的幫忙了，對我幫助很大。

Conversation 4

A: Sir, I need help using the ATM machine. Can you help me please?

B: I will come help you as soon as I am done helping this person.

A: Okay. I'll just wait here beside this nice lady. I'm sure she won't mind.

B: Why don't you go put in your bank card and enter your PIN? Then I'll come help.

A: I don't have my bank card with me. But I know my PIN number off by heart.

B: You always need your card to use the bank machine. I'll have to help you here at the counter today.

中譯

A: 先生，我不會用自動櫃員機，需要有人幫忙。你可以過來幫我嗎？

B: 我先幫這個人，弄好馬上過去幫你。

A: 好的。我就站在這位好心的小姐旁邊等，我想她不會介意才對。

B: 你可以先把金融卡插進去再輸入密碼，我馬上就過去幫你。

A: 我沒有帶金融卡，不過我有把密碼記在腦子裡。

B: 要有金融卡才能使用自動櫃員機。我等會去櫃台那邊幫你。

Conversation 5

A: I'm trying to deposit all this money. Can you help me? I haven't done this before.

B: I don't mean to be rude but you'd best be getting a teller to help you with that.

A: But I don't want to go through the teller. I want to learn how to do this at the ATM.

B: I'm sorry but I'm just not comfortable helping you. That's a lot of money.

A: I know. It's okay. I asked you to help me. Remember? Come on.

B: No. I'll go get a teller to come here and help you, but I can't help you myself.

中譯

A: 我想要存這些錢，你可以幫我嗎？我以前沒存過。

B: 我沒有冒犯之意，不過你最好找櫃臺人員幫你。

A: 可是我不想找櫃臺人員啊，我想學會怎麼操作自動櫃員機。

B: 抱歉，那是一大筆錢，幫你忙我會不安心。

A: 我知道啦，沒關係。是我要你幫我的啊，對吧？好啦。

B: 不。我還是去找櫃臺人員來幫你，我自己不能幫你。

Useful phrases and idioms
有用的片語和慣用語

You'd best be 最好

It would be best for you if you did the following

例 You'd best be handing your assignment in on time.
你最好準時交作業。

Vocabulary 字彙

living	*n.*	生存
shield	*v.*	擋住
key pad		鍵盤
behind	*adv.*	在…後面
assistance	*n.*	幫助
strip	*n.*	條；細長片
forget	*v.*	忘記

hold you up		造成你的不便
several	*adj.*	幾個
hit	*v.*	按
button	*n.*	按鈕
useful	*adj.*	有幫助的
mind	*v.*	介意
rude	*adj.*	無禮的
comfortable	*adj.*	安心的

Unit 2

Different Transactions

不同的交易

MP3-9

The banking machine or ATM can be used for most straightforward transactions. It can be used to make deposits, withdrawals, and to transfer money from one account to another. It can also be used to pay some bills. Always pay careful attention to the people standing behind you to keep yourself safe. If people know that you are watchful and paying attention to your surroundings, there is less chance of them trying to rob you.

提示　　大部分簡單交易都可以透過提存機或自動櫃員機來操作。它們可以用來存提款、在不同戶頭間轉帳，也可以用來繳款。隨時要小心站在身後的人，以保障自身安全。如果別人知道你有在注意周遭環境，想要搶你錢的機會就會變少。

Conversation 1

A: I'm going to use the bank machine.

B: You don't have to. The bank is open. You can go through a teller. Come get in line.

A: No. They charge you more for using the tellers. They want you to use the ATM.

B: I don't believe that. Why wouldn't they want you to use the tellers?

A: They don't have to pay the ATM machines. They

pay tellers. That costs money.

B: But bank machines wear out. They need repairs. I'd rather deal with a human.

中譯

A: 我要去用自動櫃員機。

B: 不用啊，銀行還開著，找櫃臺人員就好了。進來排隊吧。

A: 不。找櫃臺人員辦手續費比較貴，銀行希望你用自動櫃員機。

B: 我不相信。為什麼銀行不希望客戶找櫃臺人員辦理？

A: 銀行不用付錢給自動櫃員機，但是要付錢給櫃臺人員，所以成本比較貴。

B: 可是自動櫃員機壞了，需要修理才行。我寧可找人辦理。

Conversation 2

A: Have you ever transferred money from one account to another?

B: Yes. I do it all the time. Do you want to know how?

A: Yes please. What do you do? What buttons do you press?

B: Buttons? No. Listen. You go to the teller and tell her to transfer money for you.

A: I need to do it through the ATM and I need to do it tonight. You know that.

B: I know. A bill is coming out of checking tonight. You need to transfer money from savings.

中譯

A: 你有把錢從這個帳戶轉到別的帳戶過嗎？

B: 有啊，我常常在轉帳。你想要轉帳嗎？

A: 是啊，教一下吧。要怎麼弄？要按哪個按鈕？

B: 按鈕？不用啦，聽著，去櫃臺人員那邊叫她幫你轉帳就好了。

A: 我晚上必須用自動櫃員機操作才行，你知道的。

B: 我知道。今晚有一張帳單到期了，所以必須轉帳。

Conversation 3

A: What are you doing? What's that piece of paper for?

B: It's my credit card bill. I'm paying my credit card bill through the ATM.

A: You can do that? I thought you had to mail in a check or pay through the teller.

B: It's easy. You just need the bottom portion of your credit card statement.

A: And your bank card too, I suppose.

B: Yes. You put in the statement and say how much money to pay from which account.

中譯

A: 你在做什麼？那張紙幹嘛用的？

B: 是我的信用卡帳單啦，我正在用自動櫃員機繳交信用卡款項。

A: 可以那樣啊？我以為要寄支票或找櫃臺人員辦理才行。

B: 很簡單，用信用卡帳單下面那半張就夠了。

A: 我想金融卡也是一樣吧。

B: 沒錯。把帳單放進去，然後指定哪個帳戶要繳多少錢即可。

Conversation 4

A: Why do you print the receipt? Isn't that just a waste of paper?

B: I keep the receipts and compare them against my statement when it comes in the mail.

A: You actually read those? What for? Why? It seems like a lot of work for nothing.

B: If the bank makes a mistake I have proof of that transaction. I double check the bank.

A: You double check the bank? Isn't that a little arrogant?

B: Absolutely not. The bank makes mistakes too you know. It happens all the time.

中譯

A: 你為什麼要印交易明細表？只是浪費紙張不是嗎？

B: 保留交易明細表才可以在帳單寄來時核對是否無誤。

A: 你真的有在看哦？做什麼用？為什麼呢？好像在做很多徒勞無益的事。

B: 如果銀行弄錯了，我就有交易證明。我在覆檢銀行的作業。

A: 覆檢銀行？會不會有點自大啊？

B: 絕對不會。你知道銀行也會弄錯的。這種事老是在發生。

Conversation 5

A: Okay. I'm all done. We can go now.

B: That was sure fast. You didn't take out any money did you?

A: No I didn't. Let's go. We have shopping to do and there will be tons of people.

B: Wait a second. How come you were in such a hurry to get to the bank machine?

A: I wanted to check my account balances. My pay-check got deposited so let's go.

B: Maybe I shouldn't carry cash either. Debit might be safer. There are lots of shoppers.

中譯

A: 好了，我都弄完了，現在可以走了。

B: 真快，你沒有提款對吧？

A: 沒有，走吧。我們還要去買東西，人會很多。

B: 等一下。那你幹嘛那麼急著來自動櫃員機這裡？

A: 我想要查詢帳戶餘額啦，薪資支票已經進來了，所以我們走吧。

B: 也許我也不該帶現金，用簽帳卡比較安全。買東西的人會很多。

Conversation 6

A: What are you doing? I thought you were just going to transfer funds.

B: Right. I took out some money. I'm using an envelope to put it in another account.

A: You don't have to take money right out and put it right back in to transfer funds.

B: All right. If you're so smart then show me a better way to do this.

A: See the screen? Where it gives you the option of transferring funds? Hit that button.

B: I see. So I just follow the prompts and it does everything for me? That's much easier.

中譯

A: 你在幹嘛？我以為你要轉帳，不是嗎？

B: 是啊。我提了一些錢，正在用信封把它存進別的帳戶裡。

A: 轉帳不用先把錢提出來再存進去啦。

B: 好啊，既然你那麼行，示範一下怎麼做比較好吧。

A: 看到螢幕沒？上面有轉帳的選項看到了嗎？按下那個按鈕就行了。

B: 看到了。所以我只要跟著指示做，它就會把一切搞定對嗎？那樣簡單多了。

Conversation 7

A: You've been in here for a long time. I was beginning to worry about you.

B: Sorry. I took out some money and looked at my account balance. It looked wrong.

A: So you're printing off the statement of your account? Are there a lot of transactions?

B: Yes. That's why it's taking so long. I use debit a lot. I should start carrying cash.

A: That's the problem with debit. You have no idea how much money you're spending.

B: As I read this, I recognize every transaction. I had no idea how much money I spend.

中譯

A: 你在裡面待了好久，讓我開始擔心起來。

B: 對不起。我提了一些錢出來，但是帳戶餘額好像不太對。

A: 所以你在列印帳戶交易明細是嗎？有很多筆交易嗎？

B: 沒錯，所以才要那麼久。我簽帳太多次，應該開始帶點現金在身上才好。

A: 簽帳的確有這個問題，你不知道自己花了多少錢。

B: 明細表上每一筆交易我都認得，但是不曉得總共花了多少錢。

Useful phrases and idioms
有用的片語和慣用語

Deal with 應付，處理

to handle; to manage a situation

例 She's having a hard time dealing with her boss.

她很難搞定她老闆。

All done 完成，解決

completed

例 The bank deposit is all done now.
銀行存款的事都解決了。

Tons 很多

a lot

例 I have tons of money.
我有很多錢。

Such a hurry 匆忙

to be rushed

例 You shouldn't be in such a hurry to close your account.
你不應急著把帳戶關閉。

Vocabulary 字彙

straightforward	*adj.*	簡單的
transfer	*v.*	轉讓
watchful	*adj.*	注意的
surroundings	*n.*	環境
repair	*v.*	修理
human	*n.*	人
press	*v.*	按
piece	*n.*	一張

portion	*n.*	（一）部分
statement	*n.*	帳單
receipt	*n.*	交易明細表
waste	*n.*	浪費
compare	*v.*	比較
double check		覆檢
arrogant	*adj.*	自大的
absolutely	*adv.*	絕對地
happen	*v.*	發生
follow	*v.*	遵循
prompt	*n.*	提示
recognize	*v.*	認得

Unit 3

When Things Go Wrong
發生問題時

MP3-10

Sometimes things go wrong at the ATM. The machine does not give a bank card back or the wrong amount is punched in for a deposit. Sometimes the ATM does not give the proper amount of money during a withdrawal. If the bank is open all of these things can be reported immediately. If not it is important to contact the bank as quickly as possible the next day.

提示　　有時自動櫃員機會發生問題。可能是金融卡沒有吐回來或是按錯存款數目之類，有時候提款時自動櫃員機會吐錯鈔票。如果銀行還開著，一切問題都可以立刻反應給他們；如果關了，隔天要儘快與銀行聯繫，這點很重要。

Conversation　1

A: What's the matter? Isn't the ATM working?

B: A sign just came up on the screen. It says "temporarily out of service".

A: So go inside. Go through the teller.

B: I can't. The bank closed two minutes ago. I tried the door and it's locked.

A: Of all the rotten luck. I can't believe this. What else could go wrong?

B: I'll tell you what. The bank machine just ate my card. It won't give it back.

中譯

A: 怎麼了，自動櫃員機壞了嗎？

B: 螢幕上剛顯示「暫停服務」。

A: 那去銀行裡面找櫃臺人員辦理吧。

B: 沒用，銀行兩分鐘前關門了。我有試著把門拉開，結果鎖住了。

A: 真不敢相信會那麼倒楣，不會再背下去了吧？。

B: 我跟你說還有更衰的事。機器剛吃了我的卡，沒有吐回來給我。

Conversation 2

A: What's the matter? Take your money and let's go. We're already five minutes late.

B: I can't remember my PIN number. I'm drawing a complete blank.

A: What do you mean you can't remember your PIN? You use it all the time.

B: I know. Isn't that crazy?

A: Move over. I'll take some money out so we can get going. We'll deal with this later.

B: No wait. It's coming to me. I think I know it. Let me try.

中譯

A: 怎麼了？趕快提款走人，我們已經遲到五分鐘了。

B: 我想不起密碼，腦中一片空白。

A: 不記得密碼是什麼意思？你不是還在用嗎？

B: 我知道。很誇張對吧？

A: 閃開，我先領一些錢出來趕快走人了。密碼的事晚點再說。

B: 不，等一下，我想起來了。大概是這個號碼，試試看就

知道。

Conversation 3

A: Do you think I can take money out from this bank?

B: Is it your bank?

A: Yes, but it's not my branch. My branch is downtown.

B: I'm sure they'll let you take out money. They might want to see some ID.

A: I don't have my wallet with me. I just have my bank card.

B: Can't you just use the bank machine?

中譯

A: 你覺得這家銀行可以讓我領錢嗎？

B: 是你的開戶銀行嗎？

A: 是的，不過不是我那家分行；我那一家在市中心區。

B: 我確定你可以在這裡領錢，只不過可能需要看一些身份證明。

A: 我沒有帶錢包，只有帶金融卡。

B: 那用提款機領不就好了？

Conversation 4

A: I can only take out up to $500 a day out of the bank machine. I need $600.

B: Did you go to the teller?

A: Yes but he wants to see some ID and I don't have it on me.

B: The guy that has the painting you want to buy. Would he take a cheque for it?

A: He said he'd only take cash because people have

bounced checks with him before.

B: He can phone your bank. They can verify that you have that money in your account.

中譯

A: 我一天只能從提款機領五百塊，可是我需要六百塊。

B: 你有去找櫃臺人員嗎？

A: 有，可是他要看身份證明，我什麼都沒帶。

B: 你要向他買畫的那個人願意收支票嗎？

A: 他說他只收現金，因為以前有人付他支票結果跳票了。

B: 他可以打電話給你的銀行，銀行會跟他證實你帳戶裡有錢。

Conversation 5

A: Can you see the screen? It says "temporarily out of service". What does that mean?

B: It says that when the bank people are taking out deposits and restocking the money.

A: What a pain. How long do I have to wait?

B: This happens everyday at the same time. It usually takes about twenty minutes.

A: Twenty minutes! I don't have twenty minutes. What a hassle. What will I do?

B: Why don't you just go through a teller? The line isn't very long.

中譯

A: 你看，螢幕上出現「暫停服務」，那是什麼意思？

B: 意思是說銀行裡的人正在把客戶的存款拿出來，順便補足機器裡面的錢。

A: 真討厭，那我要等多久？

B: 每天這個時間都會暫停，通常要過二十分鐘才會恢復正常。

A: 二十分鐘！我可等不了二十分鐘。麻煩死了，該怎麼辦

才好？

為什麼不直接去找櫃臺人員辦理？排隊的人又不多。

Conversation 6

A: I don't understand what's happening here. I think I need to go get somebody.

B: What's the matter? Did the machine eat your card?

A: It says 'invalid PIN' on the screen but I know I'm using the right PIN number.

B: That's weird. Are you sure you're keying your PIN in correctly?

A: Yes. I'm positive. This has never happened to me before.

B: Is your card really old or bent up? Is the strip worn out? Maybe that's the problem.

中譯

A: 我不知道發生了什麼事。我想應該找人來看看。

B: 怎麼了？機器吃了你的卡嗎？

A: 螢幕上出現「密碼無效」，可是我知道密碼沒錯。

B: 真奇怪。你確定輸入的密碼正確嗎？

A: 對，我確定。以前沒有發生過這種事。

B: 你的卡有很舊或折到嗎？還是磁條磨損了？問題可能出在這些地方。

Conversation 7

A: The bank machine just shortchanged me. I should have got two hundred dollars.

B: How much did it give you?

A: It only gave me a hundred and eighty.

B: It shorted you a twenty. It probably got stuck inside. Lucky for you the bank is open.

A: Do you think the bank tellers can help me?

B: Of course they can. They'll be able to sort this out real quick.

中譯

> A: 自動櫃員機少給我錢，我應該拿到兩百塊才對。
>
> B: 機器吐多少給你？
>
> A: 它只給我一百八十塊。
>
> B: 那少給了二十塊，可能卡在裡面。好在銀行還開著。
>
> A: 你覺得銀行櫃臺人員可以幫我嗎？
>
> B: 當然可以啊。問題很快就會解決了。

Conversation 8

A: Okay I'm done. No, wait a minute. Where's my receipt? It didn't give me a receipt.

B: So what? We're late. We need to get going. Don't worry about it.

A: No, this is one of the machines that always automatically prints you a receipt.

B: So what's your point? Who cares about a dumb little receipt anyways? Let's go.

A: No. I want my receipt. It's the only proof I have of this transaction. I'll tell a teller.

B: We don't have time for this. I'll be in the car. Don't take too long okay?

中譯

> A: 好了，搞定了。不，等一下。交易明細表呢？機器沒有給我交易明細表。
>
> B: 那又怎麼樣？我們已經遲到，要趕快走才行，不要管它了。
>
> A: 不能不管，機器每次都會自動把交易明細表印出來給你。
>
> B: 那你的意思是？小小一張不管用的明細表有什麼好在意

A: 不行，我要拿到交易明細表才行，那是這次交易的唯一證明。我要去告訴櫃臺人員。

B: 沒有時間了啦。我先去車裡等你，不要太久好嗎？

Useful phrases and idioms
有用的片語和慣用語

運氣真差

what bad luck

例 Of all the rotten luck, I had to lock my keys in my car.

真倒楣，我把車子反鎖了。

Ate my card 吃卡

did not return my care to me; kept it

例 This bank machine just ate my bank card.

這家銀行的機器剛把我的金融卡吃掉了。

Drawing a complete blank 完全想不起來

can't remember at all

例 I'm drawing a complete blank as to what his name is.

我完全想不起來他叫什麼名字。

Guy 人，傢伙

fellow or person "male"

例 He seems like a very nice guy.

他看起來人很好。

What a hassle 真是麻煩

this is a big problem

例 What a hassle not to be able to use the ATM.
自動提款機不能用真是麻煩。

Lucky for you 好在，很幸運

it's fortunate that

例 Lucky for you I have an opening to see our Loans Officer today.
好在我今天有機會見到貸款部主任。

Sort it out 解決

fix it; solve the problem

例 The Investment Manager will be happy to sort that out for you.
基金經理人很樂意為你解決這項問題。

Real quick 很快

fast

例 I'm with a customer, but someone will be with you real quick.
我現在有客戶在談，很快有人會跟你接洽。

Dumb 愚笨的

stupid

例 Canceling your credit card was a dumb thing to do.
取消信用卡是件蠢事。

Vocabulary 字彙

proper	adj.	適當的
report	v.	報知
contact	n.	接觸
possible	adj.	可能的
temporarily	adv.	暫時地
wallet	n.	皮夾
painting	n.	畫
verify	v.	證實
restock	v.	補足
invalid	adj.	無效的
weird	adj.	奇怪的
shortchange	v.	少給
stuck	adj.	卡住
print	v.	印

TELEPHONE BANKING
電話銀行

MP3-11

Unit 1

Getting Set Up
申請

Telephone banking is a great way to transfer money and check account balances. It can also be used to pay some bills and hear a list of most recent transactions. A customer doesn't even have to leave home to do it. It is also a very secure way to conduct these transactions. Always keep your telephone access code and bank card number confidential.

提示　用電話銀行來轉帳和查詢帳戶餘額是個很棒的方法，它也可用來繳款或查詢最近交易情況。客戶不用出門即可完成所有的事。它同時也是處理上述交易一項非常安全的方法。語音密碼和金融卡號碼都是機密資料，千萬不要隨便洩露出去。

Conversation 1

A: I need to run some errands. You're not doing anything. Why don't you come?

B: I don't know. It's pretty cold outside. Where do you want to go?

A: I need to go to the bank first. I want to register for telephone banking.

B: Are you sure you need to go to the bank for that? I think you can do that from home.

A: How do I register for telephone banking from home?

B: You call the telephone banking phone number and it will prompt you as to what you do.

中譯

A: 我要出門辦些雜事。你反正沒事，要不要一起走？

B: 不知道耶，外面很冷。你要去哪裡？

A: 我要先跑一趟銀行，因為我想申請電話銀行功能。

B: 你確定要去銀行才能申請？我想在家申請就可以了。

A: 在家要怎麼申請電話銀行啊？

B: 撥打電話銀行的號碼，然後跟著指示做就對了。

Conversation 2

A: Good afternoon. How can I help you today?

B: I would like to register for telephone banking please.

A: Okay. I will give you this card. It has the telephone banking phone number on it.

B: Thanks. So do I actually register over the phone?

A: Call the number. It will ask you if you're a first time user. It will tell you what to do.

B: Okay. It sounds easy. Thanks for your help.

中譯

A: 午安。需要什麼服務嗎？

B: 我想申請電話銀行。

A: 好的。這張卡給你，上面有電話銀行的號碼。

B: 謝謝。所以我要在電話上實際申請囉？

A: 打電話後，銀行會問你是否為新用戶，然後會告訴你接下來怎麼做。

B: 好的，聽起來不難。謝謝你的幫忙。

Conversation 3

A: Have you seen my bank card?

B: No. Where did you leave it last?

A: I thought I threw it on the coffee table when I got home last night.

B: Wait a minute. I just saw it. Where did I see it? Oh right. It's on the kitchen table.

A: You were right. Thanks. Have you seen that little telephone banking card I carry?

B: The one with the telephone banking phone number on it? No. Why do you need it?

中譯

A: 你有看到我的金融卡嗎？

B: 沒。上次放哪？

A: 好像昨晚回家時放咖啡桌上。

B: 等一下，我剛有看到。在哪呢？啊，對了，在廚房餐桌上。

A: 對耶，謝了。有看到我帶回來那一張電話銀行的小卡片嗎？

B: 上面有電話銀行號碼那張嗎？沒看到耶。找那張卡片幹嘛？

Conversation 4

A: It's so cold out. I'm so tired. I don't want to go outside.

B: Then stay in. Why do you need to go out?

A: I have to go shopping. I have to go to the bank and transfer money out of my savings.

B: You don't have to go to the bank to transfer money and you can shop from home.

A: How do I do that? What are you talking about?

B: Transfer the money out of your savings by phone. Do your shopping online.

中譯

> A: 外面好冷，人又好累，實在不想出門。
>
> B: 那就待在家啊，為什麼要出門？
>
> A: 我要去買東西，還要去銀行轉帳。
>
> B: 轉帳不用去銀行，在家也可以買東西。
>
> A: 要怎麼弄？你在說什麼？
>
> B: 用電話轉帳，再去線上購物。

Conversation 5

A: I wonder if the mortgage payment has come out of our account yet.

B: I don't know. We'll have to wait for our bank statement to come.

A: No we don't. We can check today if we want to see before the statement comes.

B: Of course. How could I forget? I'll get my coat. We'll check at the ATM.

A: We don't even have to leave the house. We can check through telephone banking.

B: I haven't been doing any banking by telephone. You'll have to show me how.

中譯

> A: 不知道房屋貸款從帳戶中扣款了沒？
>
> B: 不知道耶，看來要等銀行對帳單來才會曉得。
>
> A: 不用。如果要在對帳單來之前知道情況，今天就可以查。
>
> B: 當然，我居然忘了。我去拿外套，走，去自動櫃員機查查看。
>
> A: 我們連出門都不用，用電話銀行就可以查了。
>
> B: 我沒有用過電話銀行，你要教一下。

Conversation 6

A: Are you busy? I need you to help me for a second. Come sit beside me.

B: What are you doing? What do you need help with?

A: I'm trying out this telephone banking for the first time.

B: Okay. Call the number on the telephone banking card. Are you set up already?

A: Yes. I dialed that number. Now I'm supposed to enter my bank account number.

B: Yes. Go ahead and do that. After that enter your password.

中譯

A: 你在忙嗎?我需要幫一下忙,進來坐我旁邊。

B: 你在幹嘛?要幫什麼忙?

A: 我第一次試用電話銀行。

B: 好。先打電話銀行卡片上的號碼。你有註冊了吧?

A: 有,我打了那個號碼,現在應該輸入銀行帳號對吧?

B: 對。直接輸入,然後再按密碼。

Conversation 7

A: Good afternoon, Mrs. Miller. What can I do for you today?

B: Hi. I heard some friends talking about telephone banking. Can you tell me about it?

A: It's really easy to do and you won't have to come in to the bank as much.

B: Sounds good. Does it cost any money to sign up?

A: Not at all. Registering for telephone banking is free of charge.

B: All right. Tell me more. How do I register?

中譯

A: 午安,米勒太太。需要什麼服務嗎?

B: 嗨。我有聽朋友提到什麼電話銀行,請問那是什麼?

A: 很簡單，辦好後就不用常常跑銀行了。

聽起來不錯。申請要錢嗎？

A: 完全不用。申請電話銀行是免費的。

好，那我要多了解一點。接下來要怎麼申請？

Conversation 8

A: I don't understand. How do you enter the commands? Do you tell it what to do?

No. It tells you to press a number on the phone keypad to select a specific option.

A: Like when you phone a store and you press one for the store hours.

It's really very simple. It lists options and you just hit the numbers on the phone.

A: I think I can handle that. I'll have to memorize the phone number though.

That's a good idea. That way you don't have to carry that little card around with you.

中譯

A: 我不懂，要怎麼輸入指令？跟它講就好了嗎？

不是啦，它會叫你按電話鍵盤上的數字來選擇特定選項。

A: 就像你打電話給一家店的時候，按一下就可以聽到營業時間。

很簡單啦。它會把選項列出來，你只要按電話上的數字就好了。

A: 我想應該沒問題了。不過我要記住電話號碼才行。

好主意，這樣你就不用把那張小卡片一直帶在身上了。

Useful phrases and idioms
有用的片語和慣用語

Pretty 很

very

例 I was pretty bored working at the bank.

我在銀行工作很無聊。

How could I forget 我居然忘了

I can't believe that I forgot

例 How could I forget that you were coming home early?

我居然忘了你今天會提早回家。

Vocabulary 字彙

recent	*adj.*	最近的
secure	*adj.*	安全的
conduct	*v.*	處理
access code		語音密碼
confidential	*adj.*	機密的
errand	*n.*	雜事
register	*v.*	登記
mortgage	*n.*	房屋貸款
busy	*adj.*	忙的
dial	*v.*	撥（電話）號碼
suppose	*v.*	應該
command	*n.*	指令
specific	*adj.*	特定的
memorize	*v.*	記住

Unit 2

Different Transactions
不同的交易

MP3-12

Deposits and withdrawals of course must still be made in person at the bank. They can be done through the teller or through the ATM. A list of recent transactions cannot be physically printed during telephone banking. It can only be listened to. If a customer wants a hard copy record they would have to get it from a teller or from the ATM.

提示　存提款當然得親自到銀行辦理才行，可以找櫃臺人員或用自動櫃員機辦理。電話銀行無法實際列印最近的交易明細，只能用聽的；如果客戶需要列印記錄單，必須親洽櫃臺人員或利用自動櫃員機才行。

Conversation 1

A: What are you doing? I need the phone. Give me the phone.

B: I'm doing some banking. Be quiet for a minute while I finish up.

A: Well aren't you important. What kind of banking are you doing?

B: I'm getting some account information. Didn't I just tell you to be quiet?

A: You can't tell me to be quiet. What kind of account information?

B: I just found out my account balances and now I'm

listening to my recent transactions.

中譯

A: 你在幹嘛？我要打電話，電話給我。

B: 我在處理一些銀行帳戶的事，等會就好，不要吵。

A: 很重要嗎？你在查銀行帳戶什麼？

B: 在查詢帳戶資料，不是叫你不要吵嗎？

A: 幹嘛叫我不要吵，到底是什麼資料啦？

B: 我剛查詢帳戶餘額，現在在聽最近的交易明細。

Conversation 2

A: Do you know where the phone is? I can't find it.

B: It's over here on the bed. I must have forgotten to put it back in its cradle.

A: Can you pass it to me please? Thanks. I'll hang it up when I'm done.

B: Who are you calling?

A: I'm going to pre-register my phone bill so that I can pay it from my account by phone.

B: I've never paid a bill by phone before. I never have any money in my account.

中譯

A: 你曉得電話放哪嗎？我找不到。

B: 在床這裡，一定是我忘了把它放回架子上。

A: 拿給我好嗎？謝謝。我打完會放回去。

B: 你要打給誰？

A: 我要先做電話帳單預先約定，才可以用電話從帳戶中扣款。

B: 我以前沒用電話繳過款。帳戶裡一直都沒有錢。

Conversation 3

A: Oh no! We're going to be in such trouble.

B: What's the matter? What did you do?

A: I didn't do anything. It's you who screwed up. This is all your fault.

B: Me! What did I do?

A: It's what you didn't do. You didn't pay the phone bill.

B: Relax. I pre-registered that bill last month. I'll pay it right now over the phone.

中譯

A: 啊，天啊！這下麻煩大了。

B: 怎麼了？你幹了什麼好事？

A: 我什麼都沒做，是你把事情搞砸了。都是你的錯。

B: 我！我做了什麼？

A: 就是什麼都沒做才糟糕，你沒有繳電話費啦。

不要緊張。我上個月有預先約定繳帳單，現在用電話繳就可以了。

Conversation 4

A: Honey, our house insurance is coming out tomorrow. We don't have any money.

B: That's okay. I got paid yesterday. I'll transfer money into our joint account.

A: But the bank is closed. That payment might come out as early as midnight tonight.

B: Relax. I'm set up for telephone banking. I'll transfer the money from my checking.

A: I have heard other people talking about banking by phone. It sounds so easy.

B: It is. We should get you set up for it. Let me take care of that transfer of funds first.

A: 親愛的，我們的房屋保險明天到期，可是已經沒錢了。

B: 放心，我昨天領薪水了，我再把錢轉入我們的聯名帳戶。

A: 可是銀行關了，那筆款項必須趕在今晚十二點以前入帳才行。

B: 不要緊張，我有申請電話銀行。我會從支票帳戶裡把錢轉過去。

A: 我有聽別人提過電話銀行，聽起來蠻容易的。

B: 的確。你也該申請一下，不過現在先處理轉帳的事。

Conversation 5

A: I need to borrow some money.

B: I don't know if I have any to lend you. Pass me the phone.

A: You don't have any cash on you?

B: No. I'll check my account. If I have some money I'll send it to our joint account.

A: That doesn't do me any good. I'm taking my sister out for supper tonight.

B: You can transfer it to your personal account and go to the ATM on the way to supper.

A: 我要借點錢。

B: 我不知道有沒有錢可以借你。電話給我。

A: 你身上一點現金都沒有？

B: 沒有。我查一下帳戶，如果還有錢，再把它轉入我們的聯名帳戶。

A: 那樣派不上用場啊，我今晚要帶我妹出去吃晚飯。

B: 你可以把錢轉入你的私人帳戶，路上再去自動櫃員機領出來吃晚飯。

Conversation 6

A: Has our mortgage payment come out yet?

B: I don't know. Why don't you call and see?

A: Good idea. Hand me the phone please.

B: Here you go. Do you know the number?

A: Yes. I have it memorized. I'll call and get a list of recent transactions.

B: It's nice not having to go out to the bank and check. It's too cold and dark out.

中譯

A: 我們的房屋貸款到期了嗎？

B: 我不知道，不如打電話問問看。

A: 好主意。請把電話拿給我。

B: 拿去。知道打幾號嗎？

A: 知道，我有背起來。我打去查詢一下最近的交易記錄。

B: 外面又冷又黑，不用親自去銀行查詢真是方便。

Conversation 7

A: This bill has been coming out of my account.

B: Yes I know. Why do you mention it?

A: Well, now I also have the cable bill coming out of my account.

B: That's true. It's not really fair to have both come out of your account.

A: I think we should get this bill to come out of your account from now on.

B: That's easy enough to change. Hand me the phone. I'll take care of it right now.

中譯

A: 這張帳單已經從我帳戶中扣款了。

B: 我知道啊,幹嘛提這件事?

A: 這個嘛,因為有線電視帳單也從我帳戶中扣款了。

B: 對耶,兩張帳單都從你帳戶中扣款的確不太公平。

A: 我想從現在開始,這張帳單應該從你帳戶中扣款才對。

B: 要變更很簡單,電話給我,我現在立刻處理。

Useful phrases and idioms
有用的片語和慣用語

Relax 別緊張

don't worry

例 Relax, it's just money.

別緊張,不過是錢嘛。

Vocabulary 字彙

physically	*adv.*	實際上
hard copy record		列印記錄
cradle	*n.*	架子
screw up		搞砸
insurance	*n.*	保險
borrow	*v.*	借
lend	*v.*	把…借給
cable bill		有線電視帳單

Unit 3

That's not Right
這樣不對

MP3-13

Just like anything else, banking by telephone is not **perfect**. Things can go wrong. It's important to write down the time and date of the call and what went wrong. Make sure to also write down which account the **error** was in. It's important to contact your branch as soon as possible.

提示　和其他事情一樣，電話銀行並不是完美的，還是會有出錯的時候。把打電話的時間和日期，以及哪裡出錯寫下來很重要。記得也要把出錯的帳號寫下來。務必儘快與你的分行聯絡。

Conversation 1

A: That's funny. I think something's wrong.

B: What's funny? What's wrong?

A: I don't remember having so much money in my account. Something's really wrong.

B: You have more money? Maybe you didn't spend as much this month.

A: This isn't a little more money than usual. I have thousands of dollars more than usual.

B: Really? Thousands? Have I told you lately how much I love you?

中譯

A:　真奇怪，我覺得不太對勁。

B: 什麼事很奇怪？怎麼了？

A: 我不記得帳戶裡有那麼多錢，一定哪裡弄錯了。

B: 錢變多了嗎？或許你這個月錢花得比較少。

A: 這不是一筆平常的小數目，裡面多了好幾千塊。

B: 真的嗎？好幾千塊？最近有告訴你我有多愛你嗎！

Conversation 2

A: What's the matter? You look worried. Who are you calling?

B: I'm not calling anyone. I'm just listening to my account balance.

A: Is the news that bad? Don't worry about it. You get paid tomorrow.

B: No I got paid yesterday. At least I was supposed to. But I have a negative balance.

A: What does that mean? Doesn't a negative balance mean that you're in overdraft?

B: Yes. That's absurd. It's not possible. I don't even have overdraft.

中譯

A: 怎麼了？一付心事重重的樣子，打給誰啊？

B: 我沒有打給誰，只是在聽我的帳戶餘額。

A: 情況很糟嗎？不要擔心，明天就領錢了。

B: 不，我昨天已經領了，至少昨天錢應該進來了。可是帳戶裡的餘額居然是負的。

A: 什麼意思？負的餘額代表你透支了不是嗎？

B: 對啊，真是荒謬。怎麼可能，我連透支服務都沒申請。

Conversation 3

A: Hon, can you come here for a minute? Can I get you to do something for me?

B: What do you need? You're not going to ask me

for another foot massage are you?

A: No I'm serious. I want you to listen to the list of my most recent transactions.

B: Okay. I'm listening. That's odd. Is that right? It can't be.

A: Did you hear what I heard? That there's been twenty debit transactions today alone?

B: You didn't even leave the house today. We're both home sick with the flu.

中譯

A: 親愛的,可以過來一下嗎?幫我做一件事好不好?

B: 需要什麼嗎?不會是要我幫你按摩另一隻腳吧?

A: 我是說真的啦。你幫我聽一下最近的交易記錄。

B: 好,我幫你聽。真奇怪,有沒有搞錯,怎麼可能。

A: 聽到我剛聽的嗎?光今天一天就有二十筆簽帳交易。

B: 你今天連出門都沒有啊。我們兩個都因為感染流行性感冒待在家裡耶。

Conversation 4

A: Good afternoon. What can I do for you today?

B: I've been having some problems with my telephone banking.

A: What kind of problems have you been having?

B: It tells me that I don't have an account with North West Bank.

A: I know you have an account here. You come in quite often.

B: I know I have an account here too. It's my telephone that doesn't seem to think so.

中譯

A: 午安。需要什麼服務嗎？

B: 我的電話銀行有點問題。

A: 哪一方面的問題呢？

B: 它告訴我我沒有西北銀行的帳號。

A: 我曉得你有這裡的帳號，你常來。

B: 我也知道我有這裡的帳號，可是我的電話銀行好像不這麼認為。

Conversation 5

A: Hi there. How can I help you today?

B: I was checking my bank balance by phone last night. It tells me I have no money.

A: I'll just check your account balance in our computer system.

B: I got paid yesterday so I should have lots of money in there.

A: You did have an automatic deposit yesterday. Your account balance is $3700.00.

B: The funny thing is I phoned again this morning and it still said zero dollars.

中譯

A: 你好，需要什麼服務嗎？

B: 我昨晚用電話查詢我的銀行帳戶餘額，結果它告訴我裡面沒有錢。

A: 我幫你用我們的電腦系統查詢你的帳戶餘額看看。

B: 我昨天領薪水，所以應該多了很多錢在裡面才對。

A: 你昨天的確有一筆錢自動存進來，帳戶餘額是 $3700.00。

B: 奇怪的是，我今天早上又打了一次電話，它還是告訴我餘額是零。

Conversation 6

A: I don't know about this telephone banking. I just can't get used to it.

What's wrong with it? I like it. I like it a lot.

A: I can't seem to get the information I want. It's like I'm pushing the wrong buttons.

Maybe you are. Call the number and then give me the phone. I'll listen.

A: Okay. Find out what my account balance is for my savings account.

Maybe it's aliens. Do you have a metal plate in your head?

中譯

A: 我被電話銀行弄昏了啦，就是用不慣。

怎麼了？我很喜歡耶，愛死它了。

A: 我好像得不到我要的資訊，大概按錯鍵了。

可能是。打通後把電話給我，我來聽。

A: 好。請幫我問我存款帳戶餘額有多少。

我大概遇到外星人了，你腦袋裡是不是有金屬板？

Conversation 7

A: This stupid phone. The phone's not working. Why isn't the phone working?

B: Well the phone hasn't been in its cradle all day. That battery is probably dead.

A: Oh great. Now the phone needs to recharge. I'm going to have to go to the bank.

B: Why? Can't you wait until later on tonight? It should be recharged by then.

A: I just had a great idea. Let me use your cell

phone. I'll do my banking from that.

B: My cell phone's busted. I dropped it in the toilet at Tammy's party last night.

中譯

A: 什麼爛電話，居然不能用，為什麼不能用呢？

B: 嗯，電話一整天都沒放回架子上，大概是電池沒電了。

A: 啊，這下可好了。電話現在需要充電，那我只好跑一趟銀行。

B: 為什麼？不能等到晚上嗎？那時應該充好電了。

A: 我剛想到一個好點子，不如把你的手機借我一下，我要打給電話銀行。

B: 我手機昨晚在泰咪派對上掉到馬桶裡，現在不能用了。

Conversation 8

A: I need to tell you something. You won't be very happy with me.

B: What's wrong, sweetheart? Don't worry. You can tell me anything.

A: The phone has been **disconnected**. I haven't paid the phone bill in three months.

B: What? I can't believe you. Why? Why didn't you pay it?

A: It was supposed to be pre-registered. I was supposed to be able to pay it by phone.

B: So what's your **excuse**? Why didn't you? I'm moving out.

中譯

A: 有件事我要跟你說，你可能會不太高興。

B: 怎麼了，甜心？不要擔心，你什麼事都可以告訴我。

A: 電話被斷線了，因為我三個月沒交電話費。

B: 什麼？簡直不敢相信。為什麼？為什麼你不去繳費？

A: 應該有預先申請電話繳費，照理說可以用電話繳。

那麼你的理由是甚麼？為什麼不去繳？我要搬出去了。

Useful phrases and idioms
有用的片語和慣用語

Busted 壞了

broken

例 This pen is busted.
這支筆壞掉了。

Vocabulary 字彙

perfect	*adj.*	完美的
error	*n.*	錯誤
negative	*adj.*	負的
absurd	*adj.*	荒謬的
massage	*n.*	按摩
flu	*n.*	流行　感冒
system	*n.*	系統
alien	*n.*	外星人
plate	*n.*	薄板
battery	*n.*	電池
recharge	*v.*	再充電
cell phone		手機
disconnect	*v.*	切斷（電話）
excuse	*n.*	理由

Chapter 5

BANKING ONLINE
網路銀行

Unit 1

Making it Work
開始使用

MP3-14

If you are set up for telephone banking you are also set up for banking online. Your telephone access code, which is also called a password, is what you use to access your accounts through the Internet. Some banks don't charge anything for online banking. That's why it is becoming more and more **popular**.

提示　如果你有申請電話銀行，等於也同時申請了網路銀行。你的電話語音密碼也是線上用來登入帳戶的密碼。有些銀行的網路銀行並不收費，所以才會越來越普遍。

Conversation 1

A: This Internet banking thing is so **cool**. I'm so glad I can do banking online.

B: I haven't tried it. I'm too worried about **hackers** getting my **banking information**.

A: I don't think you have to worry anymore. The banks have good **firewalls**.

B: Do you really think my banking information is safe?

A: Do you have that much money in your account that someone would want to steal it?

B: I'm almost always **broke**. By the way, do you have twenty bucks you can lend me?

中譯

A: 網路銀行這種東西太酷了，真高興有網路銀行可以用。

B: 我沒試過耶。我很擔心駭客會盜取我的帳戶資料。

A: 我覺得沒什麼好擔心的，銀行的防火牆功能都很棒。

B: 你真的覺得帳戶資料安全嗎？

A: 你帳戶裡的錢有多到有人想去偷嗎？

B: 我幾乎老是處於破產邊緣。對了，有二十塊可以借一下嗎？

Conversation 2

A: I don't want you doing any of your banking online, son. It's too dangerous.

B: I don't have much money in my account, Dad. I'm not worth a hacker's time.

A: It's not your money I worry about. Haven't you heard of identity theft?

B: Dad, I heard that it's information on paper that you should worry about.

A: That's not good. My bank statement comes in the mail each month.

B: Maybe you should sign up for online banking, Dad. It's less dangerous.

中譯

A: 兒子，不要用網路銀行好嗎？太危險了。

B: 爸，我帳戶裡沒那麼多錢啦，不值得駭客費神入侵。

A: 我不是擔心你的錢，難道你沒聽過身份盜用嗎？

B: 爸，我想書面資料才是你該擔心的。

A: 沒錯，我的對帳單銀行每個月都用寄的，的確不太好。

B: 或許你該申請網路銀行啦，爸。比較沒有那麼危險。

Conversation 3

A: Hi there. I was wondering if you could help me.

How do I go about banking online?

B: I have a brochure that you can read. It gives you our website address as well.

A: Will it explain how I do it? Does it walk me through it?

B: Everything you need to know is in the brochure. It's simple and straightforward.

A: Have you tried banking by computer yourself? Do you like it?

B: Sometimes you need to speak to someone in person, but for most things it's great.

中譯

A: 你好，可以請教一下網路銀行要怎麼用嗎？

B: 這裡有一本小冊子可以看，裡面也有我們的網址。

A: 裡面有解釋如何使用嗎？有逐步說明嗎？

B: 一切相關資訊都在小冊子裡面，簡單易懂。

A: 你自己有用電腦試過網路銀行嗎？還喜歡嗎？

B: 有時候當面洽談有其必要，但大體而言，網路銀行很不錯。

Conversation 4

A: Good morning. Can I help you?

B: Yes, please. I would like to get set up so I can do my banking on the computer.

A: Okay. Are you already set up for telephone banking?

B: No. Do I have to learn how to do that first?

A: You'll be set up for both at the same time. Which one you want to use is up to you.

B: Okay. That sounds good. Who knows? Maybe I'll

use both.

中譯

A: 早安。需要什麼服務嗎？

是的。我想申請可以在電腦上使用的網路銀行。

A: 好的。你有申請過電話銀行了嗎？

還沒。要先申請才行嗎？

A: 兩個可以同時申請，你高興用哪一個都可以。

好啊，聽起來蠻不錯的。誰知道？搞不好我兩個都用得到。

Conversation 5

A: Honey, what is the website address for our bank?

I don't know it by heart. Look on that little telephone banking card.

A: Why would I look on that?

Because it has the phone number for telephone banking and the website for online.

A: Oh. I never noticed before. But I don't know where that little card is.

Well our bank is North West Bank. Maybe just do a key word search of the name.

中譯

A: 親愛的，我們的銀行網址是什麼？

B: 我沒有記起來，看一下那張電話銀行小卡片。

A: 看它幹嘛？

B: 因為它上面有電話銀行的電話號碼和網路銀行網址。

A: 哦，我從來沒有注意到。可是我不知道那張小卡片跑哪去了。

B: 好吧，我們的銀行是西北銀行，用關鍵字搜尋名字看看。

Conversation 6

A: You've been sitting in here for a long time. What

are you doing?

B: I'm thinking. I'm sitting here trying to think.

A: No. I mean what are you doing on the computer?

B: This is the bank's website. I'm trying to sign in but I don't know my password.

A: So you're trying to think of your password?

B: I'm trying to think what it would be. I have no idea. Do you know what it is?

中譯

A: 你在這坐好久了耶,在幹嘛?

B: 我在想東西。我坐在這裡試著想一些東西。

A: 不是啦,我意思是說你用電腦在做什麼?

B: 這是銀行網站,我想要登入,但不知道我的密碼。

A: 所以你在想你的密碼囉?

B: 我想要想出密碼到底是什麼,但腦袋一片空白,你知道密碼是什麼嗎?

Conversation 7

A: Let me get this straight. I type in my account number here. Then my password here?

B: Yes. You've got it. That's all there is to it.

A: Well, that's not all there is to it. I have to figure out what to do next.

B: But it's just like telephone banking or using the ATM. You see choices on the screen.

A: And then all I do is click on the option I want, right?

B: Exactly. It's not that hard. Just think of it as an ATM screen in your own home.

中譯

A: 讓我弄清楚。在這裡輸入帳號，然後在這裡輸入密碼嗎？

B: 是的，沒錯。這樣就可以了。

A: 哪裡是，這樣還不夠啦。我想要弄清楚接下來怎麼做。

B: 它就像電話銀行，或是自動櫃員機一樣，可以在螢幕上看到不同的選項。

A: 我只要按下我要的選項就可以了，對吧？

B: 完全正確。沒那麼難的，把它想成一台自己家裡的自動櫃員機就好了。

Useful phrases and idioms
有用的片語和慣用語

Cool 酷

good

例 Banking by computer is cool.
用電腦處理銀行的事真酷。

Broke 破產

to be out of money; to not have money

例 I'm broke so can you please pay for the movie?
我破產了，可以請你幫我出電影錢嗎？

Let me get this straight 讓我搞清楚

Let me see if I understand this correctly.

例 Let me get this straight, you have no money at all?
讓我搞清楚，你什麼錢都沒了嗎？

Vocabulary 字彙

popular	*adj.*	普遍的
hacker	*n.*	駭客
banking information		帳戶資料
firewall	*n.*	防火牆
dangerous	*adj.*	危險
identity theft		身份盜用
notice	*v.*	注意
key word search		關鍵字搜尋
exactly	*adv.*	完全正確

Unit 2

Different Things to Do
不同的交易項目

MP3-15

The same transactions that can be done by phone can also be done by computer. Remember to sign out as soon as you are done your banking. If you are checking your accounts out in a public place, make sure no one can see your information by looking over your shoulder. Banking by computer is more environmentally friendly as less paper is used. That means fewer trees need to be cut down to make paper and envelopes.

提示　可以用電話完成的交易也都可以用電腦完成。網路銀行不用時記得登出。如果你在公開場合查詢帳戶資料，記得不要讓別人從背後看到你的資料。網路銀行較有環保概念，因為紙張用得少，意味著不用砍那麼多樹來製造紙張和信封。

Conversation 1

A: I want to see a list of my transactions. My statement doesn't come until Monday.

B: You can check by phone. Just do it through telephone banking.

A: I don't want to. I want to see a list. Hearing it isn't good enough.

B: I know. Why don't we try to access your account information online?

A: That's a great idea. Do you think we can figure out how to do it?

B: I bet you it's as easy as telephone banking. The website will probably prompt us.

中譯

A: 我要看交易明細，對帳單到禮拜一都還沒寄來。

B: 可以用電話查詢，利用電話銀行即可。

A: 不要啦，我想看到交易明細，聽說有點問題。

B: 我知道。不如去線上查詢帳戶資料看看？

A: 好主意，你覺得我們可以搞定嗎？

B: 一定和電話銀行一樣簡單。網站大概會提示操作步驟吧。

Conversation 2

A: Good morning. Can I help you?

B: Yes. I was wondering about banking by computer. Can I pay bills online?

A: Yes. You can pre-register a bill. Then you can pay it online each month.

B: That sounds handy and practical. How do I pre-register a bill?

A: Go to the banking website. Once you have signed in, you have it as an option.

B: Great. Then all I have to do is choose that option. That's easy. Thank you.

中譯

A: 早安。需要什麼服務嗎？

B: 是的，我想知道網路銀行的事，我可以線上繳款嗎？

A: 可以。你可以預先申請帳單，然後每個月即可線上繳款。

B: 聽起來既方便又實用。要怎樣預先申請帳單？

A: 去銀行網站登錄後，就會看到這個選項。

太好了，然後我只要選那個選項就可以對吧？真簡單，謝謝你。

Conversation 3

A: Honey, get your coat. It's time to go pay all the bills.

B: I'm not going any where.

A: What are you talking about? We need to go pay the bills.

B: No we don't. I already paid them.

A: When? You haven't been out of the house in three days.

B: I paid them online last night while you were out with your friends.

中譯

A: 親愛的，去拿外套，這些帳單不繳不行了。

B: 我哪裡都不去。

A: 你在說什麼？我們得去繳帳單才行。

B: 不用去，我已經繳過了。

A: 什麼時候繳的？你已經三天沒出門了。

B: 昨晚你和朋友出去時，我上網繳過了。

Conversation 4

A: Do you think we can look at our mortgage information on the bank website?

B: Probably. I haven't tried it before so I don't know. Let's go see.

A: Yes we can because our mortgage is at the bank we have our bank accounts at.

B: That's handy. Look at all the different things you can do.

A: Yes. There's even a listing of the bank's current interest rates for loans and accounts.

B: I'm not getting a very good interest on my savings account.

中譯

A: 你覺得銀行網站上查得到我們的房屋貸款資料嗎？

B: 應該可以。以前沒試過不知道，來試試看吧。

A: 可以耶，我們有在抵押銀行開戶，所以查得到。

B: 真方便。好多選項可以選哦。

A: 對啊。連銀行目前的貸款和帳戶利率都有列出來。

B: 我的存款帳戶利率好像不是那麼好耶。

Conversation 5

A: There's no money in our joint account. Where did it all go?

B: I transferred all of it into my personal account. Sorry. I forgot to mention that.

A: Why did you do that? That's our money. It's not all yours.

B: I had a surprise for you.

A: Oh goodie. I like surprises. So tell me. What is it?

B: I bought two tickets to Mexico...for me and my new boyfriend.

中譯

A: 我們的聯名帳戶沒錢了，都跑哪去了？

B: 我把所有的錢都轉到我的個人帳戶裡了。抱歉，忘了跟你提這件事。

A: 為什麼這麼做？那是我們的錢耶，不是你一個人的。

B: 我只是想給你一個驚喜。

A: 太棒了，我喜歡驚喜。那快告訴我是什麼？

我買了兩張到墨西哥的機票⋯替我和我新男朋友買的。

Conversation 6

A: This is really good. I'm worried that my credit card balance is unusually high.

B: So why are you on the computer? Are you going to check it out online?

A: That's right. It's so easy. I'll compare a list of recent transactions to my receipts.

B: You keep the receipt from every purchase you make? I didn't know that.

A: This is actually kind of fun. I feel like a detective. Who knows what I'll find out?

B: If there's a problem you're going to find it. I'd better confess. I used your card.

中譯

A: 太好了，我正在擔心我的刷卡金額高得不尋常。

B: 那你在電腦上幹嘛？要在線上檢查嗎？

A: 沒錯，很簡單。我要核對看看最近的交易明細和收據是否一致。

B: 你每次買東西都會留下收據？我怎麼都不知道。

A: 其實只是好玩啦，這樣感覺好像偵探一樣。誰知道我會發現什麼？

B: 有問題的話你一定會發現的。我最好先承認吧，我用了你的卡。

Useful phrases and idioms
有用的片語和慣用語

Oh goodie 太棒了

an exclamation of happiness

例　Oh goodie! I get to go home early.
　　太棒了！我得早點回去才行。

Kind of 有一點

a bit, a little

例　He's kind of hard to understand.
　　他有點讓人難以了解。

Vocabulary 字彙

environmentally	*adv.*	有關環境方面
practical	*adj.*	實用的
handy	*adj.*	便利的
mention	*v.*	提到
unusually	*adv.*	不尋常地
detective	*n.*	偵探
confess	*v.*	承認

Unit 3

Positives and Negatives
正反兩面

MP3-16

Nothing is perfect. Banking by computer is no different. The best way to bank is to use all methods. Visit the bank in person. It will keep you in touch with the people who work there. Use the ATM machine. Do some banking by phone and make some transactions online.

提示　　沒有一件事是完美的，網路銀行也一樣。和銀行交易最好的辦法就是什麼方法都用。親自跑銀行可以和在那裡工作的人當面洽談，自動櫃員機也要會用；另外記得有時用電話銀行，有時則用網路銀行進行交易。

Conversation 1

A: You should have come with me to the bank.

B: Going to the bank is for losers. I just got on the phone and took care of all my bills.

A: I'm telling you, you should have come. You'll be sorry you didn't.

B: Why would I be? I didn't even have to get out of my pajamas. This is great.

A: Listen to this. That girl you like so much? She was there. She asked about you.

B: What? Oh, I'm so stupid! Why didn't you take me to the bank with you?

中譯

A: 你應該和我去銀行的。

B: 豬頭才會去銀行，我都用電話處理所有的帳單。

A: 我跟你說，你應該和我去的，你會很遺憾沒跟我去。

B: 為什麼我會遺憾？我連睡衣褲都不用換耶，棒呆了。

A: 聽著。記得那個你很喜歡的女生嗎？她人在那兒，她有問起你。

B: 什麼？哎呀，我真是豬頭！你怎麼沒帶我去銀行啦！

Conversation 2

A: Here's your computer problem. You have spy ware on your computer.

B: So that's what's slowing it down so much. That's not good.

A: I hope you don't do a lot of banking over the internet.

B: Why?

A: There was spy ware on your computer. Who knows what that stuff can see?

B: Oh that's not good. Do you think they can get my account information? Oh dear.

中譯

A: 電腦的問題找到了，裡面有偷窺軟體。

B: 所以電腦才會那麼慢囉？這樣不行。

A: 但願你沒有常常使用網路銀行。

B: 怎麼說？

A: 你電腦裡有間諜，誰知道這種東西會偷看些什麼？

B: 哦，真不妙。你覺得它們會盜取我的帳戶資料嗎？哎呀，這下慘了。

Conversation 3

A: What's going on? What's wrong with this stupid

computer?

B: What are you yelling about? Let me see. Well here's your problem.

A: What it is?

B: The server is down. That's why you can't get to the bank website.

A: Oh no. How long do you think it'll be down?

B: I have no idea. You'd better do your banking by phone if you're in such a rush.

中譯

A: 怎麼回事？這台笨電腦有什麼毛病啊？

B: 你在叫什麼啦？我看看。嗯，原來問題出在這裡。

A: 是什麼問題？

B: 伺服器斷線了，所以你才上不去銀行網站。

A: 哦，天啊。你覺得會斷線多久？

B: 不知道。如果很急的話，你最好用電話銀行。

Conversation 4

A: The hard drive of our computer has been wiped out. We'll have to buy a new one.

B: It must have been a really bad virus. We'll have to have virus protection from now on.

A: I'm worried. Do you think we could've picked it up from the bank's website?

B: What? The virus? No. The bank website would be virus free.

A: Okay. We don't have to worry about having sent our virus to the bank website do we?

B: No. I don't think that can happen.

A: 我們電腦的硬碟毀掉了，只好買台新的。

B: 一定是中了很嚴重的病毒，從現在開始我們要加裝掃毒程式才行。

A: 我蠻擔心的。你覺得會不會是在銀行網站中毒的？

B: 什麼？病毒？不會啦。銀行網站是不會有病毒的。

A: 好。那我們也不用擔心把病毒傳染給銀行網站囉？

B: 對。我認為這種事不會發生。

Conversation 5

A: I'm on the computer every day. It's my job. I don't want to do anything by computer.

B: Do your wrists hurt? Is that it? Lots of people get wrist problems.

A: My wrists hurt. My back hurts. My eyes burn. Even my bum seems to hurt.

B: Well we need to do some banking. Maybe the drive to the bank will do you good.

A: Yes. You know what would be even better? The bank is close. Let's walk.

B: The fresh air and exercise will do us good. Shut that computer down and let's go.

A: 每天工作都坐在電腦前面，我不要再用電腦處理事情了。

B: 你手腕受傷了，對嗎？很多人都有手腕疼痛問題。

A: 我手腕痛、背痛，眼睛有灼熱感；連屁股好像都會痛。

B: 可是有些銀行的事還沒處理，或許開車去銀行比較好。

A: 是沒錯，可是你知道什麼事情更酷嗎？銀行關了，我們不如去散步吧。

B: 呼吸新鮮空氣再做些運動對身體很棒。把電腦關了，我們走吧。

Conversation 6

A: What's the matter? Why didn't the teller help you?

B: She doesn't know me. I haven't been in for so long that I don't know the staff anymore.

A: Wow. She should have asked for ID. Then she could have helped you.

B: She did. I didn't bring my wallet. I'm going to use the ATM instead. Move over.

A: Okay. Maybe you should've shaved and not worn your black leather jacket.

B: This isn't good. I can't remember my PIN. It's been too long since I used the ATM.

中譯

A： 怎麼了？櫃臺人員怎麼沒幫你？

B： 她不認識我。我好久沒來，行員都不認識了。

A： 哇，那她應該會向你要身份證明才對，然後就可以幫你了。

B： 她有，只是我沒有帶皮夾子。我要用自動櫃員機，先站一邊去。

A： 好。或許你應該刮個鬍子，不要穿你那件黑色皮夾克。

B： 真慘，我太久沒用自動櫃員機，連密碼都不記得了。

Useful phrases and idioms
有用的片語和慣用語

Oh dear 哎呀

an exclamation of worry or concern

例 Oh dear. I'm worried about money.

哎呀，我擔心錢啦。

Picked it up 得到

got it

例　This watch? I picked it up when I was in Japan.
這支手錶？我去日本時撿到的。

Bum 屁股

buttocks or butt

例　My bum hurts from sitting all day.
坐了一整天，屁股好痛。

Vocabulary 字彙

pajamas	*n.*	睡衣褲
spy ware	*n.*	偷窺軟體
stuff	*n.*	東西
yell	*v.*	叫喊
server	*n.*	伺服器
down	*adv.*	斷線
hard drive		硬碟
wipe out		消滅
virus	*n.*	病毒
wrists	*n.*	手腕
burn	*v.*	灼熱
shave	*v.*	刮（鬍子）
leather jacket		皮夾克

Chapter 6

CREDIT CARDS AND LOANS

信用卡和貸款

MP3-17

Unit 1

Credit Cards
信用卡

The best way to use credit cards is to keep the **limit** very low. Pay the card off in full every month. This helps to **avoid** paying interest and **penalty** fees. Customers need to figure out what amount they can afford to pay in full every month. They need to set that as their limit. They need to tell the **credit card company** it's not allowed to increase the limit. Credit card companies like to **increase** the limit first and tell later. Customers only read about the increase on the next statement. Often it's too late and they have already spent above their **budget**.

提示　要使用信用卡，最好的辦法就是刷卡額度要低，然後每個月都全額繳清。這樣可以避免支付利息和罰款。客戶必須清楚每個月可以負擔得起多少金額，然後把那個金額設為底限。有必要告知信用卡公司，不要調高你的可用額度。信用卡公司喜歡先幫你調高額度後再通知你。客戶收到下個月帳單時才會看到調高後的額度。不過這時通常為時已晚，而且客戶多半花的錢也已超出預算。

Conversation 1

A: Good morning. How can I help you?

B: I'd like to apply for a credit card please.

A: Okay. Please fill out this application form. I also

need your bank card please.

B: Here's my bank card.

A: Thank you. Do you also have three pieces of ID?

B: I have a driver's license and hospital card. I also have a library card. Will that do?

中譯

A: 早安。需要什麼服務嗎？

B: 我想要申請信用卡。

A: 好的。請填這張申請表，同時把你的金融卡給我。

B: 這是我的金融卡。

A: 謝謝。你有三張身份證明嗎？

B: 我有駕照和健保卡，還有一張圖書證。可以嗎？

Conversation 2

A: I got this credit card application in the mail. I'm just going to recycle it.

B: No don't put it in the recycling like that. Tear it up. Tear it up really good.

A: Why? What's the big deal?

B: It's a blank credit card application with your name and address on it. That's bad.

A: Right. What was I thinking? That's the perfect tool for identity theft.

B: That's right. Rip all of those papers up really well and throw them in the trash.

中譯

A: 我收到一封信用卡申請書的郵件，正要丟到資源回收筒。

B: 不，不要把它們資源回收。撕掉它，要把它撕爛。

A: 為什麼？有什麼大不了的嗎？

B: 那是一張空白的信用卡申請書，上面有你的名字和地

址，那樣不太好。

A: 對耶，我在想什麼？簡直是盜用身份的完美工具。

沒錯。把這些紙通通撕爛丟到垃圾筒。

Conversation 3

A: How much can you put on the credit card this month?

B: What's the minimum payment needed? I'll just pay that.

A: That's a bad idea. If you only make the minimum payment it'll take years to pay off.

B: Really? How do you know that?

A: I've seen this on talk-shows on TV many times. At least put twenty dollars more on.

B: I can afford that.

中譯

A: 你這個月的信用卡準備繳多少錢？

B: 最低應繳金額是多少？我只要付那麼多就好了。

A: 那樣不好。如果你只繳最低應繳金額，要好幾年才付得完。

B: 真的嗎？你怎麼知道？

A: 我在電視的談話詳目上看過好多次。至少多繳個二十塊。

B: 這點錢還負擔得起。

Conversation 4

A: These interest rates are horrible. I can't believe how much they are charging.

B: I know. Credit cards are only good if you can pay them off in full every month.

A: I see that now. I'm going to cut up this card.

B: Shouldn't you pay it off first?

A: Of course. I'm going to. But if it's cut up I can't use it anymore.

B: What you should do is phone the credit card company. Tell them to cancel it.

中譯

A: 這些利率真可怕。真不敢相信他們收了多少錢。

B: 我知道。除非能每個月付清信用卡，不然用信用卡沒什麼好處。

A: 我現在懂了。我要把這張卡剪掉。

B: 不用先付清嗎？

A: 當然，我會去付清的。不過只要把它剪掉，我就可以不要再用了。

B: 你應該打電話給信用卡公司，叫他們把卡片取消。

Conversation 5

A: Why are you paying by credit card? Why don't you just use your debit card?

B: I like using my credit card. I get reward miles.

A: But you also get to pay big interest rates. Doesn't that cancel the reward out?

B: Not if you pay the card off in full each month like I do.

A: I see. That's not a bad idea. What are you going to use your reward points for?

B: I'm going to take us both on a trip. We're going to go see polar bears.

A: 你幹嘛用信用卡付帳？用簽帳卡不就好了？

B: 我喜歡用信用卡，這樣可以累積紅利哩程數。

A: 但你也要負擔高利率啊，一來一往不會互相抵消嗎？

B: 只要像我一樣每個月把信用卡付清就不會。

A: 我懂了，這個主意不錯。那你的紅利點數要怎麼用？

B: 我們兩個可以去旅行，我們去看北極熊吧。

Conversation 6

A: Credit cards are out of date. Now that there are bank cards, you don't need them.

B: You need a credit card if you are shopping online.

A: Yes, I suppose.

B: You need a credit card as one of your three major pieces of ID.

A: I guess so. But you don't need to use it everyday.

B: No, you're right. But it is good if you are traveling.

中譯

A: 信用卡過時了。既然有金融卡，就不需要信用卡了。

B: 可是要信用卡才能線上購物。

A: 我想應該是。

B: 三張主要的身份證明中，也少不了信用卡。

A: 我想是吧。不過你不會每天都用得到。

B: 對，你說的沒錯。不過旅遊時信用卡蠻好用的。

Conversation 7

A: Your new credit card came in the mail.

B: Good. I'll just get rid of this old one. Will you throw this in the garbage for me?

A: You should cut it up first.

B: Okay. Good idea. Better safe than sorry.

A: Yes. Now sign the back on the new one. Sign carefully and clearly.

B: Right. I almost forgot.

中譯

A: 你新的信用卡寄來了。

B: 太好了。舊的可以丟了，幫我丟到垃圾筒好嗎？

A: 要先剪掉才對。

B: 好主意。小心駛得萬年船。

A: 沒錯。現在要在新卡背後簽名，小心簽，而且要簽清楚。

B: 對，我差點忘了。

Conversation 8

A: Good morning. How can I help you today?

B: Good morning. How can I check my credit card balance before my statement comes?

A: You can check your balance by phone. Just call this number here on this card.

B: Okay. Thank you. Can I check it at the ATM machine?

A: Yes. You can also visit the website on this card and check it there.

B: All right. Thank you. And I suppose that you would help me check it as well?

中譯

A: 早安。需要什麼服務嗎？

B: 早安。我要怎麼在對帳單寄來前查詢信用卡餘額？

A: 你可以用電話查詢，只要打這張卡上面的號碼就可以了。

B: 好的，謝謝你。我可以用自動櫃員機查詢嗎？

A: 可以。你也可以上這張卡上面寫的網站查詢。

B: 好，謝謝。我想你也可以幫我查詢吧？

Useful phrases and idioms
有用的片語和慣用語

Cut up 剪掉

use scissors to destroy

例 I'm going to cut up your credit card so you can't use it anymore.

我要把你的信用卡剪掉，你就不能再用了。

Vocabulary 字彙

limit	n.	限度
avoid	v.	避免
penalty	n.	罰款
credit card company		信用卡公司
increase	v.	增加
budget	n.	預算
hospital card		健保卡
library card		圖書證
recycle	v.	再利用
minimum payment		最低應繳金額
afford	v.	買得起
horrible	adj.	可怕
cancel	v.	取消
polar bear		北極熊
out of date		過時
carefully	adj.	小心的

Unit 2

Line of Credit
信用貸款

MP3-18

A line of credit is like a credit card and a loan combined. The bank does not give a sum of money. Rather, it gives customers an amount of credit they can use. They can use a plastic card to access their line of credit just like a credit card. Interest rates are lower than credit cards because it's treated more like a bank loan. While it's easy for almost anyone to get a credit card, it's much harder to get a line of credit.

提示　信用貸款類似信用卡和貸款兩者的結合。銀行並不是給你一筆錢，更確切地說，他們是給客戶一筆可借貸的金額。客戶可以像使用信用卡一樣，用塑膠卡片取得信用貸款。因為信用貸款更像是銀行貸款，所以利率也比信用卡低。現在幾乎人手一張信用卡，但要申請信用貸款可就難多了。

Conversation 1

A: Good afternoon. How are you today?

B: I am good. How are you?

A: I'm very good, thank you. What can I do for you?

B: I would like to get some information about a line of credit.

A: I'll make an appointment for you with our loans officer. What day is good for you?

B: I would like to see someone tomorrow morning if that's possible.

中譯

A: 午安。今天好嗎？

B: 不錯，你呢？

A: 我很好，謝謝。需要什麼服務嗎？

B: 我想了解信用貸款的相關資訊。

A: 我替你和我們的貸款部主任預約。你哪一天比較方便？

B: 可以的話，我明天早上想找人談談。

Conversation 2

A: Good afternoon. What can I do for you?

B: Yes. I have an appointment to see the loans officer about a line of credit.

A: Okay. The loans officer has not yet returned from lunch. Please have a seat.

B: What will the loans officer do in our meeting?

A: She will check to see that you have a good credit rating. You must have a good rating.

B: I think I have to go home. I think I might have left the oven on. Good bye.

中譯

A: 午安。需要什麼服務嗎？

B: 是的，我有和貸款部主任預約洽談信用貸款的事。

A: 好的。貸款部主任去吃中飯還沒回來，請先坐一下。

B: 貸款部主任會和我談些什麼？

A: 她會查詢看看你信用好不好，你一定要信用好才行。

B: 我想我必須回家一趟，烤箱好像忘了關。再見。

Conversation 3

A: With all this money I got as a Christmas bonus,

I'm going to pay off the line of credit.

B: But then we won't have it any more. We'll have to apply all over again.

A: No we won't. It just means we'll have a zero balance. We still get to keep it.

B: Oh. I thought it was a loan. I thought once we paid it back it was all done.

A: No. It's not quite the same as a loan. It's like a loan and credit card combined.

B: So it only gets cancelled when we don't want it anymore? That's great.

中譯

A: 我拿到的這筆聖誕節獎金，想要拿去還信用貸款。

B: 可是這樣一來我們就沒有信用貸款了，還要重新申請才行。

A: 不用，只不過餘額變零而已，信用貸款還是在。

B: 哦，我以為是一般貸款，一旦償還後就終止了。

A: 不是的，它和一般貸款不太一樣。比較像是貸款和信用卡合在一起。

B: 所以只有在我們想取消時才會終止對吧？那樣真好。

Conversation 4

A: How would you like to pay for this?

B: I'll use my card. Here's my card.

A: Okay. I've never seen a credit card that looked like that before.

B: It's not a credit card. It's a line of credit.

A: I don't think we can take that. I'll have to cancel the transaction.

B: No. It acts like a credit card. See? It says that the

transaction has been approved.

中譯

A: 你要怎麼付帳？

B: 我要刷卡，卡在這裡。

A: 好的。我以前沒看過信用卡長這樣子的。

B: 那不是信用卡，是信用貸款。

A: 那可能不行哦，交易必須取消才行。

B: 不會啊，它有信用卡的功能，看到沒？機器上面說交易已核准。

Conversation 5

A: What's this? Is this the statement for our credit card? It looks different.

B: It's the statement for our line of credit. That's why it looks different.

A: Oh. Why do we still have a credit card if we have this?

B: That's a good question. I guess we don't really need both.

A: I think we should pay that credit card off and just use this. The interest is much better.

B: Let's see. You're right. The interest rate is better. Say good-bye to credit cards.

中譯

A: 這是什麼？是我們的信用卡對帳單嗎？看起來不太一樣。

B: 是我們的信用貸款對帳單，所以才會看起來不一樣。

A: 喔。如果已經有信用貸款，那還要信用卡幹嘛？

B: 好問題。不管哪一個，我想我們都不一定真的需要。

A: 我覺得應該把信用卡清償掉，然後只用信用貸款就好，利率好多了。

B: 我看看。你說的沒錯，利率是比較好。那跟信用卡說再

見吧。

Conversation 6

A: Good afternoon. What can I do for you today?

B: I would like to make a payment on my line of credit.

A: No problem. Do you have your statement with you?

B: No. It hasn't come yet this month. I would still like to make a payment.

A: Certainly. You can make as many payments as you like. How much?

B: I'd like to put three hundred dollars down on it.

中譯

A: 午安。需要什麼服務嗎？
B: 我想要繳信用貸款。
A: 沒問題。你有帶對帳單嗎？
B: 沒有，這個月的還沒寄來，可是我現在想繳款。
A: 當然沒問題，你要繳幾次都可以。那現在要繳多少呢？
B: 我想要繳三百塊。

Conversation 7

A: Hi there, I'd like to make this payment please.

B: Okay Mr. Smith. You're going to make the minimum payment on your line of credit?

A: Yes. Do I have to come into the bank each time I make a payment?

B: No. You can make a payment over the internet or by phone.

A: I can? That's fantastic. But how do I get the money to you?

B: What? You have to have money in your account. Then you pay from your account.

中譯

A: 你好，我想要繳款。

B: 好的，史密斯先生。你信用貸款要繳最低應繳金額嗎？

A: 是的。每次要繳款都要跑一趟銀行嗎？

B: 不用。你也可以用網路或電話繳款。

A: 可以嗎？那太好了。可是要怎麼把錢拿給你們？

B: 什麼？你帳戶裡要先有錢，然後再從帳戶中扣款。

Conversation 8

A: I don't need this line of credit anymore. I'd like to get rid of it.

B: Sir, that's not possible. You owe four thousand dollars. You have to pay that first.

A: I know. Here's the money. I won the lottery.

B: Good for you! Now that I have made that payment for you we can cancel it.

A: Thanks. I won so much money I won't need any credit or loans anymore.

B: You won that much? Do you need a best friend? Can I be your new best friend?

A: 我不再需要這筆信用貸款了，想要取消。

B: 先生，那樣不行。你還欠四千塊，要先償還才行。

A: 我知道，錢在這裡。我中了彩券。

B: 恭喜！既然最後一筆欠款已繳清，那我們可以幫你取消了。

A: 謝謝。我贏了好多錢，任何信貸或一般貸款都不需要了。

B: 你贏很多？你有最要好的朋友嗎？我可以當你最要好的新朋友嗎？

Vocabulary 字彙

line of credit		信用貸款
combined	*adj.*	相加的
sum	*n.*	（一）筆
rather	*adv.*	更確切地說
loans officer		貸款部主任
oven	*n.*	烤箱
bonus	*n.*	獎金
approve	*v.*	批准
fantastic	*adj.*	太好了

Unit 3

Mortgages
房屋貸款

MP3-19

A mortgage is a special type of loan. It's used only to buy houses. When the bank loans money to a customer to buy property, it's called a mortgage. Customers can make one extra payment a year without penalty. That one payment goes down on the amount borrowed not on the interest owed. That helps to pay the mortgage down much faster. Some people save a little money each month so they can make that important extra payment. They can own their house and get out of debt sooner.

提示　　房屋貸款是一種只用來購屋的特殊貸款。當銀行把錢貸給客戶購置房地產時，便稱為房屋貸款。客戶每年可以額外免息還款一次。那筆款項會直接還掉本金而不用來還利息。那樣可以讓房屋貸款早點還清。有些人每個月存一些錢來付這筆重要的額外款項，以便早日擁有自己的房子並還清負債。

Conversation 1

A: What's the matter? You look upset.

B: This is the third time tonight I've had to bang on the ceiling. They just won't be quiet.

A: I know. We have very noisy neighbors.

B: I'm tired of renting. I think we should get a

house.

A: You mean you think we should buy a house?

B: Yes. We can afford to buy a house. We can handle a mortgage payment.

中譯

A: 怎麼了？你看起來很煩。

B: 我今晚已經是第三次用力敲天花板了。他們就是靜不下來。

A: 我知道，鄰居很吵。

B: 房子租到煩了，我想應該來買間房子。

A: 你是說你覺得我們應該買房子？

B: 沒錯，買房子我們還負擔得起。可以去辦房屋貸款。

Conversation 2

A: Good morning. How can I help you?

B: Yes. I'd like to get some information about mortgages.

A: Okay. Why don't I make you an appointment with our loans officer?

B: No thank you. I'm just gathering information right now. What are your interest rates?

A: This brochure will tell you what our rates are. You should talk to the loans officer.

B: I don't want to. I'm just comparing rates right now. Thank you for the brochure.

中譯

A: 早安。需要什麼服務嗎？

B: 是的。我想要了解房屋貸款的相關資訊。

A: 好的。安排你和我們的貸款部主任談談好嗎？

B: 不用了，謝謝。我現在還在收集資料。你們的利率怎麼樣？

A:　這本小冊子裡面有我們的利率表，你應該和貸款部主任談談的。

B:　不用了。我現在還在比較各家的利率。謝謝你給我這本小冊子。

Conversation 3

A: That's a nice house. It looks good from the outside. Let's call the agent and see it.

B: I don't know. How do we know we can afford a house?

A: We can get pre-approved for a mortgage. We just need to decide on a bank.

B: What does that mean?

A: They let us know how much we qualify for and how big a mortgage they'll give us.

B: That's great. I'd rather know how much we can spend before we start looking.

中譯

A:　那間房子真棒，外表看起來很不錯。不如打給仲介問問看。

B:　不曉得耶，怎麼知道我們負擔得起呢？

A:　可以先進行房屋貸款的先期作業，只要選定一家銀行即可。

B:　什麼意思？

A:　銀行會告訴我們資格條件如何，以及可以申請多少房屋貸款。

B:　太好了。我比較喜歡開始看房子之前先知道有多少錢可以花。

Conversation 4

A: What are you reading?

B: The newspaper. There's a whole section in here on mortgage rates.

A: What does it say?

B: It shows the different rates that each of the banks offer.

A: Does it show the rates for the different number of years?

B: Yes. We can get five percent at North West Bank for five years.

中譯

A: 你在看什麼？

B: 報紙啊，有一整欄在講房屋貸款利率。

A: 上面怎麼說？

B: 它列出了各家銀行所提供的不同利率。

A: 也有列出不同年限的利率嗎？

B: 有。西北銀行有提供五年期 5% 的利率。

Conversation 5

A: Good morning. How can I help you?

B: We have an appointment with the loans officer about a mortgage.

A: I am the loans officer. Please come into my office. What can I do for you?

B: We want to see if we qualify for a second mortgage. We'd like to buy another house.

A: Okay. Let me see what I can do for you. What's this house for?

B: It'll be a rental property. We want to buy close to the university so students will rent.

中譯

A: 早安。需要什麼服務嗎？

B: 我們有和貸款部主任預約洽談房屋貸款的事。

A: 我就是貸款部主任，請進來我的辦公室。哪裡需要效勞

呢？

我們想知道符不符合二次房屋貸款的條件。我們還要再買一棟房子。

A: 好的。我看看能不能幫上忙。這棟房子要用來做什麼？

B: 要用來出租。我們想要買大學附近的房子讓學生租。

Conversation 6

A: Oh no. This is very bad news. You need to take a look at this.

B: What is it? What's the matter?

A: This is a notice from the bank. It says they're going to foreclose on our mortgage.

B: What does that mean?

A: It means we owe them too much money and we haven't been making our payments.

B: Are they going to take our house away?

中譯

A: 哦，天啊。很壞的消息，你最好看看這個。

B: 是什麼？怎麼了？

A: 是銀行的通知，上面說他它們要取消所抵押房子的贖回權。

B: 什麼意思？

A: 意思是說我們欠太多錢了，又一直沒去還。

B: 那他們要把房子收回去嗎？

Conversation 7

A: Good afternoon Mrs. Smith.

B: Good afternoon. My husband and I just took out a mortgage with your bank.

A: Congratulations. What can I do for you this afternoon?

B: What is the best way for us to make our mortgage payments?

A: You can have them taken out of your bank account automatically.

B: I think that an automatic withdrawal would be best. Take it out of our joint account.

中譯

A: 午安，史密斯太太。
B: 午安。我先生和我剛拿到你們銀行的房屋貸款。
A: 恭喜。今天下午需要什麼服務嗎？
B: 怎樣繳款最好？
A: 可以自動從帳戶中扣款。
B: 我覺得自動扣款最好，那就從我們的聯名帳戶中扣款吧。

Conversation 8

A: Okay. You are approved for a mortgage. Over how many years would you like it?

B: The interest rates are very good right now. I will lock in for five years.

A: Okay. So that's five percent interest over five years. Correct?

B: Yes. I would like to get mortgage insurance please.

A: That's an extra ten dollars a month. It's good to have.

B: Yes. If something happens to me, I want the house to be paid for in full for my kids.

中譯

A: 好，你的房屋貸款已核准。要幾年期的？
B: 現在的利率很低，我要五年期的固定利率。
A: 沒問題。那就是五年 5% 的利率，沒錯吧？

B: 是的。我想辦房屋貸款保險。

A: 每個月要多付十塊，不過有保險才好。

B: 對啊。如果我發生什麼意外，我希望保險公司能替我小孩把房屋貸款全額付清。

Useful phrases and idioms
有用的片語和慣用語

Take our house away 把房子收回去

repossess, evict the current owners and sell it to make back money

例 The bank is taking our house away because we didn't make our mortgage payments.

我們的房屋貸款付不出來，銀行要把房子收回去了。

Kids 小孩

children

例 How are your kids doing in school?

你家小孩上學還好嗎？

Vocabulary 字彙

property	*n.*	房地產
debt	*n.*	負債
bang	*v.*	用力敲
ceiling	*n.*	天花板
noisy	*adj.*	喧鬧的
agent	*n.*	仲介

decide	*v.*	決定
qualify	*v.*	取得資格
section	*n.*	（文章的）段
offer	*v.*	提供
rental	*adj.*	出租的
foreclose	*v.*	取消贖回（抵押品）權
lock in		固定

Chapter 7

Transferring and Exchanging Money

轉帳和匯兌

Unit 1

Transferring to a Different Person

轉帳給不同的人 `MP3-20`

　　Close friends and family members might give their account information to each other. This enables them to deposit money into each other's accounts. This is an easy way of transferring money. People should be careful who they give their account information to. Sometimes friends or even family members can be tempted to steal. A safer way to transfer money is to write a check but this is not always practical or fast. Checks can take several days to clear. This means having to wait while the bank authorizes the release of that money. A money order is another way to get money to someone else. A money order is a check issued by the bank. The bank certifies that the money is already available. These can be cashed immediately, but they cost money and a customer has to visit the bank during bank hours to get one.

提示　　好朋友或家人之間可能彼此會有對方的帳戶資料，這樣就可以把錢存進彼此的帳戶裡。這是一種方便的轉帳方法。不過把帳戶資料給別人時要小心，有時候朋友甚至家人也會受到偷錢的誘惑。開支票轉帳比較安全，但實效性和速度可能差了一點，因為支票要幾天後才能交換。意思是說必須等到銀行授權才能拿到錢。匯票是由銀行所

開的支票，它也是一種轉帳的方法。銀行會擔保錢一定拿得到。匯票可以立即兌現，但是手續費較高，而且客戶要在銀行營業時間內，親自跑一趟銀行才行。

Conversation 1

A: Hey little brother. I need your rent. It was due yesterday.

B: I get paid tomorrow. Can I give you the rent then?

A: Okay. Don't make this a habit though. Try to be on time.

B: I will. It won't happen again. I'll leave it in your room.

A: No. Can you deposit it to my bank account like you did last time?

B: Why? Aren't you going to be here? Are you going out of town again like last month?

中譯

A: 嘿，小兄弟，租金呢？昨天就該付了。

B: 我明天領薪水，可以明天再給你嗎？

A: 好。不過不要變成習慣，最好按時給我。

B: 我會的，下次不會再這樣了。我會把錢放在你房間裡。

A: 不。可以像上回那樣把錢存進我帳戶裡嗎？

B: 為什麼？你不是會在嗎？還是跟上個月一樣又要出城去？

Conversation 2

A: Mom, you've got to send me some money. I need it fast. I just got a flat tire.

B: Why do you need money? You have a job now.

A: I don't get paid for three weeks. I didn't budget for this. I've got no groceries.

But this is the last time. You need to start saving money for emergencies like this.

A: You're the best Mom. Thanks. Grab a pen. I'll give you my account information.

A: I already have it. I just gave you money to buy an interview suit remember?

中譯

A: 媽，給我一點錢，我急著用，剛爆胎了。

B: 為什麼需要錢？不是有工作了？

A: 我三個禮拜沒拿到錢。也沒有預估到這筆錢。況且家裡也沒什麼用品了。

B: 這可是最後一次了。你要開始存錢才可以應付這類緊急狀況。

A: 你真好，媽，謝謝你。有筆嗎？我把帳號給你。

B: 我已經知道你帳號了，才剛給你錢買面試用衣服，記得吧？

Conversation 3

A: Hello. Can I help you?

B: Yes. I need to put this money in my sister's bank account please.

A: Okay. Do you have her account information?

B: No. I was hoping you could look up her name and give that to me.

A: I'm afraid I can't do that, sir. I can't give that information out.

B: Oh. Okay. I'll call her on her cell phone and get it. I'll be right back.

中譯

A: 嗨。需要什麼服務嗎？

B: 是的。我要把這筆錢存進我姐的帳戶。

A: 好的。你有她的帳號嗎？

B: 沒有。你可以幫我查一下她名字再給我她的帳號嗎？

A: 恐怕不行，先生。帳號不能外洩。

B: 這樣啊，好吧。我打她手機問她，很快就回來。

Conversation 4

A: I have such a nice Mom. She spoils me.

B: Why do you say that? What did she do this time?

A: I'm checking my recent transactions online. She just sent money to my account.

B: Isn't that nice. What a nice Mom you have. She spoils you.

A: I know. I'm going to send her an email and thank her.

B: Tell your Mom I say hi. What will you do with the money she sent you?

中譯

A: 我媽好好哦，真是寵我。

B: 怎麼說？這回她又做了什麼？

A: 我去線上查詢最近的交易明細，發現她剛存一筆錢進我戶頭。

B 好好哦，真是好媽媽。她很寵你。

A: 我知道。我要寄封電子郵件向她說聲謝謝。

B: 幫我跟你媽問好。她給你的這筆錢打算怎麼用？

Conversation 5

A: I need to give you your share of the rent. Is there any way I can do that by phone?

B: I don't know. I've never tried to transfer money to someone else's account like that.

A: Let's see. I know I can transfer money between

my own accounts.

B: It doesn't look like you can give it to someone else though.

A: I think you're right. I'll go to the bank tomorrow and take it out. How much is it?

B: Three hundred dollars.

中譯

A: 我要給你分租的錢，有沒有辦法用電話轉帳？

B: 不清楚耶，我沒試過用電話轉帳給別人。

A: 我看看。我知道我可以把錢在我兩個戶頭之間轉來轉去。

B: 看來還是沒有辦法轉帳給別人。

A: 我想你說的沒錯。我明天跑一趟銀行把錢領出來給你。是多少？

B: 三百塊。

Conversation 6

A: I really like this car. I'm so glad I saw the ad in the paper. Will you take a check?

B: Sorry, lady but I don't know you. I'd prefer cash.

A: That's a lot of money for me to carry around. I'd rather not.

B: Maybe you could get a cashier's check. I'd take one of those.

A: What's a cashier's check? Where do I get one?

B: It's a check from the bank. It certifies you have the money. I can cash it right away.

中譯

A: 我好喜歡這部車，真高興有在報紙上看到廣告。你們收支票嗎？

B: 抱歉，小姐，我並不認識你。我想現金會比較好。

A: 那可是一大筆錢耶，不適合帶在身上。我寧可不帶比較安全。

B: 或許你可以給我銀行本票，本票我就收。

A: 什麼是銀行本票？要去哪裡拿？

B: 那是銀行開的支票，銀行保證錢一定拿得到。我可以馬上兌現。

Conversation 7

A: I'm sorry honey, but I've tried transferring money to you by phone and online.

B: Doesn't that work?

A: No. I need your account information. Then I can do it online, but not by phone.

B: Oh. I didn't know that. I'll give you my account information.

A: We should really think about getting a joint account. I could transfer money into it.

B: And then I can transfer it out into my own account. Good idea.

中譯

A: 抱歉，甜心，我已經試過用電話轉帳給你，現在要線上轉帳。

B: 電話轉帳不能用嗎？

A: 不行。給我你的帳號，我要用線上轉帳，不用電話了。

B: 哦，我不知道會那樣。我把帳號給你。

A: 我們應該考慮弄個聯名帳戶，這樣我就可以把錢轉進去。

B: 然後我再去把錢轉到個人帳戶裡。好主意。

Conversation 8

A: Good morning. Can I help you?

B: Yes. I'd like to transfer some money to my brother.

He lives in a different country.

A: Okay. That's not a problem. Do you have his account information?

B: Yes. It's all on this piece of paper. Please take it.

A: Thank you. This will only take a minute. How much do you want to send him?

B: Thirty thousand dollars please. He's trying to bribe a lawyer.

中譯

A: 早安。需要什麼服務嗎？

B: 是的。我要轉帳給我弟弟，他住在別的國家。

A: 好的，沒問題。你有他帳號嗎？

B: 有。都寫在這張紙上，拿去。

A: 謝謝，請稍待片刻。你要轉多少給他？

B: 請幫我轉三萬塊。他想要賄賂律師。

Conversation 9

A: Good afternoon. How can I help you?

B: I would like to send some money to my father's account.

A: Okay. Do you have his account information?

B: It's all right here. You can take it.

A: Thanks. This won't take long. Oh, there's a problem. This account is closed.

B: Oh dear. Are you sure? Maybe I wrote the information down wrong.

中譯

A: 午安。需要什麼服務嗎？

B: 我要轉一些錢到我爸帳戶裡。

A: 好的。你有他帳號嗎？

B: 都在這裡，拿去。

A: 謝謝，請稍待片刻。啊，有點問題，這個帳戶已經停用了。

B: 哎呀，你確定嗎？可能是我把帳號寫錯了。

Useful phrases and idioms
有用的片語和慣用語

Spoil 寵壞

to treat someone too well. To give someone too much

例 Every birthday, my mother spoils the kids.

我媽每年生日那天都很寵小孩。

Vocabulary 字彙

tempt	*v.*	誘惑
authorize	*v.*	授權
certify	*v.*	擔保
flat	*adj.*	洩了氣的（輪胎）
emergency	*n.*	緊急狀況
interview suit		面試用衣服
ad	*n.*	廣告
bribe	*v.*	賄賂

Unit 2

Transferring Money to a Different Account
轉帳到不同的帳戶

MP3-21

Transferring money to and from different accounts owned by the same person is easy. It can be done by phone or by computer. It can be done in person with a teller or at the bank machine. There are bank charges for transferring. It's best to keep it to a minimum. Try to have the right money going directly into the right accounts instead of moving it yourself. This will keep bank charges to a minimum.

提示　　同一個人的不同帳戶互相轉帳很簡單，可以用電話或電腦來處理，也可以親洽櫃臺人員或使用自動櫃員機辦理。轉帳要收手續費，所以記得讓手續費降到最低。儘量用自動轉帳讓正確金額直接轉進希望的帳戶，而不要手動轉帳；這樣可以讓手續費降到最低。

Conversation 1

A: Good morning. Can I help you?

B: Yes please. I'd like to transfer four hundred dollars from my savings to my checking.

A: No problem. Can I have your bank card please?

B: Oh dear. I seem to have misplaced it. It's not in my wallet. Oh dear.

A: Do you know your account numbers? If you have some ID, I can do that transfer.

B: I have some ID here in my wallet but I don't know my account numbers.

中譯

A: 早安。需要什麼服務嗎？

B: 是的。我想從存款帳戶中轉四百塊到支票帳戶。

A: 沒問題。請把金融卡給我好嗎？

B: 哎呀，好像忘了放哪，沒有在我皮夾子裡，真糟糕。

A: 記得帳號多少嗎？如果有帶身份證明，我可以幫你轉。

B: 皮夾子裡是有一些身份證明，但我不知道帳號多少。

Conversation 2

A: Good morning. How can I help you today?

B: I'd like to transfer some money out of my checking account into my savings.

A: Okay. I can do that for you. I'll need your bank card.

B: Here's my bank card. You know I find it so hard to get here.

A: Have you tried transferring funds over the phone or on the computer?

B: No I haven't. I'll have to try that. That would save me a trip on my lunch hour.

中譯

A: 早安。需要什麼服務嗎？

B: 我想從支票帳戶轉帳到存款帳戶。

A: 好的，我幫你。請給我金融卡。

B: 這是我的金融卡。你知道嗎？你們這裡好難找。

A: 你有用電話或電腦轉帳過嗎？

B: 沒有，不過我會試試看。這樣午飯時間就可以少跑一趟銀行了。

Conversation 3

A: Honey, I ran out of checks. Can you pay the rent this month?

B: Okay. I'll have to transfer some money into my checking.

A: Sorry about this. I'll get some money to you later and you can put it in your savings.

B: Sounds good. Can I have the checks for a minute? I'll just do that online.

A: Oh. Okay. I was just ordering checks. It'll take six weeks for them to get here.

B: So, it looks like I'll be mailing in the rent check next month too I guess.

中譯

A: 親愛的,我支票用完了。這個月的房租你可以先付嗎?

B: 好。我要先轉一些錢到支票帳戶裡。

A: 真抱歉。我會再把錢給你,讓你存到戶頭裡去。

B: 好啊。我可以用一下電腦嗎?線上轉一下就好了。

A: 哦,沒問題。我正在訂支票,六個禮拜後就會送來。

B: 這樣啊,看來下個月的房租我也要開支票先付了。

Conversation 4

A: You look happy. What's the good news?

B: I got a promotion. I also get a big raise to go with that promotion.

A: Good for you. What are you going to do with your big raise?

B: First I'm going to go on that cruise I've been saving up for.

A: A cruise. I wish I could go. That's expensive.

B: I can afford it now. I'm going to get all the money out of my savings and go.

中譯

A: 你看起來蠻開心的，有什麼好消息嗎？

B: 我升官了，加薪幅度也大大增加。

A: 太好了。加薪那麼多有沒有想要幹嘛？

B: 存了一陣子的錢，我想先去坐船旅行。

A: 坐船旅行？真希望我也可以去，不過好貴哦。

B: 我現在付得起了。我要把存款提光然後旅行去。

Conversation 5

A: Can I have the phone when you're done?

B: Yes. I won't be long.

A: Who are you talking to?

B: Nobody. I'm transferring some money into my savings account.

A: You've been putting a lot of money into your savings lately.

B: I'm saving up to buy us a second phone. Then you won't bug me for it all the time.

中譯

A: 電話打完後換我打好嗎？

B: 好，我不會打太久的。

A: 你打給誰啊？

B: 沒有打給誰，我只是把錢轉入存款帳戶。

A: 你最近存了好多錢進去。

B: 存錢才能再買一支電話，這樣你就不會老愛煩我，跟我搶電話了。

Conversation 6

A: Do you want to come to the bank with me?

B: That doesn't sound like much fun. Why are you going to the bank?

A: I have to transfer some money out of my savings into my checking.

B: The bank's closed. It's after midnight.

A: I know. It doesn't matter. I'll do it through the ATM.

B: Oh right. I forgot. Sorry, but I'm really tired. I'm just going to stay here.

中譯

A: 你要和我去銀行嗎？

B: 好像不怎麼好玩，你要去幹嘛？

A: 我要從存款帳戶轉帳到支票帳戶。

B: 銀行關了啦，已經過午夜了。

A: 我知道啊，那有什麼關係，用自動櫃員機就好了。

B: 哦，對耶，我忘了。抱歉，我真的好累，只想待著不想出門。

Conversation 7

A: I need to make a payment on my line of credit please.

B: Of course. Can I have your statement? I'll also need your bank card as well please.

A: Here's my bank card and my line of credit statement. I'd like to pay fifty dollars.

B: All right. And how will you be paying?

A: Please take the money out of my checking account.

B: Okay. That transaction is completed. Here's your bank card. Thank you.

中譯

A: 我要繳信用貸款。

B: 沒問題，請問有對帳單嗎？還有金融卡也要。

A: 金融卡和信用貸款對帳單在這。我要繳四十塊。

B: 好的。你要怎麼繳？

A: 請從支票帳戶中扣款。

B: 好。交易完成了，金融卡還你。謝謝。

Conversation 8

A: Can I help you?

B: Yes. I'd like to make a payment on my credit card please.

A: Of course. How much do you want to put on your card?

B: I'd like to put fifty-five hundred dollars down on it please.

A: And how would you like to make that payment?

B: Pay it from my savings account. If there isn't enough money there, use my checking.

中譯

A: 需要幫忙嗎？

B: 是的。我要繳信用卡。

A: 沒問題。你要繳多少錢？

B: 我想繳五千五百塊。

A: 你要怎麼繳？

B: 從存款帳戶中扣款，如果錢不夠，就從支票帳戶中扣。

Useful phrases and idioms
有用的片語和慣用語

Save me a trip 少跑一趟

To help me by not needing to go anywhere.

例 Doing my banking online will save me a trip to the bank.

用網路銀行可以少一趟銀行。

Ran out of 用完

have no more of

例 I ran out of time and didn't get the banking done.

我時間不夠，來不及去銀行。

Bug 煩

bother or disturb

例 Stop bugging me. I'm trying to watch TV.

不要煩我，我想要看電視。

Vocabulary 字彙

minimum	*adj.*	最低的
misplace	*v.*	遺忘
promotion	*n.*	升職
raise	*n.*	加薪
cruise	*n.*	（坐船）旅行

Unit 3

Exchanging Money

匯兌

MP3-22

The best place to exchange currency is at the bank. The bank will always be the most reliable and honest. When you travel, many places that exchange money charge heavily for that service. There are lots of websites where you can compare the value of different currencies at no charge. This is good information to have before you decide to have money changed.

提示　　要兌換外幣最好去銀行，因為銀行最可靠也最有誠信。出門旅行時，很多匯兌的地方手續費都很貴。有很多網站都可以免費比較不同貨幣間的匯差，在你決定兌換外幣之前，這是一項值得參考的資訊。

Conversation 1

A: Good morning. Can I help you?

B: Yes. I am going to be doing some traveling. I need to exchange some money.

A: What kind of currency do you need?

B: I'm going to Canada on business. I need Canadian dollars.

A: All right. The exchange rate for Canadian dollars and New Taiwan dollars is good.

B: That's good. Then I will exchange lots of money.

中譯

A: 早安。需要什麼服務嗎？

B: 是的。我要出門旅行，想要兌換一些外幣。

A: 你需要哪一種貨幣？

B: 我要去加拿大談生意，需要加幣。

A: 好的。加幣對新台幣的匯率不錯。

B: 真好，那我要換多一點。

Conversation 2

A: Good afternoon. How can I help you?

B: I need to exchange some money please. Did I come to the right place?

A: Yes. What currency do you want?

B: I'm going to India. I need Indian money, but I don't know what that is.

A: Okay. What you need is called Indian Rupees. We will have to order those for you.

B: What do you mean? You don't carry those here?

中譯

A: 午安。需要什麼服務嗎？

B: 我要兌換一些外幣，是在這裡兌換嗎？

A: 是的。你需要哪一種外幣？

B: 我要去印度，需要印度貨幣，可是不知道是哪一種。

A: 好的。你需要的貨幣叫做印度盧比，我們會幫你調。

B: 什麼意思？這裡沒有嗎？

Conversation 3

A: Good morning. Can I help you?

B: Good morning. Yes. I need to change some money. Can you do that?

A: Yes. What do you need?

B: I need a fifty for this twenty. Just kidding. I need some United Kingdom Pounds.

A: We have some but not much. If you need a lot we'll have to order more.

B: Well get ready to order more because I need three thousand pounds.

中譯

A: 早安。需要什麼服務嗎？

B: 早安。是的，我要兌換外幣，可以嗎？

A: 可以。你需要什麼外幣？

B: 我要把二十塊換成五十塊。開玩笑啦，我需要一些英磅。

A: 英磅雖然有但數量不多。如果你要兌換的數目很大，我們要先多調一些進來才行。

B: 嗯，那就多調一點吧，因為我需要三千英磅。

Conversation 4

A: Does the bank exchange money? I'm going on a trip and I've never traveled before.

B: Yes. When are you going away?

A: Not for several months. I don't need to exchange any money yet.

B: What kind of currency are you going to need?

A: I don't know. I'll be going to Jamaica.

B: Start watching the Jamaican dollar. Change your currency when the price is good.

中譯

A: 你們這家銀行可以換外幣嗎？我要出國旅行，以前沒有出去過。

B: 有。那你何時啟程？

A: 幾個月後，所以現在還不需要兌換外幣。

B: 你未來需要哪一種貨幣？

A: 不知道耶，我要去牙買加。

B: 那要開始注意牙買加幣。等價格不錯時再來兌換吧。

Conversation 5

A: I would like to get some information on having money changed please.

B: Yes? I can help you. What do you want to know?

A: Is it better to get all cash or all traveler's checks?

B: It's best to get some of each. Checks are safer and don't get stolen like cash does.

A: I suppose there will be some places that will take the checks and some that won't.

B: That's right. Most places will take the checks, but some will prefer cash.

中譯

A: 我想了解一些匯兌相關資訊。

B: 是嗎？我可以幫你，你想知道什麼？

A: 全部帶現金還是全部帶旅行支票比較好？

B: 最好每種都帶一點。支票比較安全，不會像現金那樣遭竊。

A: 我想有些地方會收支票，有些地方可能不收。

B: 沒錯。大部分地方都會收支票，但有些則偏好現金。

Conversation 6

A: I've started watching the Canadian dollar. My firm wants to do business there.

B: So, what's the dollar doing these days?

A: It's the strongest it's been in over eleven years.

B: I don't understand. What makes the dollar become weak or strong?

A: The things that affect the strength of currency are major world events.

B: I see. I didn't know that politics could affect money so much.

中譯

A: 我開始在注意加幣。我們公司要去哪裡做生意。

B: 這樣啊，那最近匯率如何？

A: 十一年來首度升值創新高。

B: 我不懂。貨幣升貶的原因是什麼？

A: 影響貨幣強勢與否的關鍵在於重大國際事件。

B: 我懂了。我還不曉得原來政治對貨幣的影響那麼大。

Conversation 7

A: How often can the market value of a foreign currency change?

B: It changes every day.

A: So how does the bank know what the worth is when I come in to change money?

B: That's decided before they open for business each morning.

A: Do people do that for a living? Pay attention to the value of different currencies?

B: Of course. How do you think the rest of us normal people find out?

中譯

A: 外幣牌價多久會變一次？

B: 每天都在變。

A: 那我要來兌換外幣時，銀行怎麼知道當時的利率？

B: 每天早上開門營業時便已事先決定。

A: 有人天天在注意匯市漲跌，靠這行吃飯嗎？

B: 當然有啊。不然你覺得一般人是怎麼知道的？

Conversation 8

A: I need to change some money for British pounds but the exchange rate is not good.

B: Some business people will exchange money two or even three times.

A: Really? That's a great idea.

B: They watch the markets and change currency more than once to get the best return.

A: My goodness. I'll try that. Hopefully our little local bank will let me.

B: You won't know until you ask. Do some research before you go there.

中譯

A: 我需要換些英磅，可是匯率不太好。

B: 有些生意人會兌換兩次甚至三次。

A: 真的嗎？這個主意真棒。

B: 他們會盯著市場，不只一次進行匯兌，以謀取最佳報酬率。

A: 我的天，我也要試試看。希望我們當地的小銀行也可以讓我這麼做。

B: 你要問才知道。去之前先研究一下。

Conversation 9

A: I have just returned from my vacation. I need to change this money back please.

B: How much money do you have left over from your trip?

A: I have thirty two dollars and thirty three cents. It's all in change.

B: I'm sorry. We can only exchange bills. We can't exchange coins.

A: What will I do with all these Canadian coins?

B: Why don't you hang on to them for the next time you go?

中譯

A: 我剛渡完假回國，要把這些錢換回來。

B: 旅行完還剩多少錢？

A: 三十二塊三十三分，都是零錢。

B: 抱歉，我們只能兌換鈔票，不能換硬幣。

A: 那這些加幣要怎麼辦？

B: 不如先留著，下回去加拿大時可以用。

Useful phrases and idioms
有用的片語和慣用語

Hang on to 保留

to keep

Hang on to those papers for me.
幫我把那些資料拿著。

Vocabulary 字彙

exchange	*v.*	兌換外幣
currency	*n.*	貨幣
rupee	*n.*	盧比
pound	*n.*	英磅
price	*n.*	價格
traveler's checks		旅行支票
prefer	*v.*	更喜歡
firm	*n.*	公司

major world events		重大國際事件
politics	*n.*	政治
market value		牌價
foreign	*adj.*	外國的
research	*n.*	研究
vacation	*n.*	休假
change	*n.*	零錢
coin	*n.*	硬幣

Chapter 8

INVESTING

投資

Unit 1

Retirement Savings Plans

退休儲蓄計畫

MP3-23

There are all sorts of different ways to invest money. There are Registered Retirement Savings Plans which are called RRSPs. There are GICs. You can buy bonds or invest in stocks. Many people invest in properties or in businesses like restaurants. The most common way to invest for retirement is the RRSP. Money can be put into this fund on a monthly basis. It can be taken out of your bank account by automatic withdrawal.

提示　投資管道五花八門。有所謂的 RRSP －註冊退休儲蓄計畫，也有所謂 GIC （政府基金）。你可以買債券或投資股票。許多人投資房地產或是餐廳這類的生意。RRSP 是最普遍的退休投資計畫，錢會自動從你銀行帳戶中扣除，每個月存入這個基金裡面。

Conversation 1

A: Good morning. What can I do for you today?

B: I would like to talk to someone about saving up for my retirement.

A: Okay. I'm sorry but can I ask you a question? How old are you?

B: I don't mind. I'm twelve years old.

A: Maybe it's none of my business, but aren't you

too young to be worried about retiring?

B. I like to think ahead.

中譯

A: 早安。需要什麼服務嗎？

B: 我想要找人談談退休儲蓄計畫。

A: 好的。抱歉，想問你一個問題，請問你幾歲？

B: 我不介意你問，我今年十二歲。

A: 或許這不干我事，但是你那麼年輕，現在就擔心退休問題會不會太早了？

B: 我喜歡未雨綢繆。

Conversation 2

A: Good afternoon. How can I help you?

B. I'd like to talk to someone about saving some money in RRSPs.

A: Okay. Why don't I make an appointment for you with our Investments Manager?

B. Okay. There won't be any pressure though will there? I'm just trying to learn.

A: No problem. She'll be more than happy to meet with you and answer your questions.

B. That's great. When can I see her?

中譯

A: 午安。需要什麼服務嗎？

B: 我想要找人談談註冊退休儲蓄計畫。

A: 好的。安排你和我們的投資部經理談談好嗎？

B: 好啊。不會有什麼壓力吧？我只是想知道一下。

A: 放心。她會非常樂意和你見面並回答你的問題。

B: 太好了。那什麼時候可以見她？

Conversation 3

A: I would like to open a savings account please.

B: Okay. I'll get an application form for us to fill out.

A: I have a question. What is the interest rate on a savings account?

B: We have a very competitive rate. It's around one percent.

A: That's it? That's terrible. That won't do at all. I'll never be able to retire.

B: To save for retirement, you should put your money in RRSPs, not a savings account.

中譯

A: 我想要開存款帳戶。

B: 好的。我去拿申請表給你填。

A: 我有個問題。請問存款帳戶利率多少？

B: 我們的利率很有競爭性，大約 1%。

A: 就這樣？太差了啦，一點用都沒有，那我永遠都退休不了。

B: 要為退休儲蓄的話，你應該把錢放在註冊退休儲蓄計畫，而不是存款帳戶。

Conversation 4

A: We have GICs and Mutual Funds. Those are what we're using to save for retirement.

B: Don't forget. You also have money in savings bonds.

A: Yes. That's right. I forgot about those. Don't we have some RRSPs?

B: No. Why do you ask?

A: Those are supposed to be the best way to save for retirement.

B: Maybe we should roll all of our different savings into some RRSPs then.

中譯

A: 我們已經有用來為退休儲蓄的政府基金和共同基金。

B: 不要忘了還有儲蓄債券的錢。

A: 對,沒錯。我忘了那個。我們沒有註冊退休儲蓄計畫嗎?

B: 沒有,問這個幹嘛?

A: 註冊退休儲蓄計畫應該是為退休儲蓄的最好方法。

B: 或許我們應該把各類不同存款整合到註冊退休儲蓄計畫才對。

Conversation 5

A: We're thinking about buying a house. We would use it as a rental property.

B: That might be a good investment. What would you use for the down payment?

A: We have money in RRSPs. Maybe we could cash them in to get the money out.

B: I don't think it's a good idea to liquidate one investment to get another.

A: Then what do we do? We can't afford the down payment on another house.

B: Start saving a little money each month. Then you can put a down payment down.

中譯

A: 我們想再買一棟房子,當做出租用的房地產投資。

B: 這項投資可能不錯,那你們要用什麼來付頭期款?

A: 我們有錢在註冊退休儲蓄計畫裡面,或許可以把錢領出來用。

B: 我覺得把一項投資變現,再拿來投資另一項不是個好主意。

A: 那我們要怎麼辦?多買一棟房子的話,我們負擔不起頭

期款。

B: 開始每個月存點錢，很快就付得出來了。

Conversation 6

A: Why would I need to save my money in some sort of bank account or investment?

B: You can get interest on your money. It can grow even if you're not adding to it.

A: I'll keep my money in a hole in my mattress. That's where it's been for fifty years.

B: You've had the same mattress for fifty years? That's disgusting.

A: Don't be silly. This mattress is almost brand new. I bought it in 1970.

B: Forget about bank accounts for now. I think you should invest in a new mattress first.

中譯

A: 為什麼要把錢存到銀行或是拿去投資？

B: 你的錢可以生利息啊。即使沒有再存錢進去，原本的錢也會變大。

A: 我把錢都放在床墊的破洞裡面，已經放了五十年了。

B: 你一張床墊睡五十年？有夠噁心。

A: 少呆了。這張床墊幾乎是全新的，是我在 1970 年買的。

B: 先不管銀行帳戶的事了，我想你應該先投資買張新床墊。

Conversation 7

A: If you want to save some money for your retirement, you need to put it in a RRSP.

B: What's an RRSP? Is that some fancy name for a bank account?

A: It's not really a bank account. It stands for

Registered Retirement Savings Plan.

B: Where do you buy one of those? How big is it? Do I just keep it in my house?

A: No. You give money to the bank and they put it in an RRSP for you.

B: So it is a kind of bank account after all isn't it? Sounds like it to me.

中譯

A: 如果你想要為將來退休存點錢，必須把錢放在註冊退休儲蓄計畫。

B: 註冊退休儲蓄計畫是什麼？是銀行帳戶的花俏名稱嗎？

A: 也不真的算是銀行帳戶啦。它的意思是「註冊退休儲蓄計畫」。

B: 要去哪裡買？規模有多大？放在家裡就可以了嗎？

A: 不是啦。你拿錢給銀行，銀行會幫你把錢存進註冊退休儲蓄計畫。

B: 所以它畢竟還是一種銀行帳戶，不是嗎？我聽起來就像銀行帳戶啊。

Conversation 8

A: What are you doing? You've been on the computer for a long time.

B: I'm just checking out my investments.

A: I don't invest with the bank so I can't do that. I wish I could.

B: If your investment firm has a website, you won't have to wait for your statements.

A: I don't know. I never asked. When you're done with the computer I'll see if they do.

B: It's nice to be able to see what your investments are doing whenever you want.

A: 你在幹嘛？你電腦用好久了。

B: 我只是在查詢我的投資情況。

A: 我沒有向那家銀行投資，所以不能查。真希望我也可以查。

B: 如果你的投資公司有網站的話，就不用等對帳單來才知道情況了。

A: 我不知道耶，從來沒問過他們。等你電腦用完後，我再上網看看有沒有網站。

B: 查的時候就可以知道目前投資情況如何，真的很棒。

Useful phrases and idioms
有用的片語和慣用語

It's none of my business 不干我的事

It might not be my place to comment; it doesn't concern me

例 I know it's probably none of my business, but your dog is about to bite your son.

我知道這可能不干我的事，不過你家的狗想要咬你兒子。

Fancy 花俏，別緻

sophisticated; very nice; formal

例 This is a very fancy restaurant.

這家餐館很別緻。

Vocabulary 字彙

bond	*n.*	債券

stock	*n.*	股票
monthly basis		每個月
retirement	*n.*	退休
pressure	*n.*	壓力
competitive	*adj.*	競爭性的
terrible	*adj.*	極差的
GICs		政府基金
Mutual Funds		共同基金
down payment		頭期款
liquidate	*v.*	將…變換成現金
mattress	*n.*	床墊
disgusting	*v.*	使作嘔
brand new		全新的

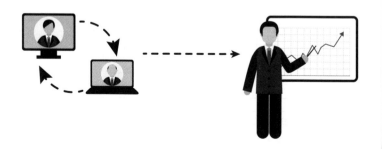

Unit 2

Saving for a Big Ticket Item
存錢買昂貴的東西

MP3-24

RRSPs are not the best way to save for a shorter term. RRSPs are best for a long term. Short term investments are good to use to save money for a big purchase like a house, boat, or trip. A short term GIC is a good choice. A savings bond is also a good choice. They will both have better interest rates than a savings account. They are also harder to get at. That means there's less temptation to take the money out as you're saving.

提示　　註冊退休儲蓄計畫 並不是短期儲蓄最好的方法，長期投資才能發揮效益。短期投資適合用來存一筆大錢買東西，例如房子、小船或用來旅行之類。短期政府基金是不錯的選擇。另外儲蓄債券也不錯。這兩者的利率都比存款帳戶好，但同時也較難申購，意思就是你存錢後，比較不會有變現的誘因。

Conversation　1

A:　I think this is the best boat we've seen. I don't like any other boat as much as this one.

B:　I agree. This boat is perfect. We've seen a lot of boats. None are as good as this.

A:　Do you know how much it costs?

B:　The price tag is over here. Oh my goodness. I think I'd better sit down.

A: Why? Is it that bad? Is the price that high? How much is it?

B: This boat is going to cost fifty thousand dollars. Time to cash in those savings bonds.

中譯

A: 我覺得這是我們看過最棒的小船，其他的都沒有像這艘那麼讓人喜歡。

B: 我同意，這艘船真是完美。我們看過那麼多艘船了，沒有一艘比它好。

A: 你知道這艘船多少錢嗎？

B: 這裡有標價。哦，天啊。我想坐著比較不會頭暈。

A: 怎麼了？有那麼糟嗎？很貴嗎？多少錢？

B: 買這艘船要花五萬塊。看來該是把儲蓄債券變現的時候了。

Conversation 2

A: I'm a school teacher and I need to talk to someone about investment strategies please.

B: Yes. Are you looking to start saving for your retirement?

A: No. I already have money in RRSPs. I'm looking to save for a big purchase.

B: The best place for your investment depends on how much you need to save.

A: I want to buy a tropical island. I think it'll take at least five years to save for that.

B: Yes. I think you're right. It'll probably take you at least five years to save for that.

中譯

A: 我是學校老師，想要找人談談投資策略的事。

B: 好的。你希望開始為退休存錢嗎？

A: 不，我已經參加註冊退休儲蓄計畫了，我希望存一筆大

錢買東西。

最好的投資管道要看你需要存多少錢來決定。

A: 我想要買一座熱帶小島。我想至少要花五年才存得到那筆錢吧。

B: 對,我想你說的沒錯。大概至少要花五年才存得到。

Conversation 3

A: You know what'd be nice to have? A cabin at the lake.

B: Yes. It'd be really nice to have a cabin to go to. We could get away from the city.

A: Yes. I think we should start saving for a cabin.

B: It's going to take forever. The interest rates on a savings account are terrible.

A: We won't use a savings account. We'll get a GIC. We'll get it for a five year term.

B: We should have enough saved for a good sized down payment by then.

中譯

A: 你知道擁有什麼東西很棒嗎?就是湖邊小屋。

B: 對啊。有間小屋可以去住真的很棒,那我們就可以遠離城市了。

A: 沒錯。我想我們該開始存錢買小屋了。

B: 存款帳戶的利率那麼差,要存到什麼時候啊。

A: 不要用存款帳戶,去買五年期的政府基金。

B: 到時就可以存夠錢付那筆數目龐大的頭期款了。

Conversation 4

A: I want to go to Africa. I want to go on a safari. We should go for at least three weeks.

B: What a wonderful experience. The thought is nice but we can't afford it.

A: We're going to start saving for it now. By the time we retire, we'll be able to go.

B: That takes care of my next question which was how will we get the time off work?

A: Tomorrow I'll go to the different banks and compare their investment accounts.

B: Okay. Let's do it. I think this will be great. I'll be happy to save for this trip.

中譯

A: 我想要去非洲參加狩獵旅行，至少要去三個禮拜才夠。

B: 這種經驗多美好啊。想法是很棒，但我們負擔不起。

A: 我們現在開始存錢，等我們退休後就可以去了。

B: 本來還要問你我們在工作要怎麼請那麼多天假，結果你已經回答了。

A: 明天我會去各家銀行比較看看各種投資計畫。

B: 好，我們開始進行吧。我覺得這樣很棒，可以很高興地存這筆旅行的錢。

Conversation 5

A: Excuse me. Can you help me? I need some information on investment accounts.

B: We have several different kinds of investment accounts. What are you saving for?

A: I'm saving for a big expense. My family wants to make a big purchase.

B: Okay. How many years will you be saving for?

A: I think it'll take us about five years to save for this.

B: A GIC might be a good choice for you and your family. Let me find a brochure.

中譯

A: 對不起，可以麻煩你嗎？我想了解一下投資計畫的相關資訊。

B: 我們有各種不同的投資計畫，你要存錢做什麼用？

A: 我要存一大筆錢，因為家人要買貴的東西。

B: 好的。你要存幾年？

A: 我想大概五年才夠。

B: 政府基金應該是你和你家人不錯的選擇。我找本小冊子給你。

Conversation 6

A: I think we should just get a loan and buy it on loan.

B: I think we should save for it. It will cost us less money in the long run.

A: Yes it'll cost less because we don't have to pay interest on a loan. I agree.

B: On the other hand, by the time we have the money saved, the price will have gone up.

A: That's what I was thinking. That why we should get a loan and buy it now.

B: Let's talk to someone at the bank. They will be able to help us compare.

中譯

A: 我覺得我們應該貸款把它買下來就好。

B: 我覺得應該存錢買。長期而言會比較省。

A: 對啊，不必付貸款利息會比較省，這點我同意。

B: 不過，等我們存夠錢，那時的價格也變貴了。

A: 我就是這麼想啊，所以才說應該現在去貸款來買。

B: 我們去銀行找人談談吧，他們會幫我們看怎樣比較划算。

Vocabulary 字彙

temptation	*n.*	誘惑
price tag		標價
strategy	*n.*	策略
tropical island		熱帶小島
cabin	*n.*	小屋
lake	*n.*	湖
safari	*n.*	非洲的（狩獵）旅行
expense	*n.*	經費

Unit 3

Investing for University
大學投資計畫

MP3-25

Parents can start saving for their children's secondary education when the children are young. They can save money in a RESP. RESP stands for Registered Education Savings Plan. University gets more expensive every year. The more money parents are able to save, the less it will cost when it's time for university.

提示　　父母可以在子女還小時，開始為他們未來的中等教育存錢。父母可以參加 RESP，即是所謂的「註冊教育儲蓄計劃」。大學每年的學費比較貴，存越多錢的話，子女上大學時的負擔就會越輕。

Conversation 1

A: Honey I've been thinking. I want our daughter to be able to go to university.

B: University? Why are you thinking about that now? She's only four days old?

A: I know. But I want to be a good father and give her every opportunity.

B: Okay. We'll put a little money aside in a savings account each month.

A: No. I heard about this thing called an RESP. It's made for saving money for school.

B: All right. You do some research on that. If it's a

good idea we'll do it.

中譯

A: 親愛的，我一直在想一件事。我希望我們的女兒將來可以上大學。

B: 大學？為什麼現在就在想？她才出生四天耶？

A: 我知道，我只是希望當個好父親，幫她爭取未來每個可能的機會。

B: 好吧。我們每個月都幫她存一點錢進戶頭。

A: 不用。有個叫做註冊教育儲蓄的計畫，是專為存錢上學用的。

B: 好，你先去研究一下，好的話我們就參加。

Conversation 2

A: Good morning. What can I do for you?

B: I need some help. I want to save some money for my children's education.

A: No problem. Our investment officer will be glad to discuss your options with you.

B: Have you ever heard of a plan that's designed for saving for children's education?

A: I think it's called a Registered Education Savings Plan. But I don't know for sure.

B: Okay. You'd better make an appointment for me to see that investment officer.

中譯

A: 早安。需要什麼服務嗎？

B: 我想替小孩的教育費存點錢，需要你們幫忙。

A: 沒問題。我們的投資部主任很樂意和你討論各種適合的方案。

B: 你有聽過一種專為子女教育儲蓄而設計的方案嗎？

A: 我想那叫做註冊教育儲蓄計劃，不過我不確定。

B: 好吧。那你最好安排我和投資部主任見個面。

Conversation 3

A: Are you done with the computer?

B: Yes. What are you doing?

A: I'm going to check out our investments online.

B: Okay. Check out what the RESP is doing while you're at it.

A: Yes. I'm glad we are investing in our kids and their education.

B: Yes. Then they can get good jobs and take care of us when we get old.

中譯

A: 你電腦用完了嗎？

B: 好了。你要做什麼？

A: 我要上網查詢我們的投資狀況。

B: 好。待會查一下那個註冊教育儲蓄計劃現在怎麼樣了。

A: 好。真高興我們能替小孩和他們的教育投資。

B: 對啊。那他們以後就可以找個好工作，等我們老的時候也可以照顧我們。

Conversation 4

A: I can help whoever is next down here please. Hello sir.

B: Hello. I need to save some money for education.

A: Okay. You're talking about an RESP.

B: That's a Registered Education Savings Plan right? Then yes.

A: How many children do you have?

B: Oh, I don't have any children. I wanted to save for an education for myself.

中譯

A: 請問再來是哪位需要服務？先生你好。

B: 你好。我想要存教育費用。

A: 好的，你說的是 RESP。

B: 申請教育儲蓄計劃對吧？那沒錯。

A: 你有幾個小孩？

B: 哦，我還沒有小孩，我是想替我自己存教育費用。

Conversation 5

A: Our investment officer helps you figure out what you can afford to save each month.

B: Great. I don't want to go into debt because I'm putting too much money aside.

A: She'll also help you figure out how much you need to save to reach your goal.

B: Yes. I want at least twenty thousand dollars saved by the time he leaves high school.

A: Yes. Who knows how much university will cost fifteen years from now?

B: Hopefully, twenty thousand dollars will be a good start.

中譯

A: 我們的投資部主任會幫你算出你每個月有能力存多少錢。

B: 太好了。要存的錢太多了，我可不想負債。

A: 她也會幫你算出要存多少錢才能達到目標。

B: 好。我希望他高中畢業時，至少可以存到兩萬塊。

A: 好的。誰知道十五年後上大學要花多少錢呢？

B: 但願兩萬塊會是個好的開始。

Conversation 6

A: Hi there. I want to be able to see how my

investment account is doing.

B: You get a statement mailed to you once a month.

A: I'd rather be able to check it whenever I feel like it.

B: I see. We should get you set up for telephone and online banking.

A: Online banking. That's sounds hard. It also sounds exciting.

B: Yes. It's like getting a bank statement whenever you want one.

中譯

A: 你好。我想知道投資計畫現在進行得怎麼樣了。

B: 每個月的對帳單都會寄給你。

A: 我是希望可以想查的時候就可以查。

B: 我懂。那我們幫你申請電話和網路銀行。

A: 網路銀行啊，聽起來有點難，又好像很刺激。

B: 沒錯。就好比想要看銀行對帳單的時候，隨時都可以看。

Conversation 7

A: I seem to be having a problem viewing my investment accounts online.

B: What's the matter?

A: The screen is just black. It doesn't matter how much I click on the mouse.

B: Try hitting some keys on the keyboard.

A: Nothing is working. Come here and see if you can figure out what's wrong.

B: First of all the computer monitor should be turned on. Maybe that's the problem.

中譯

A: 我想上網查詢我的投資計畫狀況，可是好像有問題。

B: 怎麼了？

A: 螢幕黑漆漆的，不管我怎麼按滑鼠都沒有用。

B: 按幾個鍵盤上的鍵試試看。

A: 沒有用，來幫我看看哪裡出了問題。

B: 電腦螢幕要先打開才行。問題大概出在那裡。

Vocabulary 字彙

secondary education		中等教育
expensive	*adj.*	昂貴的
design	*v.*	設計
click on		點擊
mouse	*n.*	滑鼠
monitor	*n.*	螢幕

Characters 人 物 介 紹

Jean Jean is 14 years old. She goes to school with Billy.
珍十四歲，她都和比利一起去上學。

Billy Billy is 17 years old. He is friends with both Jean and Jack.
比利十七歲，他是珍和傑克共同的朋友。

Jack Jack is 17 years old. He likes to travel.
傑克十七歲，喜歡到處旅遊。

Sarah Sarah is older than the others. She works in a bank as a bank teller. Sarah has a daughter named Patti who is the same age as Jean.
莎拉比他們的年紀都大，她在一家銀行擔任銀行櫃員。莎拉有一個女兒，名叫派蒂，她和珍的年紀一樣大。

Part 2 銀行金融英語會話應用

Chapter 1

In the Beginning
剛開始時

Unit 1

First Job
第一份工作

MP3-26

Jean and Billy are walking to school.

Jean	Hey, Billy, I've got some good news.
Billy	What is it, Jean?
Jean	I got a job.
Billy	That's great. I'm happy for you.
Jean	Thanks. I'm very excited.
Billy	Where will you be working?
Jean	I got a job at the bookstore.
Billy	That's a good place for you to work. I know that you like to read books.
Jean	I do love to read books. I think it'll be fun to work in a bookstore.

Billy asks Jean questions about her new job.

Billy	When do you start?
Jean	I start work tomorrow.
Billy	Tomorrow is Saturday. Will you also be working during the week?
Jean	I'll only work on Saturdays. I don't want this job to cause a problem with my schoolwork.

Billy	That's a good idea. School is important.
Jean	Yes. I'm excited about my new job but I always want to do well in school. I need time to study.
Billy	Will I be able to come visit you at work?
Jean	You can come to visit me when I have my lunch break.
Billy	What time will you have your lunch break?
Jean	I get to take a lunch break at twelve o'clock.
Billy	I'll come see you tomorrow at noon.
Jean	Okay.
Billy	Where do you want to go for lunch?
Jean	There is a bank down the street from the bookstore. Right beside the bank is a good restaurant.
	I'll meet you in that restaurant at noon tomorrow.

Billy and Jean make a date to
open a bank account.

Billy	Okay. Have you opened a bank account yet, Jean?
Jean	No, I haven't. Maybe tomorrow we can go to the bank. We can find out what I need to do to open a bank account.
Billy	We will have to eat quickly so that we have time to go to the bank after lunch. Then you can go back to work.
Jean	Okay.
Billy	You need a bank account for your paycheck. You will need to have a bank account or the bank

cannot cash your paycheck for you.

Jean   I won't get my first paycheck for two weeks. I'll get paid every two weeks.

Billy   Good. That gives us time to get everything ready at the bank.

Jean   Do you think that we will have enough time to get everything done tomorrow?

Billy   I don't know, Jean, but at least we can get started.

Jean   I've never needed a bank account before. I feel important.

Questions

1) Who needs a bank account?

A) Billy
B) Jean
C) Billy and Jean
D) None of the above

2) Where is the restaurant?

A) Beside the book store
B) Beside a tree
C) Beside Billy
D) Beside the bank

3) What is Jean's good news?

A) She is in love with Billy.
B) She has a new bank account.
C) She has a new restaurant.
D) She has a new job.

4) Where is Billy working?

    A) At the bank

    B) At the book store

    C) At the restaurant

    D) We do not know where Billy is working.

Vocabulary 字彙

bank account	*n.*	銀行（活期）帳戶
paycheck	*n.*	付薪水的支票

會話中譯

> 珍和比利正走路前往學校。

珍　嘿！比利，我有好消息喔。

比利　什麼好消息啊，珍？

珍　我找到一份工作了。

比利　太好了，我真替妳感到高興。

珍　謝啦，我好興奮呢。

比利　妳要在哪裡工作？

珍　我會在書店工作。

比利　對妳來說，那是一個很好的工作場所。我知道妳喜歡看書。

珍　我的確喜歡看書。我想，在書店工作應該會很有趣。

比利向珍詢問新工作的事情。

| 比利 | 妳什麼時候開始上班？ |

珍　我明天就開始了。

比利　明天是星期六。那妳星期一到五也要上班嗎？

珍　我只有星期六才上班。我不想讓這份工作影響到學校功課。

比利　這是個好辦法。學校課業比較重要。

珍　對啊。雖然我對新工作感到很興奮，但還是想把學校課業顧好，我需要時間唸書。

比利　我可以在妳上班時探訪妳嗎？

珍　你可以在我午餐休息時間來看我。

比利　那妳的午餐休息時間是幾點？

珍　我十二點時就可以休息吃午餐了。

比利　那我明天中午去找妳。

珍　好啊。

比利　妳想去哪裡吃午餐？

珍　書店再過去下一條街，有一家銀行，銀行隔壁有一家不錯的餐館。

我明天中午和你在那家餐館碰面。

比利和珍相約去銀行開戶。

比利　好的。珍，妳在銀行開過戶嗎？

珍　我沒開過戶頭。也許明天我們可以去一趟銀行，看看需要什麼資料來開戶。

比利　那我們午餐就要吃快一點，才有時間在吃飽後，去一趟銀行，之後妳才能回去上班。

珍 好的。

比利 妳需要為薪資支票開個銀行帳戶，不然銀行沒辦法兌現妳的支票。

珍 我工作兩個禮拜後，才會拿到第一張薪資支票。我每兩個星期支薪一次。

比利 很好。這樣子我們就有時間辦好銀行的事。

珍 你覺得我們明天有足夠的時間，把所有手續都辦好嗎？

比利 我不知道，珍。但至少可以開始辦那些手續。

珍 我以前從來都不需要銀行帳戶。現在覺得很重要。

Answers

B 1) 誰需要一個銀行帳戶？

D 2) 餐館位於哪裡？

D 3) 珍的好消息是什麼？

D 4) 比利在哪裡工作？

Unit 2

Getting Ready
準備就緒

MP3-27

Billy and Jean meet at a restaurant.

Billy	Hi, Jean.
Jean	Hi, Billy. Have you been waiting long?
Billy	No. I arrived only five minutes ago. Are you ready to eat?
Jean	Yes. I'm starving.
Billy	Sit down. I ordered for you. I thought that if I ordered for you, it would give us more time at the bank.
Jean	That was a good idea, Billy. What did you order?
Billy	I'm going to have a roast beef sandwich and some cream of mushroom soup.
Jean	What did you order for me?
Billy	I ordered the same thing.
Jean	I like mushroom soup. Thanks.

Jean chats about her first day at work.

Billy	No sweat. How was your first morning at work?
Jean	It was fun. I was busy. I helped people choose books. When a book was sold, I would put another book out on the shelf. I put books that people bought into bags for them

to take home.

Billy	Are there other workers in the bookstore?
Jean	Yes.
Billy	Are they nice?
Jean	Yes, they are nice. I know that I'm going to like working with them.
Billy	Good for you. Here comes our food.
Jean	That was fast. This mushroom soup tastes good.
Billy	Yes, it does. I'm glad that I ordered it.

Jean wonders what kind of account to open.

Jean	What kind of bank account should I get?
Billy	There are a few different kinds of accounts to choose from. There are savings accounts. Those are good for people who just want to use cash. There are checking accounts for people who need to write a lot of checks.
Jean	I've never written a check before.
Billy	Maybe you should start off with a savings account. It will be the easiest to start with.
Jean	Can I change the type of account later on if I need to?
Billy	Yes. The bank can close your account if you want. You can open a different kind of account later on if you need to.
Jean	What else do I need to know?
Billy	There is a lot to know about banking. You will

learn it as you need to. Don't worry right now about knowing everything.

Questions

1) Where are Billy and Jean?

A) At the book store
B) At the restaurant
C) At home
D) At the bank

2) What are Billy and Jean doing?

A) They are talking.
B) They are eating.
C) They are talking and eating.
D) They are not doing anything.

3) Who had mushroom soup for lunch?

A) Billy and Jean
B) Billy
C) Jean
D) Neither Billy nor Jean had mushroom soup.

4) When will Jean go to the bank?

A) Tomorrow
B) When she gets back to work
C) After she is done eating supper
D) After she is done eating lunch

Vocabulary 字彙

starve	*adj.*	飢餓的
No sweat		毫不費力；不用擔心

會話中譯

比利和珍在一家餐館碰面。

比利 嗨！珍。

珍 嗨！比利。你等很久了嗎？

比利 沒有，我才剛到五分鐘而已。妳準備好要吃東西了嗎？

珍 想啊，我餓死了。

比利 坐下吧，我已經幫妳點餐了。因為我想如果我先幫妳點餐，就能多爭取一點時間，去銀行辦事。

珍 這個主意不錯，比利。你點了什麼？

比利 我點了烤牛肉三明治和奶油蘑菇湯。

珍 那你幫我點了些什麼？

比利 點一樣的東西囉！

珍 我喜歡蘑菇湯，謝啦！

珍聊起她第一天的工作情況。

比利 不用客氣，小事一椿。妳第一天的工作情況怎麼樣？

珍 蠻有趣的。我忙著幫顧客選書，當書賣出去時，我就再拿另一本書，放在書架上。

我把顧客買的書放在袋子裡，讓他們好帶回家。

比利 書店裡還有其他同事嗎？

| 珍 | 有啊。 |

| 比利 | 他們人好嗎？ |

| 珍 | 他們人很好。我知道我會喜歡和他們一起工作的。 |

| 比利 | 不錯嘛。我們的食物來囉。 |

| 珍 | 還蠻快的嘛！這蘑菇湯很好喝。 |

| 比利 | 沒錯，真的很好喝。我很高興點了這道湯。 |

珍不曉得該開哪一種銀行帳戶。

| 珍 | 我應該開哪一種銀行帳戶？ |

| 比利 | 有幾種不同帳戶可以選擇。像是存款帳戶，這對只想用現金的人來說，蠻好用的。也有支票帳戶，這對需要開支票的人來說，比較好用。 |

| 珍 | 我以前從沒有開過支票。 |

| 比利 | 也許妳該從存款帳戶開始。這是剛開始時最容易使用的一種帳戶。 |

| 珍 | 那以後有需要的話，可以更改帳戶種類嗎？ |

| 比利 | 可以的，如果妳有需要，銀行可以幫妳關閉帳戶。等妳有需要時，可以再開一個不同種類的帳戶。 |

| 珍 | 我還需要知道哪些事情？ |

| 比利 | 銀行服務有很多，等妳需要其中一種時，自然就會學到。現在不需要擔心或想要全盤了解。 |

Answers

B 1) 比利和珍在哪裡？

C 2) 比利和珍在做什麼？

A 3) 誰在午餐時點了蘑菇湯？

D 4) 珍什麼時候會去銀行？

Unit 3

At the Bank
在銀行

MP3-28

Jean and Billy arrive at the bank.

Jean	Whom do I need to talk to about opening a bank account?
Billy	Let's get in the line up. We will ask a bank teller.
	If she cannot help us, she will be able to tell us who we need to talk to.
Jean	Thank you again for lunch. It was delicious.
Billy	You're welcome.
Jean	I'm the one who just started a new job. I should have paid for your lunch.
Billy	You can buy lunch for me when you get your first pay check.
Jean	Okay. I will.

Jean notices an ATM.

Jean	Look at that machine. People are getting money out of it. Maybe I don't need a bank account. Can I just use that machine?
Billy	That's an automated teller machine. All of the people who are using it have bank accounts.
	Everyone who uses the bank machine needs to have an account at the bank.

Jean	An automated teller machine. That's a long name.
Billy	They are also called ATMs.
Jean	What does an ATM do?
Billy	You can do a lot of your banking at an ATM. That way, you don't have to get in this long line.
Jean	Yes. This line is taking a long time to move. There are nine people in line ahead of us. Are all of them waiting to talk to a bank teller?
Billy	Yes.
Jean	They should use the ATM. It would be faster.
Billy	They might have questions like we do. It's best to talk to a bank teller if you have questions.
	If you have a simple and easy transaction, you can save a lot of time by using the ATM.

Jean and Billy wait in the line-up.

Jean	What is a transaction?
Billy	A transaction is any business that you are doing at the bank. When you are doing banking, you are making transactions.
Jean	I've a lot to learn about banking. Maybe I should buy a book about banking.
Billy	I'll help you. The tellers will help you so you don't need a book.
Jean	But I do need to get back to work soon.
Billy	This line up is not moving very quickly.
Jean	I think that we should go. Maybe we can go to the bank tomorrow.

Billy	The banking hours are on the door. When is the bank open tomorrow?
Jean	It says here that the bank is not open on Sundays.
Billy	Oh, well, then I guess we can come back Monday after school.
Jean	Too bad we didn't open an account, but thanks for your help anyway Billy.
Billy	No problem, Jean. Can I walk you back to work?
Jean	I would like that.

Questions

1) Why did Billy and Jean leave the bank?

A) They were done their banking.
B) They didn't like that bank.
C) Jean had to get back to work.
D) Billy had to get back to work.

2) Who paid for lunch?

A) The bank teller
B) The ATM
C) Jean
D) Billy

3) How many people were ahead of Billy and Jean in the bank line up?

A) Nine
B) Ten
C) Eleven
D) Twelve

4) When will Billy and Jean come back to the bank?

A) Tomorrow
B) Tonight
C) Sunday
D) Monday

Vocabulary 字彙

bank teller		銀行櫃員
delicious	*adj.*	美味的
automated teller machine		自動櫃員機
line-up		人（或）物的列隊

會話中譯

珍和比利到了銀行。

珍	我需要找誰開銀行帳戶？
比利	來排隊吧，我們去問銀行櫃員。
	如果她不能幫我們，也該能夠告訴我們需要做哪些事。
珍	謝謝今天的午餐。真的很好吃。
比利	不客氣。
珍	我是剛找到新工作的人。我應該幫你付午餐費用才對。
比利	當妳拿到第一張薪資支票時，就可以請我吃午餐啦！
珍	好啊，我會的。

珍注意到一台自動櫃員機。

珍	看看那台機器，大家都從那裡領到錢。也許我不需要一

個銀行帳戶，我可以只用那個機器嗎？

比利　那是自動櫃員機，所有使用它的人都有銀行帳戶。每一個使用銀行櫃員機的人，都必須先在銀行開戶。

珍　　自動櫃員機，好長的名字啊。

比利　大家也叫它 ATM。

珍　　ATM 可以做哪些事？

比利　妳可以用 ATM 進行很多種銀行服務，這樣的話，妳就不用排這麼長的隊啦！

珍　　對啊，排隊要等好久才會前進。我們前面還有九個人，他們都要找銀行櫃員嗎？

比利　是的。

珍　　他們應該用 ATM，這樣會比較快。

比利　他們可能跟我們有相同的疑問吧。如果妳有問題，最好是問銀行櫃員。

　　　如果妳只是要處理簡單又容易的交易手續，用 ATM 就可以省下很多時間。

珍和比利在排隊隊伍中等待。

珍　　什麼是交易手續？

比利　交易手續指的是妳要在銀行處理的任何一種金融服務。當妳進行銀行金融服務時，就等於在進行一項交易手續。

珍　　銀行方面的事，我還有好多要學喔。也許我該買一本關於金融業務的書。

比利　我會幫妳，銀行櫃員也會幫妳，所以妳不需要買書。

珍　　但是我很快就得回去上班了。

比利　這個隊伍移動的蠻緩慢。

珍	我想我們該走了，也許明天再來吧。
比利	大門上有說明銀行的營業時間。明天幾點開始營業？
珍	上面寫說銀行星期天不營業。
比利	喔，嗯，那我想我們星期一放學時再來吧。
珍	真可惜，我們沒開成銀行帳戶。但還是謝謝你的幫忙，比利。
比利	沒問題，珍。我陪妳一起走回書店好嗎？
珍	好啊，我也想和你一起走回去。

Answers

C　1) 比利和珍為什麼離開銀行？

D　2) 誰付了午餐的費用？

A　3) 比利和珍在銀行時，有多少人排在他們前面？

D　4) 比利和珍什麼時候會再來銀行？

Chapter 2

Getting Started

新手上路

MP3-29

Unit 1

Telling the Teller
告知銀行櫃員

Jean and Billy meet after school.

Jean	Hi, Billy. How was school?
Billy	It was good, Jean. How about you?
Jean	I wrote a test today.
Billy	How do you think you did?
Jean	It was easy. I have a feeling that I did well on it.
Billy	Well, I hope that you are right.
Jean	We will see. I'll get that test back on Wednesday.
Billy	Do you want to go to the bank now?
Jean	If you can still come, I'm ready to go.
Billy	Okay.
Jean	I'm going to tell the teller that I need to open a bank account.
Billy	That's right.
Jean	I'm also going to tell the teller that I want a savings account.
Billy	Yes.
Jean	What else am I going to tell the teller?
Billy	I don't think that you have to tell her anything else. She will know what to do. She will give you a bankcard.

Billy answers questions about banking.

Jean	What is a bankcard?
Billy	Your bankcard is what you show to the teller when you are doing banking. It's what you show to the teller when you are making a transaction.
	They use it to keep track of all your banking transactions in the computer.
Jean	How will I keep track of my banking transactions?
Billy	The bank will mail a statement to you. You will receive it once a month. It will have all of your transactions in the last month written on it.
Jean	How will I know if the statement is correct? What if they missed something?
Billy	Each time you see a teller to do some banking, she will give you a receipt. On your receipt will be written what banking you did.
	You can keep your receipts. You can compare them to your monthly statement.
Jean	What if I use the ATM?
Billy	The ATM will also give you a receipt. It does not matter if you give your bankcard to the real teller or to the ATM. Every time you do business with the bank, you will get a receipt.
Jean	You should be a bank teller because you are telling me many things about the bank. Get it? Bank teller telling me things?
Billy	Yah, I get it. You're a real comedian.

Questions

1) Why does Jean want Billy to come with her to the bank?

    A) Jean does not know very much about banking.
    B) Billy does not know very much about banking.
    C) Jean does not go anywhere by herself.
    D) Jean thinks that Billy is in love with her.

2) Who will know what to do at the bank?

    A) Billy
    B) The Teller
    C) Jean
    D) Billy and Jean

3) What will the teller give to Jean?

    A) She will give her a job.
    B) She will give her a cold.
    C) She will give her a bank card.
    D) She will give her a cookie.

4) What time of day is it?

    A) It is noon.
    B) Billy and Jean just finished school.
    C) It is time to go to bed.
    D) There is no time to go to the bank.

Vocabulary 字彙

bankcard	n.	銀行金融卡
transaction	n.	交易
receipt	n.	收據

comedian	*n.*	喜劇演員

會話中譯

珍和比利在放學後碰面。

珍	嗨！比利。今天在學校還好嗎？
比利	不錯啊，珍。妳呢？
珍	我今天有考試。
比利	妳覺得考得怎麼樣？
珍	題目很簡單，我覺得應該考得很好。
比利	嗯，希望妳是對的。
珍	再看看囉。星期三我就可以拿回試卷了。
比利	妳現在想去銀行嗎？
珍	如果你還是可以和我一起去的話，我就準備好了。
比利	好啊。
珍	我要跟銀行櫃員說，我需要開一個銀行帳戶。
比利	沒錯。
珍	我還要跟銀行櫃員說，我想要一個存款帳戶。
比利	是的。
珍	我還需要告訴銀行櫃員什麼事呢？
比利	我想妳不用說其它事了。她會知道該怎麼做。她會給妳一張銀行金融卡。

比利回答銀行的相關問題。

珍	什麼是銀行金融卡？
比利	妳的銀行金融卡是用來在進行金融服務時，給銀行櫃員核對

的東西。妳在進行金融交易時，要把這張卡交給銀行櫃員核對。

他們用這張卡來追蹤妳在電腦裡所有的銀行交易紀錄。

珍　那我自己要怎樣追蹤我的銀行交易紀錄呢？

比利　銀行會寄結算單給妳，每個月都會收到一次。上面會寫妳上個月所有的交易紀錄。

珍　那我怎麼知道結算單的內容是否正確？萬一他們漏掉了一些紀錄呢？

比利　妳每一次和銀行櫃員處理銀行業務時，她都會給妳一張明細表。明細表上會寫著妳進行了什麼樣的金融服務。

妳可以保存明細表，然後將這些明細表和每月結算單比對。

珍　如果我用 ATM 呢？

比利　ATM 也會給妳一張明細表。不管妳把銀行金融卡交給銀行櫃員，或在 ATM 進行交易，每一次和銀行進行交易後，妳都會拿到一張明細表。

珍　你應該當銀行櫃員，因為你跟我講了好多銀行的業務。懂了嗎？「告知銀行業務的人」（「bank teller」字面意義的直接詮釋可說成「告知銀行業務的人」，但其實「bank teller」是銀行櫃員的意思，而珍以此揶揄比利）…因為你告訴我很多事。

比利　是啊，我懂妳的意思。妳真像一個喜劇演員。

Answers

A　1) 珍為什麼要比利和她一起去銀行？

B　2) 銀行裡知道該怎麼處理業務的人是誰？

C　3) 銀行櫃員會給珍什麼東西？

B　4) 以上對話的時間背景是什麼時候？

Learning the Basics
學習基本事項

MP3-30

Waiting in the line up.

Billy	It's your turn, Jean.
Jean	What? I wasn't paying attention.
Billy	That teller is ready to see you now. Go up to the counter. She will help you.
Jean	Aren't you going to come with me?
Billy	No. I'll go sit down in the waiting area.
Jean	But I don't know what to do. I need you to come with me.
Billy	Don't worry. It's the teller's job to help you.
Jean	Okay, Billy. I'll come get you when I'm done.
Billy	Okay. Good luck.

Jean meets Sarah the bank teller.

Sarah	Can I help you?
Jean	Yes, please. My name is Jean.
Sarah	It's nice to meet you, Jean. My name is Sarah. How can I help you today?
Jean	I would like to open a bank account.
Sarah	Okay, Jean. Do you know what kind of bank account you want to open?

Jean	Yes. I would like to open a savings account.
Sarah	We need your name, address, phone number, and date of birth.
Jean	Okay.
Sarah	We also need to see two pieces of ID. I'll put all of your information on this form. It will go in your file here at the bank.
	I'll photocopy your identification. The photocopies will also go in your file.
Jean	Here is my ID and all of my contact information.
Sarah	Thank you. We also need your signature. Will you please sign here?
Jean	Yes.
Sarah	Good. Thank you. Now that we have completed your application for a bank account, I'll give you your bankcard.
Jean	Thank you.

Jean learns how to use the bankcard.

Sarah	If you are making a deposit or withdrawal, it's easy to use the ATM. Since you only have one account, you won't need to do transfers.
	If you decide you want to open another account, we can talk about transfers at that time.
Jean	Okay.
Sarah	Here is your PIN. It's your secret code. You will need it to do banking through the ATM. Don't show anyone your secret number.
Jean	Okay.

Sarah	I've given you your bankcard and your PIN number. Your account is now open for you to use. Do you have any questions?
Jean	Yes. Can I go now?
Sarah	I'm sorry. I didn't know that you are in a hurry. Do you want to make a deposit before you go?
Jean	No.
Sarah	Okay. Thank you for opening a bank account here today.
Jean	You're welcome.
Sarah	Have a good afternoon.
Jean	Thank you. You, too. Good-bye.
Sarah	Good-bye.

Billy is waiting for Jean.

Billy	How did it go, Jean?
Jean	What is a deposit?
Billy	That's when you want to put money in your account.
Jean	What is a withdrawal?
Billy	That's when you take money out of your account.
Jean	What is a transfer?
Billy	That's when you move money from one account to another account. You have not told me how it went with the bank teller.
Jean	I think that I just learned some of the basics.

Questions

1) Why did Billy leave Jean?

    A) He wanted to sit down.
    B) He was mad at her.
    C) He didn't like the teller.
    D) He had to go to the bank.

2) Where did Billy go?

    A) He sat in a chair by the door.
    B) He went to the book store.
    C) He went to the restaurant.
    D) He didn't go anywhere.

3) What is Jean's PIN?

    A) 1234
    B) 5678
    C) 3456
    D) We do not know.

4) How much money did Jean deposit into her account?

    A) Four hundred dollars
    B) Five hundred dollars
    C) Zero dollars
    D) Five dollars

Vocabulary 字彙

| pay attention | 注意 |

counter	*n.*	櫃臺
waiting area		等待區
savings account		存款帳戶
identification	*n.*	身份証
contact information		聯絡資料
application	*n.*	申請
deposit	*n.*	存款
withdrawal	*n.*	提款
transfer	*n.*	轉帳
secret code		密碼

會話中譯

他們正在隊伍裡排隊等候。

比利	輪到妳了，珍。
珍	什麼？我剛剛沒專心注意。
比利	銀行櫃員已經可以和妳討論事情了。去櫃檯那邊吧，她會幫妳的。
珍	你不跟我一起去嗎？
比利	不了，我在等候區這裡坐著就好。
珍	可是我不知道該怎麼做，我需要你跟我一起過去。
比利	不用擔心，銀行櫃員的職責就是幫忙妳解答疑惑。
珍	好吧，比利。我處理好了就過來你這裡。
比利	好。祝妳好運！

珍和銀行櫃員莎拉談話。

莎拉	我能幫妳什麼忙？
珍	是的，麻煩您了。我的名字叫珍。
莎拉	很高興見到妳，珍。我的名字叫莎拉，今天需要我幫妳

什麼忙呢？

珍　我想開一個銀行帳戶。

莎拉　好的，珍。妳知道妳想開什麼種類的銀行帳戶嗎？

珍　我知道，我想開一個存款帳戶。

莎拉　我們需要妳的姓名、地址、電話號碼，還有出生年月日。

珍　好的。

莎拉　我們還需核對兩種身分識別證。我會把妳所有資料都填在這張表上，它會是妳在銀行檔案的一部分。我還會影印妳的身分證，身分證副本也會存在妳的檔案裡。

珍　這是我的身分證，還有我的所有聯絡資料。

莎拉　謝謝妳，我們還需要妳的簽名。可以請妳在這裡簽名嗎？

珍　好的。

莎拉　好的，謝謝妳。我們現在已完成了妳銀行帳戶的申請手續，我會給妳妳的銀行金融卡。

珍　謝謝妳。

珍學習如何使用銀行金融卡。

莎拉　如果妳想存款或提款的話，使用簡易 ATM 就可以了。因為妳只有一個帳戶，所以不需使用轉帳服務。

　　　如果妳決定要開另一個帳戶，我們到時候再談轉帳的相關事宜。

珍　好的。

莎拉　這裡是妳的 PIN 碼，它是妳的密碼。妳在使用 ATM 進行金融服務時，會需要它。不要把妳的密碼告訴任何人。

珍　好的。

莎拉　我已經給了妳銀行金融卡和 PIN 碼。妳的帳戶現在已經啟用了。有沒有其它問題呢？

珍	沒有，我現在可以離開了嗎？
莎拉	真是抱歉，我不曉得妳在趕時間。妳想要在離開之前，存一筆款項嗎？
珍	不了。
莎拉	好的。謝謝妳今天在這裡開戶。
珍	不客氣。
莎拉	祝妳有個愉快的下午！
珍	謝謝妳，妳也是。再見！
莎拉	再見！

比利正在等候珍。

比利	進行得怎麼樣，珍？
珍	什麼是存款啊？
比利	那是指妳要把錢放進帳戶裡的意思。
珍	什麼是提款？
比利	那是指妳要把錢提出帳戶裡的意思。
珍	什麼是轉帳？
比利	那是指妳要把錢從一個帳戶轉到另一個帳戶。妳還沒跟我說，妳和銀行櫃員談得怎麼樣？
珍	我想我剛學了些基本的東西。

Answers

A 1) 比利為什麼離開珍？

A 2) 比利去哪裡了？

D 3) 珍的 PIN 碼是多少？

C 4) 珍在她的帳戶裡存了多少錢？

Putting it All Together
整合所有事項

MP3-31

Jean talks with her coworker Jack at the bookstore.

Jack	Hi, Jean.
Jean	Hi, Jack.
Jack	It's nice outside today.
Jean	Yes, It is.
Jack	It's too bad that we have to spend the day inside working.
Jean	I don't mind.
Jack	Do you like your new job here at the bookstore?
Jean	Yes, I do. I like books. Everyone who works here seems to be nice. How long have you worked here?
Jack	I've worked here for two months.
Jean	Do you like it?
Jack	Yes. I like books too. I also think that everybody who works here is nice. Will you help me?
Jean	What are you doing?
Jack	I have to put these three piles of books all together on one shelf.
Jean	I can help you.

Jack	Thanks. I'm happy that today is payday.
Jean	Me too. This will be my first pay check ever.
Jack	Are you ready for it?
Jean	What do you mean?
Jack	Have you opened a bank account?
Jean	Yes. My friend Billy and I are putting it all together at the bank.
Jack	That's good.
Jack	Which bank do you go to?
Jean	The one down the street. It's right beside the restaurant.
Jack	Hey, that's the same bank that I go to!
Jean	Oh yah? I'm going after work.
Jack	Can I walk down to the bank with you?
Jean	Yes. I'll be happy to have the company. Besides, you can help me.
Jack	Okay. We will make our deposits at the ATM.
Jean	We will have to because the bank will be closed by the time we get off work. All of the tellers will be done for the day.
Jack	That's right. Banks have such bad hours.
Jean	I know. It seems like they are never open.
Jack	That's because they want you to use the ATM. They don't have to pay the ATM but they do have to pay the human tellers. It saves them money.
Jean	Of course.
Jack	Let's get back to work and deal with these books.

Jean   Okay.

Questions

1) How long has Jack worked in the book store?

- A) Two weeks
- B) One week
- C) One month
- D) Two months

2) Why is Jean happy that Jack will walk to the bank with her?

- A) She is will be glad to have the company.
- B) She does not feel safe.
- C) Jack does not feel safe.
- D) He can carry her books for her.

3) Where will they make their deposits?

- A) At a different bank
- B) At the teller
- C) At the automated teller machine
- D) At the book store

4) How many piles of books are there?

- A) One
- B) Two
- C) Three
- D) Four

會話中譯

珍和她在書店的同事傑克談話。

傑克 嗨！珍。

珍 嗨！傑克。

傑克 今天天氣很好喔！

珍 對啊，沒錯。

傑克 太可惜了，我們必須把一天時間花費在室內工作。

珍 我不在意。

傑克 妳喜歡書店這份新工作嗎？

珍 是的，我喜歡。因為我喜歡書。而且在這裡工作的每一個人似乎都很好。你在這裡工作多久了？

傑克 我在這裡工作兩個月了。

珍 那你喜歡這份工作嗎？

傑克 喜歡啊，因為我也喜歡書。而我也覺得在這裡工作的每一個人都很好。妳可以幫我一個忙嗎？

珍 你在做什麼？

傑克 我必須把這三疊書一起放到書架上。

珍 我可以幫你。

傑克 謝啦。我好高興今天是領薪水的日子。

珍 我也是，這將是我人生的第一份薪水。

傑克 妳準備好了嗎？

珍 什麼意思？

傑克 妳去開戶了嗎？

珍 我開過了，我朋友比利和我把銀行的所有事項都辦好了。

傑克	那很好。
傑克	妳去哪一家銀行？
珍	位於下一條街的那家。就在餐廳隔壁。
傑克	嘿！那跟我去的銀行是同一家。
珍	真的嗎？我下班後會去一趟。
傑克	我可以和妳一起走去銀行嗎？
珍	可以啊！我很高興你跟我作伴。而且，你還可以幫我的忙。
傑克	好的，我們就在 ATM 存款吧。
珍	我們必須這樣做，因為銀行在我們下班時，也已經關門了，所有的銀行櫃員都下班了。
傑克	沒錯。銀行的營業時間不太好。
珍	我知道，好像銀行一向都是關著的。
傑克	那是因為他們想要妳用 ATM。他們不用付薪水給 ATM，可是要付薪水給真正的銀行櫃員。這樣子做可以省錢。
珍	我想也是。
傑克	我們繼續工作，去處理那些書吧。
珍	好的。

Answers

D 1) 傑克在書店工作多久了？

A 2) 珍為什麼會因為傑克可以和她一起去銀行而感到高興？

C 3) 他們會在哪裡存款？

C 4) 要處理的書有幾疊？

Chapter 3

First Steps

第一步

Unit 1

Pins and Needles
關於密碼的笑話

MP3-32

Jack asks Jean some trivia on the way to the bank.

Jack	Do you know why the ATM machines are inside the bank doors?
Jean	No.
Jack	They used to have ATMs on the outside of the bank. They were attached to the outside wall.
Jean	Really?
Jack	Yes.
Jean	Maybe they moved them inside because people didn't like to get rained on when they were doing their banking.
Jack	Nice idea, actually it's because people were stealing the machines. They would pull them off of the wall.
Jean	With their hands?
Jack	No. That's not possible. They would use trucks and machines. They would do it late at night when there was no one around.
Jean	I can't believe that.
Jack	It's true. Here we are.
Jean	The bank is closed just like I thought it would be.

Jack and Jean arrive at the bank machine.

Jack	You need to use your bankcard to unlock the door. Put it in this slot by the door.
Jean	Okay. The door just opened all by itself.
Jack	That's right. Now, here we are at the bank machine. Put your card in that slot. Do it just like you did at the door.
Jean	Okay.
Jack	On the screen, it is asking for your PIN. Punch in your PIN number on the keypad.
Jean	I cannot remember my PIN. I wrote it down. It's in my pocket.
Jack	It's not safe to keep your password on paper. You must memorize it and throw away that paper. Someone could steal that paper from you.
	If they took your bankcard from you, they could steal money out of your bank account.
Jean	That would be horrible. Who would do something so horrible?
Jack	There are bad people who steal bank cards. It's best to be careful.
Jean	You are right. I want to be safe. I'll rip up this paper.
Jack	There is a garbage can. Throw that ripped up paper in there.

Jean makes a big mistake.

Jean	Okay. I'm putting my card in the ATM slot.
Jack	Yes.

Jean	I'm putting it in the same way that I put it in the slot at the door.
Jack	Right.
Jean	Now, what do I do?
Jack	Type in your PIN. What is wrong?
Jean	I didn't memorize my PIN number before I ripped up that paper.
Jack	Well, you will have to come back to the bank tomorrow.
Jean	Tomorrow is Sunday. The bank won't be open.
Jack	Well, you'll have to come back to the bank on Monday. You'll need to see the teller. She will give you a new PIN.
Jean	What if I use your PIN number?
Jack	It won't work for your bankcard.
Jean	With all these rules, no wonder people rip the machines off the wall.

Questions

1) Where are Jack and Jean?

A) Inside the book store
B) On the way to the bank
C) In front of the bank
D) Inside of the bank

2) When will Jean be able to see a teller?

A) Tomorrow

B) The day after tomorrow
C) Three days from now
D) Two days from yesterday

3) Why can't Jean use the ATM?

A) She doesn't know how.
B) She isn't smart enough.
C) She ripped up her PIN.
D) She ripped up her bank card.

4) What does Jean want to use from Jack?

A) His money
B) His PIN number
C) His bank card
D) His job

Vocabulary 字彙

attache	*v.*	裝上
slot	*n.*	插槽
password	*n.*	密碼
horrible	*adj.*	可怕的
rip up		撕碎
memorize	*v.*	背熟

會話中譯

傑克在走去銀行的途中，問珍一些小事情。

傑克 妳知道為什麼自動櫃員機設在銀行大門內嗎？

珍 不知道。

傑克 以前 ATM 是設在銀行外面的。自動櫃員機就嵌附在外

牆上。

珍　真的嗎？

傑克　真的。

珍　他們之所以把櫃員機移進去，可能是因為大家不喜歡在進行金融服務時被雨淋到吧。

傑克　不錯的想法。但其實是因為有人偷櫃員機，他們把櫃員機從牆上扯下來。

珍　徒手把櫃員機扯下來？

傑克　不，那當然不可能。他們會用卡車和機械設備，然後在夜深人靜時行動。

珍　我不敢相信有這種事。

傑克　這是真的。我們到了。

珍　跟我想的一樣，銀行已經關門了。

傑克和珍抵達櫃員機。

傑克　妳必須用金融卡解開門鎖，把卡片放進門邊的插槽吧。

珍　好。門自己開了。

傑克　沒錯，現在我們來到櫃員機前面了。把妳的卡片放進那個插槽，就像剛剛在門邊做的動作一樣。

珍　好的。

傑克　螢幕上會詢問妳的個人識別碼。在鍵盤上鍵入妳的個人識別碼吧。

珍　我記不住我的個人識別碼，我寫下來了，在我的口袋裡。

傑克　把密碼記在紙上很不安全。妳必須把密碼背起來，然後把紙扔掉。因為有人可能會從妳這偷走那張紙。

如果他們又拿到了妳的金融卡，他們就可以把妳帳戶裡的錢偷走。

珍	這真是太可怕了。誰會做這種可怕的事？
傑克	有壞人專門偷金融卡，所以最好是小心一點。
珍	你說得沒錯，為了安全起見，我還是把這張紙撕掉。
傑克	那邊有一個垃圾桶。把妳撕掉的紙丟進那裡吧。

珍犯了一個天大的錯誤。

珍	好了。我現在要把我的卡片放進 ATM 插槽裡。
比利	是的。
珍	我用剛剛把卡片插入門邊插槽一樣的方法，把卡片插入這個插槽。
比利	沒錯。
珍	現在，我該怎麼做呢？
比利	把妳的 個人識別碼鍵入啊。怎麼了？
珍	把紙撕掉前，我忘了要先把 個人識別碼背起來了。
比利	好吧，妳明天必須再來銀行一趟。
珍	明天是星期天，銀行不營業。
比利	好吧，那妳得星期一再過來一趟。妳需要找銀行櫃員處理，她會再給妳一個新的個人識別碼。
珍	如果我用你的個人識別碼呢？
比利	那對妳的金融卡起不了作用。
珍	這麼多的規則，難怪有人想把櫃員機從牆上扯下來。

Answers

D　1) 傑克和珍人在哪裡？

B　2) 珍什麼時候才可以見到銀行櫃員？

C　3) 珍為什麼沒辦法使用 ATM？

B　4) 珍想要使用傑克的什麼東西？

Unit 2

Back to the Bank

回到銀行

MP3-33

Jean goes back to the bank to get a new PIN.

Sarah	Can I help you?
Jean	Yes. My name is Jean.
Sarah	Hello, Jean. How can I help you today?
Jean	I just opened a bank account here two weeks ago.
Sarah	Yes?
Jean	I tried to deposit my first pay check in the bank machine on Saturday. I couldn't do it.
Sarah	Is the bank machine broken?
Jean	No. I ripped up the paper that you wrote my PIN on.
Sarah	Okay. You don't need to keep the paper.
Jean	I didn't memorize the PIN before I ripped up that paper.
Sarah	Oh. I understand. I can help you with that. Do you have your bankcard?
Jean	Yes, I do. Here it is.
Sarah	Thank you. Will you please show me some identification?
Jean	Yes.

Sarah	I need to make sure that you are Jean. I need to be sure that this is your bankcard.
Jean	Sometimes people steal bank cards.
Sarah	That's correct.
Jean	Here is my ID.
Sarah	Thank you, Jean.

Sarah finds Jean a new PIN.

Sarah	Here is your bankcard back.
Jean	Thank you.
Sarah	I have a new PIN for you. I'll write it down on a piece of paper.
Jean	I think that you should just tell me what it is. I don't want to have this problem happen again.
Sarah	Okay. Your password is seven seven two one.
Jean	Seven seven two one.
Sarah	Right.
Jean	Seven seven two one.
Sarah	That's correct. But don't say it out loud. Someone might hear it. You need to keep that password private and safe.
Jean	But that's the only way that I'll remember it. I need to repeat it to memorize it.
Sarah	In that case, I'll write it down on a piece of paper. When you get home, you can repeat it out loud until you remember it. Then you can rip up the piece of paper.
Jean	Okay. I'll memorize it when I get home.

Sarah	Just make sure that you memorize it before you rip up the paper this time.
Jean	You are very funny, Sarah.
Sarah	Bye, Jean. Thank you for banking with us.
Jean	Bye, Sarah.

Jean makes a deposit.

Sarah	Oh, wait. I think that we are forgetting something.
Jean	What?
Sarah	Don't you want to make a deposit while you are here?
Jean	Yes. I almost forgot.
Sarah	Please fill out this deposit slip. Write your bank account number, the date, and your name.
Jean	Okay.
Sarah	Sign the deposit slip at the bottom.
Jean	Okay.
Sarah	Now you can give the deposit slip to me.
Jean	Here you go.
Sarah	Thank you. I also need your deposit.
Jean	What?
Sarah	What are you depositing?
Jean	My paycheck.
Sarah	Sign it and give it to me.
Jean	Here it is.

Sarah	And here is your receipt. Thank you for banking with us.
Jean	Thank you for your help, Sarah.
Sarah	Bye, Jean.

Questions

1) What does Jean need to memorize?

    A) Her account number
    B) Her PIN
    C) Her receipt
    D) Her deposit

2) What did she almost forget to do?

    A) Wash her hands
    B) Sign the deposit slip
    C) Deposit her pay check
    D) Say thank you

3) How did Sarah act when Jean told her that she ripped up her PIN?

    A) She was angry.
    B) She made a joke about Jean ripping it up again.
    C) She asked her out for lunch.
    D) She started to cry.

4) Why did Jean go to the bank?

    A) To make a deposit
    B) To get a new password
    C) To talk to the teller
    D) all of the above

Vocabulary 字彙

sign	*v.*	簽名

會話中譯

珍回到銀行，申請一個新的 PIN 碼。

莎拉	我可以幫妳什麼忙？
珍	是的。我的名字叫珍。
莎拉	哈囉！珍。我今天可以幫妳什麼忙呢？
珍	我兩個星期前在這裡開了一個帳戶。
莎拉	然後呢？
珍	星期六時，我試著把我第一份薪水存入櫃員機，但沒辦法完成手續。
莎拉	櫃員機壞掉了嗎？
珍	不是的。我把妳寫給我個人識別碼的那張紙撕掉了。
莎拉	沒關係的。妳不需要保留那張紙。
珍	但我把紙撕掉之前，沒有把個人識別碼背起來。
莎拉	喔，我明白了。我可以幫妳。妳有帶金融卡過來嗎？
珍	有。在這裡。
莎拉	謝謝妳。可以請妳給我看一下身分證嗎？
珍	好的。
莎拉	我必須確認妳就是珍本人，也必須確認這張是妳的金融卡。
珍	因為有人會偷金融卡。
莎拉	沒錯。

珍	這是我的身分證。
莎拉	謝謝妳，珍。

莎拉幫珍設了一個新的 PIN 碼。

莎拉	這是妳的金融卡。
珍	謝謝妳。
莎拉	我幫妳設了一個新個人識別碼。我會把它寫在一張紙上。
珍	我想妳就把號碼告訴我吧。我不想再發生同樣的問題。
莎拉	好的。妳的密碼是七七二一。
珍	七七二一。
莎拉	對。
珍	七七二一。
莎拉	沒錯，但是不要說得太大聲，可能有人會聽見。妳必須把密碼記在隱密和安全的地方。
珍	但這是我唯一可以記得住的方法。我必須重複唸到記住為止。
莎拉	這樣的話，我把它寫在一張紙上，妳回家時就可以大聲重複唸，直到記住為止。然後妳就可以把紙撕掉了。
珍	好的。我回家的時候再背。
莎拉	但這次在撕掉紙之前，要先確定妳記住密碼了喔。
珍	妳真風趣，莎拉。
莎拉	再見，珍，謝謝妳到行裡來處理金融業務。
珍	再見，莎拉。

珍進行存款事宜。

莎拉	喔，等等。我想我們忘了一件事。

珍	什麼事？
莎拉	妳難道不想趁妳在這裡時，順便存款嗎？
珍	對，我差點忘了。
莎拉	請把這張存款單填寫好。填上妳的銀行帳戶號碼、存款日期和姓名。
珍	好的。
莎拉	並在最底下簽名。
珍	好的。
莎拉	妳現在可以把存款單給我了。
珍	拿去吧。
莎拉	謝謝妳。我還需要妳的存款款項。
珍	什麼意思？
莎拉	妳想存什麼款項呢？
珍	我的薪資支票。
莎拉	請在支票上簽名，再交給我就可以了。
珍	好的，支票在這裡。
莎拉	這是妳的明細表。謝謝妳到行裡來進行金融業務。
珍	謝謝妳的幫忙，莎拉。
莎拉	再見，珍。

Answers

B 1) 珍需要記住什麼東西？

C 2) 她差點忘了做什麼事？

B 3) 當珍告訴莎拉，她把寫上個人識別碼的紙條撕掉時，莎拉作何反應？

D 4) 珍為什麼要去銀行？

What's Next?
接下來呢？

MP3-34

It is Jean's turn to pay for lunch.

Billy	I'm excited that you are taking me for lunch today, Jean.
Jean	It's my turn to buy you lunch. Last time you bought me lunch.
	I said that when I got my first paycheck that I would take you for lunch.
Billy	You have now been at your new job for three weeks. Do you still enjoy it?
Jean	I like it more than ever. I'm getting to know the other people who work at the bookstore. They are all friendly.
	I'm also getting to know some of the customers. Some of them come into the store every weekend.
Billy	I would like to be able to buy a book every weekend. I don't have enough money.
Jean	What are you going to order for lunch?
Billy	I would like to have the cream of tomato soup and an egg salad sandwich. What are you going to have?
Jean	I think that I'll get the same. That sounds good.
Billy	Okay. What else is new, Jean?

Jean	My bank account is new.
Billy	How do you like having a bank account?
Jean	It's not easy. There is a lot to remember.
Billy	You will learn all you need to know. You will get used to it.
Jean	I made a deposit at the bank the other day.
Billy	Have you made a withdrawal yet?
Jean	No.
Billy	Does that mean that you don't have any money with you?
Jean	No. My mom gave me some money so that I could buy you lunch.
Billy	Why didn't you use some money from your paycheck?
Jean	I don't know how to get it out of my account.
Billy	That's called withdrawing. That's making a withdrawal.
Jean	Is that what you will teach me next?
Billy	Yes. That's what's next. But first, let's eat this delicious lunch.
Jean	It looks so good.

The food arrives.

Jean	Wait a minute. This does not look like cream of tomato soup. It's not red. It's white.
Billy	So, what's next?
Jean	I better try it. This does not taste like cream of tomato soup. It tastes like mushroom soup.

Billy	What are you going to do?
Jean	I'm going to eat it. I love cream of mushroom soup. When we are done eating, will you come with me to the bank?
Billy	Yes. I'll show you how to make a withdrawal.
Jean	Do I have to fill out a slip?
Billy	When you go through a teller, most of them want you to fill out a withdrawal slip. Some of them don't mind if you don't.
	When you go through the ATM, you don't need to fill out a withdrawal slip.
Jean	Okay. So, I go up to the ATM. I put in my card. I type in my password. What's next?
Billy	The banking machine will show you what to do next. It's easy. You will see. Now, eat your soup before it gets cold.

Questions

1) What kind of soup does Billy order?

    A) Cream of mushroom
    B) Cream of tomato
    C) Egg salad
    D) He does not order soup.

2) What kind of soup does Jean get?

    A) Cream of mushroom
    B) Cream of tomato
    C) Egg salad
    D) She does not get soup.

3) Who has never done a withdrawal before?

A) The ATM
B) The teller
C) Billy
D) Jean

4) What are Billy and Jean going to do next?

A) They are going to order lunch.
B) They are going to go back to the book store.
C) They are going to go to the bank.
D) They are going to get married.

Vocabulary 字彙

| customer | n. | 顧客 |
| fill out | | 填寫 |

會話中譯

輪到珍請吃午餐了。

比利 珍，我好興奮妳今天要請我吃午餐。

珍 輪到我請你吃午餐啦，因為上次你請過我了。

我說過當我拿到第一張薪資支票時，就會請你吃午餐。

比利 妳已經工作三個星期了。仍然喜歡這份新工作嗎？

珍 我比之前更喜歡這份工作了。我漸漸認識在書店工作的其他人員，他們都很友善。

我也逐漸認識一些顧客，有些人每個星期都會來我們的店呢。

比利 我也很想每星期都買一本書。可是錢不夠。

珍	你午餐想點些什麼呢？
比利	我想點番茄奶油湯和蛋沙拉三明治。那妳想吃什麼？
珍	我想點一樣的好了，因為你點的東西聽起來不錯。
比利	好的。還有什麼其它新鮮事，珍？
珍	我的新銀行帳戶囉。
比利	妳覺得有一個銀行帳戶，感覺怎樣？
珍	不太容易處理。要記住好多東西。
比利	妳以後就會學到所有需要知道的事，妳會習慣的。
珍	我前些天在銀行存款了。
比利	那妳提過款了嗎？
珍	還沒。
比利	妳的意思是妳現在身上沒有錢？
珍	不是的。我媽媽給了我一點錢，所以我才能請你吃午餐。
比利	為什麼不從妳的薪資支票領一點錢來用呢？
珍	我不知道要怎麼把錢從帳戶領出來。
比利	那就叫提款。把款項提出來使用。
珍	接下來你要教我這件事嗎？
比利	是的，那就是我接下來要教妳的。但首先，我們先把美味的午餐吃完吧。
珍	看起來真的很好吃呢。

食物送達。

珍	等一下，這看起來不像奶油番茄湯，它不是紅色的，是白色的。
比利	所以妳想幹嘛？

珍　我最好試一下味道。這嚐起來不像奶油番茄湯，倒像是蘑菇湯。

比利　那妳要怎麼做？

珍　我就把它吃掉囉，反正我喜歡奶油蘑菇湯。我們吃完飯後，你會跟我一起去銀行嗎？

比利　會的，我會教妳怎麼提款。

珍　我需要填寫單子嗎？

比利　當妳和銀行櫃員提款時，大部分銀行櫃員都會要求妳填寫提款單。有些銀行櫃員則不介意妳有沒有填寫提款單。

如果妳用 ATM 提款的話，就不需要填寫提款單。

珍　好的，那我就去 ATM。我要把卡放進去，然後鍵入我的密碼，接下來呢？

比利　櫃員機會顯示接下來的步驟，很簡單的，妳等一下就會了解。現在趁妳的湯還沒冷掉，先把它喝完吧。

Answers

B　1) 比利點什麼種類的湯？

A　2) 珍拿到的是什麼種類的湯？

D　3) 誰從未提款過？

C　4) 比利和珍接下來要做什麼事？

Chapter 4

Learning More
學習更多事務

Unit 1

What it's Called
怎麼稱呼這個東西

MP3-35

Jean and Billy are back at the bank. There is a long line up.

Billy	Do you want to get in line or do you want to try using the bank machine?
Jean	Bank machine, definitely.
Billy	Okay.
Jean	I know that I put my bankcard in this slot.
Billy	Yes.
Jean	I also know that I punch in my password.
Billy	That's right.
Jean	Why is it called a password? It's not a word. It's a number.
Billy	Some people call it a password. Most people call it a code.
Jean	Okay. I'll type in my code.
Billy	Now, type in the amount that you want. It will show you right on the cash machine screen what you are typing.
Jean	Why do you call it a cash machine?
Billy	It has many names. Bank machine, cash machine, ATM, automated teller. It's called all of those things.

The machine makes a strange noise.

Jean	What is that strange noise?
Billy	The machine is counting out your money. There is your money now. Just grab it. The machine will let go of your money when you pull it out.
Jean	Will it give me back my card?
Billy	Here comes your card now. It's being pushed out. Grab your card and the machine will let go of it.
Jean	Will it give me a receipt?
Billy	Here comes your receipt now. Grab your receipt and the bank machine will let go.
Jean	That's it?
Billy	That's it. Congratulations. You have just made your first ATM withdrawal.
Jean	That was easy.
Billy	I told you that it would be.
Jean	People might have different names for this machine but I know what I want to call it.
Billy	What? Cash machine?
Jean	No.
Billy	Bank machine?
Jean	No.
Billy	What do you want to call it?
Jean	It gives me money when I ask. Getting money out of it was so easy. I like this machine.

I like this bank machine so much. I'm going to call it my new best friend.

Questions

1) What is another name for the password?

A) It can also be called a word.
B) It can also be called a number.
C) It can also be called a code.
D) All of the above

2) What is another name for ATM?

A) It can be called a bank machine.
B) It can be called a cash machine.
C) It can be called an automated teller.
D) All of the above

3) How does Jean feel about the ATM?

A) She likes it.
B) She hates it.
C) She loves it.
D) She wants to ask it out for lunch.

4) Why didn't Jean go through the line up?

A) She didn't want to.
B) The line was too long.
C) Billy didn't want to.
D) Jean was too long.

Vocabulary 字彙

code	*n.*	密碼
grab	*v.*	抓取

會話中譯

珍和比利回到銀行，而等候的隊伍很長。

比利　妳想去排隊，還是想試試櫃員機呢？

珍　當然是櫃員機。

比利　好的。

珍　我知道要把提款卡放進這個插槽裡。

比利　是的。

珍　我也知道要鍵入密碼。

比利　沒錯。

珍　為什麼密碼要叫作「password」？它並不是一個字，而是一個號碼啊。（「word」的中文意思是「文字」，如果直接照「password」的字面來解釋的話，意思為「通行所使用的文字」，但中譯都以單字的意義來解釋，因此我們直接將其稱為「密碼」。）

比利　有人叫它「password」。但大多數的人則叫它密碼（code）。

珍　好吧，我要鍵入我的密碼。

比利　現在，鍵入妳想提領的金額。妳鍵入的數字會馬上顯示在櫃員機的螢幕上。

珍　為什麼你叫它「cash machine」（在中文裡，也是櫃員機的意思。）？

比利　它有很多種名稱。例如 「bank machine」、「cash machine」、「ATM」、「automated teller」。這些都是自動櫃員機的意思。

櫃員機發出奇怪的聲音。

珍　這個奇怪的聲音是什麼？

比利　櫃員機正在計算妳要提領的金額。妳的錢出來囉。把鈔票從櫃員機取出來吧，在妳拿取鈔票時，櫃員機的取鈔處就會鬆開。

珍　它會把我的卡還給我嗎？

比利　妳的卡出來了。櫃員機會把金融卡吐出來。取卡處同樣會打開，讓妳拿取卡片。

珍　它會給我明細表嗎？

比利　妳的明細表出來了。櫃員機的明細表出口會打開，讓妳拿取明細表。

珍　就這樣子？

比利　就是這樣。恭喜妳，妳剛完成第一次的 ATM 提款手續。

珍　真簡單。

比利　我早就跟妳說過，就是這麼簡單啊。

珍　大家可能會用很多不同的英文名稱，稱呼櫃員機，但我知道我要怎麼稱呼它。

比利　妳要怎麼稱呼它？「cash machine」？

珍　不是。

比利　「bank machine」嗎？

珍　不是。

比利　那妳想叫它什麼？

珍　我需要錢時，它就會給我錢。而從它這裡領錢又這麼簡單。

我喜歡這台機器。因為我太喜歡這台櫃員機，所以我要叫它「我的新好朋友」。

Answers

C　1)「password」密碼的另一個名稱是什麼？

D　2) ATM 的另一個名稱是什麼？

A　3) 珍對 ATM 的感覺如何？

B　4) 珍為什麼不去排隊？

Unit 2

Running Behind

來不及

MP3-36

Jean and her coworker Jack talk at the start of the workday.

Jack	Did you bring your lunch to work today, Jean?
Jean	No, I didn't, Jack. I didn't have time to make lunch this morning. I was running behind because I slept in.
Jack	Why did you sleep in?
Jean	My alarm clock didn't go off. I don't know why. I was sure that I set it last night before I went to bed.
Jack	Maybe it's broken.
Jean	It's an old alarm clock. I've had it for as long as I can remember.
Jack	Maybe you need to replace it with a new one.
Jean	Maybe. I'll go look at alarm clocks on my lunch break. I'll see how much they cost. Maybe now that I have money in the bank I'll be able to afford one.
Jack	Can I come with you?
Jean	Sure.
Jack	Good. I didn't bring a lunch either today. I'll buy something to eat while we shop.

Jean	You never bring a lunch to work.
Jack	I was running behind this morning too. I was looking at my bank account.
Jean	You have already been to the bank this morning?

Jack fills Jean in about online banking.

Jack	No. I went on my computer. The bank has a website. You can look at your account information on your computer.
Jean	That's interesting.
Jack	You can even do some of your banking online.
Jean	I can do a deposit or a withdrawal from home?
Jack	You can see all of your transactions. It is a good way to keep track of them. You can transfer money from one account to another. You can send money to people. You can pay bills.
Jean	I'm not ready to do any of that. What were you doing?
Jack	I have a second savings account. I'm saving money to travel to Newfoundland when I finish high school. I've always wanted to go there.
Jean	My sister went. She loves Newfound land.
Jack	I was transferring money from my regular account to my savings account. My regular account is the one I use all of the time. My savings account is the one where I'm saving money for my trip.
Jean	Do you have a lot of money saved already?
Jack	I don't have as much as I thought I would by now. I'm running behind. I need to catch up.

Jean	Maybe you need to work more hours. The bookstore might give you more hours if you asked.
Jack	I don't need to work more hours. I need to spend less money.
Jean	You go out for lunch a lot. You would spend less money if you weren't running behind in the morning.
Jack	I would not be running behind in the morning if I weren't always checking to see how much money I have.

Questions

1) **Why was Jack running behind this morning?**

A) He slept in.
B) He made lunch.
C) He was checking his bank account online.
D) He was trying to find a new alarm clock.

2) **Where does Jack do some of his banking?**

A) Through the teller at the bank
B) Through the bank machine at the bank
C) Through Jean at the book store
D) Through the bank website on the computer

3) **How did Jean sleep in?**

A) Her alarm clock did not go off.
B) She was checking her bank account online.
C) She was making lunch.
D) All of the above

4) What is Jack saving for?

A) A new alarm clock
B) A trip
C) A computer
D) Lunch

Vocabulary 字彙

running behind		趕不及
sleep in		睡過頭
replace	*v.*	以…代替
online	*adj.*	線上的

會話中譯

珍和同事傑克在一開始上班時聊天。

傑克 妳今天有帶午餐來嗎，珍？

珍 沒有，傑克。我今天早上沒時間做午餐，我趕著來上班，因為睡過頭了。

傑克 為什麼妳會睡過頭？

珍 我的鬧鐘沒有響，我也不曉得為什麼。我確定昨天晚上睡覺前，我有把鬧鐘設定好啊。

傑克 它可能壞了吧。

珍 它是一個很舊的鬧鐘。從我有記憶開始，就有這個鬧鐘了。

傑克 妳可能需要買一個新的鬧鐘來替換它。

珍 也許吧，我在午餐休息時間，會去逛逛鐘錶店，看看需要多少錢。現在我有銀行存款了，所以可以有能力買一個鬧鐘。

傑克	我可以跟妳一起去嗎？
珍	當然可以。
傑克	很好。我今天也沒帶午餐，等我們去逛逛的時候，我再買點東西來吃。
珍	你從來沒帶午餐來過。
傑克	我今早也趕著來上班。因為我在查詢我的銀行帳戶。
珍	你今天早上已經去過銀行了？

傑克告訴珍關於線上金融服務的資訊。

傑克	不是的，我用電腦上網查的。銀行有自己的網站，妳可以上網去查看自己的帳戶資訊。
珍	真有趣。
傑克	妳甚至可以進行一些線上金融交易。
珍	我可以在家裡存款或提款嗎？
傑克	妳可以看到所有的交易紀錄。這是一個很好的追蹤方法。妳可以把錢從一個帳戶轉到另一個帳戶、匯款給別人及支付帳單。
珍	我還沒準備好要做你剛說的那些事。你在網路銀行做些什麼？
傑克	我有第二個存款帳戶。等我高中畢業後，我要去紐芬蘭旅遊，所以我正在存這筆旅費，我一直很想去那裡。
珍	我姐姐去過了。她很喜歡紐芬蘭。
傑克	我都從一般帳戶轉一些金額到存款帳戶。我的一般帳戶就是我經常使用的帳戶，而存款帳戶是用來存旅費的帳戶。
珍	你已經存了很多錢了嗎？
傑克	我現在的存款比我預期中要少。我存款進度有點落後，必須加緊腳步，趕上自己的計畫進度。

珍	也許你需要多工作幾個小時。如果你要求的話，也許書店會讓你多工作幾個小時。
傑克	我不需要多工作幾個小時。我需要少花一點錢。
珍	你常在外面吃午餐。如果你早上不趕著上班的話，就可以少花一點錢了。
傑克	如果我不要老查我還有多少錢的話，早上就不需要趕著上班了。

Answers

C 　1) 傑克今天早上為什麼趕著去上班？

D 　2) 傑克在哪裡處理一部分的金融交易？

A 　3) 珍怎麼會睡過頭？

B 　4) 傑克正在存款做什麼用？

Unit 3

Finding Balance

找到平衡

MP3-37

Jean goes to the bank to find out about her statement.

Sarah	Good afternoon. Can I help you?
Jean	Hello, Sarah. My name is Jean.
Sarah	Oh, yes. I remember you, Jean. What can I do for you?
Jean	Can you please explain this bank statement to me? This is the first bank statement that I have received.
Sarah	I would be glad to help you with that. May I see it?
Jean	Yes. Here it is.
Sarah	Thank you. Here is your account number and your name.
Jean	Yes.
Sarah	Here is the list of all transactions that you have made in the past month. (Sarah yawns.) Please forgive me for yawning like that. I'm very tired.
Jean	Why are you so tired?
Sarah	I have lots to do at home. When I'm finished working here at the bank, I go home and work there.

The house needs to be cleaned. Supper needs to be prepared. The children need help with their homework. I haven't found a way to balance work and home.

Jean offers a tired Sarah some polite words.

Jean It's not good for your health to have to work so hard.

Sarah Thank you for your kind words. I'm sorry to bother you with my personal life.

Jean I don't mind.

Sarah Getting back to your monthly statement, it shows that you opened this account a month ago.

It shows that you have made two deposits and one withdrawal. You have not made any transfers.

Jean I have kept all of my receipts. I'll compare them to this statement. I'll see if it's accurate.

Sarah The bank keeps very accurate records of all customer transactions. But it's still a good idea to check.

Jean Is that where it tells me how much money I have?

Sarah Yes, that's where it tells you your balance.

Jean My balance?

Sarah Yes. The amount of money that you have in your account is called your account balance. Your balance will change every time you make a transaction.

Jean Too bad the balance you're looking for wasn't this easy.

Questions

1) What is wrong with Sarah?

A) She is tired.

B) She needs to find balance between work and home.

C) The children need help with their homework.

D) All of the above

2) How does Jean know that Sarah is tired?

A) Sarah tells her.

B) Jean guesses.

C) Someone told Jean.

D) She read it in the newspaper.

3) How long has Jean had the bank account?

A) One day

B) One week

C) One month

D) One year

4) What were Jean's transactions?

A) Two deposits, one withdrawal

B) Two withdrawals, one transfer

C) Two transfers, one deposit

D) Two deposits, one transfer

Vocabulary 字彙

yawn	v.	打呵欠
balance	v.	使平衡

bother	*v.*	打擾
personal life		私生活
accurate record		正確的記錄
balance	*n.*	結餘；收支平衡

會話中譯

珍到銀行詢問關於結算單的問題。

莎拉	午安。我能幫您什麼忙呢？
珍	哈囉，莎拉。我的名字叫珍。
莎拉	喔，對。我記得妳，珍。我能為妳做些什麼呢？
珍	可否請妳解釋一下這份銀行結算單？這是我收到的第一份銀行結算單。
莎拉	我很高興能幫妳這個忙。我可以看一下嗎？
珍	可以的，在這裡。
莎拉	謝謝妳，這邊是妳的帳戶號碼和姓名。
珍	是的。
莎拉	這邊是妳上個月所有的交易紀錄清單。（莎拉打哈欠。）不好意思，請原諒我打哈欠，我很累。
珍	妳為什麼這麼累？
莎拉	我要做很多家事。當我從銀行下班後，回家還要繼續工作。
	我需要打掃房子、準備晚餐，孩子們需要我幫忙教功課。我還沒在工作和家庭之間找到平衡點。

珍對疲憊的莎拉提出一些禮貌性的建言。

| 珍 | 妳這麼忙碌於工作，對健康不太好。 |

莎拉	謝謝妳的關心。我很抱歉講我的私生活來打擾妳。
珍	我不介意。
莎拉	回到妳每月結算單的話題吧。它顯示妳在一個月前開戶，也顯示妳已經進行過兩次存款和一次提款，但並且尚未進行任何轉帳交易。
珍	我把所有的明細表都留起來了，要和這份結算單比對，到時我會檢查看看結算單是否正確。
莎拉	銀行將所有客戶的交易都做了非常正確的紀錄保存。不過妳想比對這個想法也很好。
珍	這裡顯示的是我還有多少存款嗎？
莎拉	是的，那裡顯示的是妳的收支平衡金額。
珍	我的收支平衡金額？
莎拉	是的，妳帳戶裡的金額叫作帳戶收支平衡金額。每進行一筆交易，收支平衡金額就會跟著改變。
珍	真可惜，妳想要的平衡並不像收支平衡這樣容易。

Answers

A 1) 莎拉怎麼了？

A 2) 珍怎麼知道莎拉很累？

C 3) 珍的銀行帳戶已經使用多久了？

A 4) 珍的交易紀錄為何？

Chapter 5

Making Progress
有進步

Unit 1

Trying New Things
嘗試新事物

MP3-38

Billy goes to the bookstore to ask Jean out for lunch.

Billy	Hello, Jack.
Jack	Hi, Billy. What are you doing here?
Billy	I'm looking for Jean. Is she working today?
Jack	No. She said that she has a big test in school on Monday. She wanted to stay home and study. The manager of the store gave her the day off.
Billy	Okay. I was going to ask her to have lunch with me. I'll go see her later.
Jack	What were you doing this morning?
Billy	I was at the bank. I wanted some information about credit cards.
Jack	Why would you need a credit card?
Billy	I thought a credit card would be convenient. Some stores don't take cash and many stores don't take checks.
Jack	That's because people bounce checks. They write a check when there is not enough money in their account.
Billy	That's one reason why checks are used less and less.

Jack	What do you want to buy that you need a credit card for?
Billy	I want to buy Christmas presents. It's near the end of October. It's time to start doing my Christmas shopping.
	I have many friends and family members to buy for but I don't have enough money. If I could use a credit card, I could pay it off a little at a time.
Jack	That's helpful for your shopping but it's expensive. You will pay money in interest.
Billy	Yah, maybe, but I want to buy nice gifts this year.
Jack	You know, there is a job open here at the book store. You could make some extra money. That way you would not need the credit card.
Billy	I haven't worked in a book store before but I would like to try.
Jack	Why don't you go talk to the manager?
Billy	I will. Where is she?
Jack	I'll take you to her. I'll introduce you. She's nice. I'm sure that she will like you.
Billy	Thanks a lot.

Questions

1) Why did Billy go to the bank?

    A) To do some banking
    B) To talk to Sarah
    C) To find out about credit cards

D) To find Jean

2) Where is Jean?

A) At work
B) At the bank
C) Studying
D) In the bathroom

3) What month is it?

A) October
B) November
C) It is Christmas
D) Christmas is coming

4) How will Billy make more money?

A) He will take Jean's job.
B) He will take the manager's job.
C) He will take Jack's job.
D) He will take a job at the book store.

Vocabulary 字彙

credit card		信用卡
convenient	*adj.*	方便的
bounce	*v.*	（支票）被拒付 而退還給開票人
manager	*n.*	經理

會話中譯

比利去書店問珍要不要一起去吃午餐。

比利	哈囉，傑克。
傑克	嗨，比利。你在這裡做什麼？
比利	我在找珍。她今天有上班嗎？
傑克	沒有，她説星期一有個很重要的考試要準備，所以想在家唸書。書店經理就讓她休假。
比利	好吧，我本來想問她要不要和我一起吃午餐，我待會再去找她好了。
傑克	你今天早上在做什麼呢？
比利	我在銀行，想問一些關於信用卡的資訊。
傑克	你為什麼需要信用卡？
比利	我想説信用卡應該蠻方便的，有些商店不收現金，而很多商店又不收支票。
傑克	那是因為很多人的支票都跳票。他們開了支票，結果帳戶裡沒有足夠的存款，來支付支票。
比利	這也是為什麼現在越來越少人使用支票的原因。
傑克	你想買什麼東西，所以需要用到信用卡嗎？
比利	我想買聖誕節禮物，現在已經快十月底了，也是開始採 聖誕節禮品的時候了。
	我要買禮物給很多朋友和家人，但現在錢還不夠，如果我有信用卡的話，就可以一次償還一點款項。
傑克	對你想採購的東西，這是蠻有幫助的，但使用信用卡是很昂貴的，你必須支付利息。
比利	對啊，也許吧。但是我今年想買好一點的禮物。
傑克	你知道嗎？書店這裡有一個缺，你可以賺點外快，這樣

	你就不需要信用卡了。
比利	我沒在書店工作過，不過很想試試看。
傑克	你去跟經理談談吧？
比利	我會的，她在哪裡？
傑克	我帶你去見她，然後向她介紹你。她人很好，我知道她一定會喜歡你的。
比利	謝謝你囉。

Answers

C　1) 比利為什麼去銀行？

C　2) 珍在哪裡？

A　3) 對話中的月份是幾月？

D　4) 比利要如何賺得更多錢？

Unit 2

How Interesting

真有意思

MP3-39

Jean enters the staff room at work.

Jean	Hi, Jack. I haven't seen you for two weeks. It feels like I've been away from the store for such a long time.
Jack	Hi, Jean. Excuse me for a minute.
Jean	I'm sorry. I did not realize that you were on the phone.
Jack	That's okay. I won't be long. I'm doing some telephone banking.
Jean	You can do banking over the phone?
Jack	Yes. You can do the same sorts of banking transactions that you can do by computer. I'm checking my account balance.
Jean	That's neat.
Jack	You just call the phone number for telephone banking. You will hear a voice.
	It will list different things you can do and it will tell you which numbers to push on your phone.
Jean	Can you ask it questions? Is it Sarah on the phone?
Jack	No. You are not phoning the bank. It's an automated voice recording. You must press numbers on the phone to move through the list.

Jean	It's so easy to do banking. Doing your banking over the phone would save a lot of time.
Jack	Yes.

Jack gets off the phone.

Jack	What is new with you, Jean?
Jean	I have some news. My mom and dad want to buy a house.
Jack	That would be nice.
Jean	Yes. They don't have enough money. I don't know what they can do.
Jack	They can get a loan from the bank. The bank will lend them money and they can pay it back slowly over many months.
Jean	I wonder if they know about this.
Jack	When that loan is for a house, it's called a mortgage.
Jean	I heard them talking about mortgages. They are going to go to several banks to see who will give them the best mortgage.
Jack	There might be a bank that will charge less interest.
Jean	That's interesting.
Jack	That's a bad joke, Jean
Jean	I thought it was funny. Are you done with your telephone banking?
Jack	Yes. It's time to get to work. Unlock the door so that customers can come in.

Jean	Okay. Did you know that Billy got a job here at the book store?
Jack	Yes. I introduced him to the manager.
Jean	That was nice of you.
Jack	She liked Billy. I told her that I know him and that he would be a good worker.
Jean	That's interesting.
Jack	Are you still trying to be funny?
Jean	Not any more.

Questions

1) Who is looking for a mortgage?

    A) Jack is looking for a mortgage.
    B) Jean is looking for a mortgage.
    C) Jack's parents are looking for a mortgage.
    D) Jean's parents are looking for a mortgage.

2) Why does Jean unlock the door?

    A) To let Jack in
    B) To let customers in
    C) To let the manager in
    D) To let Billy in

3) How can someone buy a house when they do not have enough money?

    A) They can get a mortgage from a bank.
    B) They can get a mortgage from a book store.
    C) They can get a mortgage from a manager.
    D) They can use a credit card.

4) What is Jean doing that Jack wants her to stop?

A) She is unlocking the door.
B) She is talking about her parents.
C) She is making bad jokes.
D) She is not being interesting.

Vocabulary 字彙

automated voice recording		自動錄音
loan	*n.*	貸款
pay back		償還
mortgage	*n.*	抵押貸款
interest	*n.*	利息

會話中譯

珍在工作時進入職員室。

珍　嗨，傑克，我兩個星期沒見到你了，覺得好像離開書店很久了。

傑克　嗨，珍。先等我一下。

珍　不好意思，我沒發現你在講電話。

傑克　沒關係的，我不會講太久。我只是在用電話查金融交易。

珍　你可以藉由電話進行金融交易？

傑克　對啊。妳可以用電話進行一些用電腦也可以進行的銀行交易事項。我正在查帳戶結存餘額。

珍　真不錯。

傑克	妳只要撥打銀行的號碼，就會聽到語音。
	它會列出可以進行的不同金融交易種類，並告訴妳該按下哪個數字，來進入交易事項。
珍	你也可以問它問題嗎？是不是莎拉接聽的電話？
傑克	不可以的，妳不是撥電話到銀行。這是自動語音，妳必須按下號碼鍵，來點選清單。
珍	銀行金融交易好容易喔。用電話進行金融交易，能節省好多時間。
傑克	沒錯。

傑克結束電話銀行查詢。

傑克	妳最近有什麼新鮮事嗎，珍？
珍	我有個新消息，我爸媽想買一間房子。
傑克	那很好啊。
珍	對啊，但他們錢不夠，我不知道他們要怎麼打算。
傑克	他們可以向銀行貸款，銀行會借錢給他們，他們可以分好幾個月，慢慢償還款項。
珍	我在想他們是否知道這個。
傑克	當房子需要貸款時，就叫作「房屋抵押貸款」。
珍	我有聽到他們在討論抵押貸款的事，他們打算去好幾家銀行查詢，看哪一家能提供最好的抵押貸款。
傑克	也許有銀行收取較低的利息吧。
珍	真有趣。
傑克	這是個很差的笑話，珍。（「interest」這個單字會因詞性不同而有不同意思，「less interest」的「interest」是名詞，意思是「利息」，而「interesting」是形容詞，意思是「有趣的」，而珍總是喜歡以文字表面的意思，開些雙關語玩笑。）

珍	我以為這樣講蠻好玩的。你電話銀行的事情處理完了嗎？
傑克	處理完了，也是時候開始工作了，去把門打開，這樣顧客才能進來書店。
珍	好的。你知道比利在我們書店應徵到一個工作嗎？
傑克	我知道。是我向經理介紹他的。
珍	你人真好。
傑克	她喜歡比利。我跟她說我認識比利，而比利會是一個很稱職的員工。
珍	真有意思啊。
傑克	妳還想裝風趣嗎？
珍	再也不想了。

Answers

D　1) 誰在找抵押契約？

B　2) 珍為什麼要把門打開？

A　3) 當人們想買房子，卻又沒足夠的錢時，該怎麼做？

C　4) 珍做了什麼事，讓傑克想叫她不要再做了？

Unit 3

Branching Out
銀行事務的延伸

MP3-40

Jack from the bookstore goes to the bank.

Sarah　Can I help you?

Jack　Yes. My name is Jack and I have two bank accounts with your bank.

Sarah　Hello, Jack. My name is Sarah. How can I help you today?

Jack　I don't understand something on my bank statement. Can you please explain it to me?

Sarah　Do you have your statement with you?

Jack　Yes, I do. Here it is.

Sarah　What do you not understand?

Jack　Can you please explain this charge to my account?

Sarah　Yes. That's a service charge. There is a charge of four dollars and fifty cents to your account each month.

Jack　Why does the bank charge me that money each month?

Sarah　There are services that you use that the bank charges for. You use telephone banking and internet banking. You use the ATM machine.

That's why the bank takes a service charge out of your account each month.

Jack	I see.
Sarah	Some people pay much more each month in bank service charges. People who write a lot of checks will have more services charges. People who bounce checks will have to pay more.
Jack	I took a check from a customer last week and it bounced.
Sarah	Where do you work?
Jack	I work at the book store. It's just down the street from here.
Sarah	I've walked by that book store but I haven't been in.
Jack	I have visited you at your job. You will have to come and visit me at my job.
Sarah	I will, Jack. Is there anything else that I can do for you today?
Jack	No. I just had that one question. You answered it. Thanks for your help.
Sarah	Thank you for banking with us. Come again soon.
Jack	I will. Bye, Sarah.
Sarah	Bye, Jack.

Questions

1) How many accounts does Jack have?

A) One

B) Two

C) Three
D) Four

2) Why does Jack go to see Sarah?

A) He wants to know what a service charge is.
B) He does not understand a charge to his account.
C) He wants to give her some cookies.
D) He wants her to visit him at work.

3) When has Sarah been to the book store?

A) She goes there all of the time.
B) She goes there every Saturday.
C) She has never been there.
D) She goes to the book store whenever Jack invites her.

4) Where does Jack see the service charge?

A) He sees it on the computer.
B) He reads about it in a book.
C) He heard about it at the restaurant.
D) He saw it on his monthly statement.

Vocabulary 字彙

service charge | 服務費

會話中譯

傑克從書店出門，並走到銀行。

莎拉 我能幫您什麼忙？

傑克 是的，我的名字叫傑克。我在這裡有兩個銀行帳戶。

| 莎拉 | 哈囉，傑克，我的名字叫莎拉。今天能幫您什麼忙？ |

| 傑克 | 我不太了解銀行結算單上的某些項目。可以請妳解釋一下嗎？ |

| 莎拉 | 你有將結算單帶來嗎？ |

| 傑克 | 有的，在這裡。 |

| 莎拉 | 哪些項目你不了解？ |

| 傑克 | 可以請妳解釋一下我帳戶的這筆費用嗎？ |

| 莎拉 | 好的，那是服務費。銀行每個月都會收取四點五元的費用。 |

| 傑克 | 為什麼銀行每個月都會跟我收取這項費用？ |

| 莎拉 | 因為你所進行的交易事項中，有些依照銀行規定必須另收服務費。例如你使用電話銀行和網路銀行，還有ATM。 |

因此銀行每個月會從你的帳戶扣取服務費。

| 傑克 | 我懂了。 |

| 莎拉 | 有些人每個月支付更多的銀行服務費。例如常開支票的人就需支付更多服務費，而跳票的人也需支付更多服務費。 |

| 傑克 | 我從一個顧客收了一張支票，而支票跳票了。 |

| 莎拉 | 你在哪裡工作？ |

| 傑克 | 我在書店工作，離這裡只有一條街。 |

| 莎拉 | 我曾經經過那家書店，但沒進去逛過。 |

| 傑克 | 我已經來妳工作的地方探訪妳了，所以妳也必須到我工作的地方探訪我。 |

| 莎拉 | 我會的，傑克。今天還有其它事需要幫忙嗎？ |

| 傑克 | 沒有了，我只有一個問題，而妳已經回答我了。謝謝妳 |

的幫忙。

莎拉　謝謝你到本行進行銀行金融業務。希望很快能再見到你。

傑克　我會的，再見，莎拉。

莎拉　再見，傑克。

Answers

B　1) 傑克有幾個帳戶？

B　2) 傑克為什麼去找莎拉？

C　3) 莎拉什麼時候去過書店？

D　4) 傑克在哪裡看到服務費項目？

Chapter 6

The Possibilities
可能性

Good Idea
好主意

MP3-41

Billy goes to work to pick up his paycheck.

Billy	Hi, Jack. How are you?
Jack	Hi, Billy. What are you doing here? You don't work today. Today is Saturday.
Billy	It's payday. I've come to pick up my paycheck.
Jack	Right. How could I forget? This is your first paycheck, isn't it?
Billy	Yes. I've been working here at the bookstore for two weeks.
Jack	Good for you. What are you going to do with your check?
Billy	I'm going to cash it at the bank then I'm going to start buying Christmas presents.
	With this job, I'll have enough money this year to buy good Christmas presents. Where is Jean?
Jack	She's helping a customer to find a book. Did you get a credit card?
Billy	No. I decided not to. With this job, I don't need a credit card any more.
Jack	I learned of something different. There is a different kind of loan. It's not like a normal loan. It's different from a credit card. It's called a line of credit.

Billy	Line of credit? What is it?
Jack	It's like a credit card and a loan combined. It has the interest rate of a loan.
Billy	That's good. Credit cards have higher interest rates than loans do.
Jack	That's right. You get a card with your line of credit. It's like a bankcard. You can even use it in a bank machine. But it has the interest rate of a loan.
Billy	That's a good idea.
Jack	I'm going to get one. It will help me with my trip. I can phone to Newfoundland and use my line of credit number to book a hotel room. I can use my line of credit number to go online and book my flight to Newfoundland. I can use it just like a credit card.
Billy	What a good idea.
Jack	Yes.

Billy talks to Jack about his good idea.

Billy	Jack, I have another good idea.
Jack	What is it?
Billy	Do you have a book on Newfoundland?
Jack	I don't have a book about Newfoundland. I should. There are good books about Newfoundland right here in this store. Let's look for them.
Billy	Okay. Here is another good idea. Can I buy you lunch today? We will celebrate my first paycheck

from this job.

Jack You are full of good ideas today. I would be happy to let you buy me lunch. Can we take Jean with us?

Billy Of course. That's also a good idea. I have one more good idea for you, Jack.

Jack What is that?

Billy You will need company when you visit the province of Newfoundland. Why don't I come with you?

Jack That's not a good idea. That's a great idea.

Questions

1) When will Jack go on his trip?

A) Today
B) Tomorrow
C) Tuesday
D) We do not know.

2) How will Jack pay for his trip?

A) Line of credit
B) Credit card
C) Pay check
D) He will not pay for his trip.

3) Why is Billy buying Jack's lunch?

A) To celebrate Jack going away
B) To celebrate Billy's first pay check at his new job
C) To celebrate Billy going away

D) To celebrate Billy, Jack, and Jean going away

4) Who is going for lunch?

A) Jack
B) Billy
C) Jean
D) All of the above

Vocabulary 字彙

pick up	提取；接
a line of credit	信用貸款

會話中譯

比利去書店，領取他的薪資支票。

比利 嗨！傑克，你好嗎？

傑克 嗨！比利。你在這裡做什麼？你今天不用上班啊，今天是星期六。

比利 今天是發薪日。我來領取薪資支票。

傑克 對喔！我怎麼會忘記呢？這是你的第一張薪資支票，對吧？

比利 是啊，我已經在書店工作兩星期了。

傑克 很好啊。你打算怎麼處理你的薪資支票？

比利 我打算去銀行兌換成現金，然後開始採購聖誕節禮物。

　　因為這份工作，我有足夠的錢去買聖誕節禮物。珍在哪裡？

傑克 她在幫一位顧客找一本書。你有信用卡了嗎？

比利	不，我決定不申請了。因為現在有這份工作，就不需要信用卡了。
傑克	我發現不同的資訊。有一種貸款類型不同，它不像一般貸款，也和信用卡不一樣，它叫作信貸。
比利	信貸？那是什麼？
傑克	它像是信用卡和貸款的結合。具有和貸款相同的利率。
比利	那很好。信用卡的利率都比貸款的利率高。
傑克	沒錯，你申請一張擁有信貸的卡，它就像金融卡一樣，你甚至可以在櫃員機使用它，但是它卻擁有和貸款一樣的利率。
比利	這是個不錯的好主意。
傑克	我打算要申請一張，它可以幫我達成旅行的願望。我可以撥打電話到紐芬蘭，然後用信貸卡號在飯店訂房。
	也可以用信貸卡號在網路上訂飛往紐芬蘭的機票，還可以將它當作信用卡一樣使用。
比利	這真是一個好主意。
傑克	沒錯。

比利和傑克談論他的好主意。

比利	傑克，我還有另外一個好主意。
傑克	什麼好主意？
比利	你有沒有介紹紐芬蘭的書？
傑克	我沒有關於紐芬蘭的書，我應該要有一本才對。書店裡有很多關於紐芬蘭的好書，我們一起去找找看吧。
比利	好啊。我還有另一個好主意，今天可以請你吃午餐嗎？一起慶祝我從這份工作得到的第一張薪資支票。
傑克	你今天真是滿腦子的好主意。我很高興你要請我吃午餐。我們可以帶珍一起去嗎？

比利	當然可以，那也是一個好主意。我又幫你想到另一個好主意了，傑克。
傑克	什麼好主意？
比利	你到紐芬蘭省的時候會需要一個夥伴，我可以和你一起去啊。
傑克	那不只是一個好主意。那主意棒呆了。

Answers

D　1) 傑克什麼時候要去旅行？

A　2) 傑克要怎麼支付他的旅費？

B　3) 比利為什麼要請傑克吃午餐？

D　4) 誰要去吃午餐？

Unit 2

I Don't Know

我不知道

MP3-42

Jack goes to the bank to get some help.

Sarah Good afternoon and welcome. How may I help you today?

Jack Hi. My name is Jack.

Sarah Hello, Jack, my name is Sarah. What can I do for you?

Jack I don't know. I need something but I don't know what it is.

Sarah What do you need?

Jack I'm going to take a trip to out of the province when I finish high school.

Sarah Congratulations.

Jack Thank you.

Sarah Where will you go?

Jack Newfoundland.

Sarah I would love to go to Newfoundland. I've never been to that province before.

Jack Neither have I. I've heard such nice things about it.

Sarah How long before you go?

Jack I'll go when I graduate from high school.

Sarah How long is that?

Jack	I'm in grade twelve this year. This is my last year in high school.
Sarah	You will be graduating at the end of June?
Jack	Yes.
Sarah	That's less than nine months from now.
Jack	Yes. That's not much time.
Sarah	So, you will be taking a trip to Newfoundland. You need something but you don't know what.
Jack	Right. I don't know.
Sarah	Does it have something to do with your trip?
Jack	Yes. I have a friend who will be coming with me. We're both saving money for this trip.
	Is there a bank account that we can both put our money into? Can I have a savings account to share with my friend?
Sarah	Yes and no. There is a type of bank account called a joint account. A joint account is an account that two people can both use. It's normally only used by married couples.

After an uncomfortable pause,
Jack continues to talk.

Jack	Billy and I are not married.
Sarah	I hope not. If he's also in school, both of you are too young to be married.
Jack	Anyway, what can we do?
Sarah	You can have a savings account. You can give Billy the account information. He can transfer money from his account into this savings account.

You can transfer money from your account into this account for your trip.

Jack	That sounds good. That sounds simple and easy.
Sarah	Yes. Would you like to open that account today?
Jack	I don't know. I should talk to Billy about it first.
Sarah	Do you know when you will talk to your friend?
Jack	I don't know. He's working this afternoon. I hope that I can talk to him tomorrow. Maybe we will be able to talk about this tomorrow at school.
Sarah	Do you study a lot before you write your exams at school?
Jack	Yes, I do. Why do you ask?
Sarah	Because you don't seem to know very much.
Jack	Do you talk like that to all of the bank customers?
Sarah	I don't know.

Questions

1) Which friend is saving for the trip with Jack?

A) Sarah
B) Jack
C) Jean
D) Billy

2) What is an account shared by married people called?

A) A joint account
B) A joint

C) An account
D) I don't know.

3) Where is Billy?

A) He is at the bank.
B) He is at work.
C) He is in Canada.
D) He is talking to Sarah.

4) In how many months will Jack go on his trip?

A) Two months
B) Ten months
C) Nine months
D) Three months

Vocabulary 字彙

province	*n.*	省
graduate	*v.*	畢業
a joint account		聯名帳戶

會話中譯

傑克到銀行去尋求幫助。

莎拉　午安，歡迎您。我今天可以幫您什麼忙？

傑克　嗨，我的名字叫傑克。

莎拉　哈囉，傑克，我的名字叫莎拉，能為您做些什麼呢？

傑克　我不知道，我需要一些資料，但我不知道該怎麼說。

莎拉　你需要什麼資料呢？

傑克	我打算高中畢業時,要出外旅行。
莎拉	恭喜你。
傑克	謝謝妳。
莎拉	你要去哪裡旅行呢?
傑克	紐芬蘭。
莎拉	我好想去紐芬蘭,從來沒有去過那個省份。
傑克	我也是,我已經聽過很多關於紐芬蘭的好評。
莎拉	還有多久你就要去了?
傑克	就等我高中畢業以後。
莎拉	離你畢業還有多久?
傑克	我今年十二年級,這是我高中的最後一年了。
莎拉	你六月底就要畢業了?
傑克	是的。
莎拉	離現在不到九個月的時間。
傑克	沒錯,沒有多少時間了。
莎拉	所以你將到紐芬蘭旅行,你需要一些資訊,但不知道該怎麼敘述。
傑克	沒錯,我不知道。
莎拉	和你的旅行有關嗎?
傑克	是的,我朋友會和我一起去,我們兩個都在為這個旅行存錢。 有沒有帳戶可以讓我們把錢存在一起?我可以和朋友合開一個存款帳戶嗎?
莎拉	有一種可以把錢存在一起的帳戶,但你和朋友沒辦法使用這種帳戶。這種銀行帳戶叫作聯名帳戶,可以讓兩個人共用一個帳戶,但通常都只能讓夫妻使用。

傑克傻眼了一會兒，然後繼續講話。

傑克 比利和我都沒有結婚。

莎拉 我想也是，如果他也還在唸書，你們兩個都太年輕，還不到適婚年齡。

傑克 那我們該怎麼辦？

莎拉 你可以開個存款帳戶，然後告訴比利這個帳戶的資料，他可以從他的帳戶將錢轉帳到這個帳戶，你也可以從你的帳戶轉帳到這個帳戶，當作旅費。

傑克 聽起來不錯，蠻簡單、方便的。

莎拉 是的，那你今天想要開這個存款帳戶嗎？

傑克 我不知道，我應該先和比利討論一下。

莎拉 你什麼時候要和朋友討論？

傑克 我不知道，他今天下午在上班，希望明天能有機會和他討論。或者我們明天能夠在學校討論這件事。

莎拉 你考試前都有用功唸書嗎？

傑克 有啊。為什麼妳會這麼問？

莎拉 因為你知道的事情好像不多。

傑克 妳都和所有銀行客戶這樣講話嗎？

莎拉 我不知道。

Answers

D　1) 哪個朋友和傑克一起存旅費？

A　2) 夫妻共同使用的帳戶叫作什麼？

B　3) 比利在哪裡？

C　4) 還有幾個月，傑克就要去旅行了？

Unit 3

What If?

萬一 ?

MP3-43

Billy goes to eat lunch at a local restaurant. The place is very busy.

Billy	Excuse me. Is this seat taken?
Sarah	No, it isn't.
Billy	May I sit there?
Sarah	Yes, you can.
Billy	Thank you.
Sarah	You're welcome.
Billy	It's very busy in the restaurant today.
Sarah	Yes, it is.
Billy	There was nowhere else that I could sit down. Thank you for letting me share your table.
Sarah	I'm glad to have someone to talk to. I don't like to eat alone.
Billy	I think I know you. Do you work somewhere on this street?
Sarah	Yes, I do.
Billy	I think that I've talked to you before. Do you work at the bank right beside this restaurant?
Sarah	Yes, I do. My name is Sarah.
Billy	I do know you. My name is Billy. That's my

bank. I do all of my banking there.

Sarah Hello, Billy. It's nice to meet you. Do you work on this street?

Billy Yes. I work at the bookstore.

Sarah I haven't been in that bookstore. I want to go in there one day. I like books.

Billy So do I. It's a great job.

Sarah wonders if Billy has ever met Jack.

Sarah Do you know a boy named Jack?

Billy Jack is my good friend.

Sarah You must be the friend who is going to Newfoundland with him.

Billy Yes. How did you know that?

Sarah Jack came into the bank. He was asking me about savings account. He said that the two of you are saving for a trip to Newfoundland.

Billy Yes. I'm excited to go. I can't wait. But I'm also afraid. What if we cannot get enough money saved in time?

Sarah You will. You both have jobs. You are both saving money. You will need less money if you go together.

You can share hotel rooms, which will save a lot of money.

Billy You're right but what if our money gets stolen?

Sarah You can buy traveler's checks from the bank before you go.

Billy   Please tell me about traveler's checks.

Sarah   Traveler's checks are like money. Almost any store, restaurant or hotel will take them. They are safer than money because you must sign them.

You sign them in front of the worker when you are paying for something. The worker can ask to see identification. People don't like to steal traveler's checks.

Billy   That sounds like a really good idea. It sounds safer than carrying cash.

Sarah   It is.

Billy   But what if someone does steal them?

Sarah   You will be given a phone number. If your check is stolen, you call that phone number. That check will be stopped. No one will be able to use it. The bank will send you a new check to use.

Billy   That's a great idea.

Sarah   Yes. Traveler's checks will get rid of all of your what if questions.

Billy   What if Jack drives me crazy in Newfoundland?

Sarah   That's one "what if" question that a travelers' check cannot help you with. Newfoundland is an island.

Billy   Yes.

Sarah   You can throw him in the water.

Questions

1) Why is a travelers' check better than cash?

A) It can be replaced.
B) You need to sign it to use it.
C) You may have to show ID to use it.
D) All of the above

2) Where does Billy see Sarah?

A) At the bank
B) In the restaurant
C) In Canada
D) In the book store

3) Who was telling Sarah about Billy?

A) Someone in the restaurant
B) Billy
C) Jack
D) Sarah

4) Why is traveling with another person less expensive?

A) You can share travelers' checks.
B) You can share a table.
C) You have a place to sit.
D) You can share hotel rooms.

Vocabulary 字彙

share	v.	分享

比利在一家餐館吃午餐。餐館的生意非常好。

比利	不好意思，請問這個位子有人坐嗎？
莎拉	沒有。
比利	我可以坐這裡嗎？
莎拉	可以。
比利	謝謝妳。
莎拉	不客氣。
比利	今天餐館裡的生意真好。
莎拉	是啊。
比利	我找不到其他位子。謝謝妳讓我和妳共用一張桌子。
莎拉	我很高興有人和我聊天。我不喜歡一個人吃飯。
比利	我想我認識妳。妳工作的地方在這條街上嗎？
莎拉	是的。
比利	我想我以前和妳講過話。妳在這間餐館隔壁的銀行上班嗎？
莎拉	是的。我的名字叫莎拉。
比利	我的確認識妳，我的名字叫比利。我都去妳工作的那家銀行辦事，我在那處理所有的金融業務。
莎拉	哈囉，比利，很高興遇見你。你工作的地點在這條街上嗎？
比利	是的，我在那家書店上班。
莎拉	我還沒進去過那家書店，我想找一天進去逛逛。我喜歡書。
比利	我也是，這份工作真的很棒。

莎拉在想比利是不是曾經遇見過傑克？

莎拉	你認識一個叫傑克的男孩嗎？
比利	傑克是我的好朋友。
莎拉	那你一定是那個要和他一起去紐芬蘭的朋友。
比利	對啊，妳怎麼知道？
莎拉	傑克來過銀行，他問我關於存款帳戶的事。他說你們兩個正在存要去紐芬蘭旅行的旅費。
比利	是的，我對於要去紐芬蘭旅行感到很興奮，也等不及了，但我也怕說萬一我們來不及存夠錢，該怎麼辦？
莎拉	你們會存夠錢的。你們兩個都有工作，也都在存錢，而且兩人一起旅行的話，需要的費用也比較少。 你們在飯店時可以共住一間房，這樣就可以省不少錢。
比利	妳說的沒錯，但萬一我們的錢被偷了，該怎麼辦？
莎拉	你們去旅行前，可以到銀行購買旅行支票。
比利	請跟我說明一下旅行支票的用途。
莎拉	旅行支票就像金錢一樣，幾乎任何一家商店、餐廳或飯店都接受旅行支票。它們比金錢還安全，因為你必須在支票上簽名。 當你要支付某樣東西時，就在店員面前，在支票上簽名，店員可以詢問、核對你的身分證。人們不喜歡偷旅行支票。
比利	聽起來真的個不錯的主意，也比帶現金還安全。
莎拉	是這樣沒錯。
比利	但是萬一真的被人偷走了，怎麼辦？
莎拉	銀行會給你一個電話號碼，如果你的旅行支票被偷，就撥打這個號碼，支票的效用就會中止，這樣就沒有人能使用旅行支票了。然後銀行還會再寄一張新的支票給

你。

| 比利 | 這主意太棒了。 |

| 莎拉 | 是啊，旅行支票可以解決你所有「萬一怎麼樣，該怎麼辦」的問題。 |

| 比利 | 萬一傑克在紐芬蘭把我逼瘋了，怎麼辦？ |

| 莎拉 | 這個「萬一」問題是旅行支票沒有辦法解決的，紐芬蘭是一個島。 |

| 比利 | 沒錯。 |

| 莎拉 | 你可以把他丟到水裡。 |

Answers

D   1) 為什麼旅行支票比現金好用？

B   2) 比利在哪裡看見莎拉？

C   3) 誰和莎拉講過比利的事？

D   4) 為什麼和另一個人一起旅遊，旅費會比較便宜？

Chapter 7

Coming Along

一起來吧

Unit 1

More Good Ideas
更多的好主意

MP3-44

Jack goes to the bank to get more help

Sarah Hi, Jack. How can I help you today?

Jack I'm here to see you.

Sarah Yes?

Jack I was talking to Billy. He said that you had some good ideas that could help us on our trip. Can you tell me your ideas?

Sarah I'm happy to help. Save as much money as you can. With the money that you save, buy traveler's checks. Take very little cash with you.

Jack That sounds like a good idea.

Sarah It is. Also, get a credit card before you leave home. You don't have to use it. It can be used in case of emergency. It can be used to reserve hotels and rental cars.

Jack Good idea.

Sarah Give your parents your account information. That way if you run out of money they can transfer some money to your account.

Jack I see. Thanks a lot. Hey, I have a good idea.

Sarah What is that?

| Jack | Let me buy you a coffee. I'll take you out for your coffee break to thank you for helping me. |
| Sarah | That's a good idea. Let me get my coat. |

Questions

1) What were some of Sarah's good ideas?

    A) Get a credit card.
    B) Take very little money.
    C) Take a rain coat and a fishing rod.
    D) Both (A) and (B)

2) Why is Jack taking Sarah for coffee?

    A) He wants to date her.
    B) He misses his mother.
    C) He wants to thank her.
    D) He wants her to buy him a coffee.

3) When are they going for coffee?

    A) Tomorrow
    B) Right now
    C) Tonight
    D) This morning

4) Who needs Canadian money?

    A) People traveling to Canada
    B) People traveling in Canada
    C) People living in Canada
    D) All of the above

Vocabulary 字彙

emergency	*n.*	緊急情況
reserve	*v.*	預訂
rental	*adj.*	租賃的
run out		被用完

會話中譯

傑克去銀行找莎拉，以尋求更多的幫助。

莎拉 嗨，傑克。我今天能幫你什麼忙？

傑克 我是來這裡找妳。

莎拉 怎麼了？

傑克 我之前和比利在聊天。他說妳有一些好主意，對我們的旅行有幫助，妳可以告訴我妳的想法嗎？

莎拉 我很樂意幫助你們。你們盡量存錢，然後用這些存款去購買旅遊支票，去旅遊時，只要攜帶一點現金就好了。

傑克 聽起來真的是個好主意。

莎拉 是啊。還有，離家之前記得帶信用卡，你不必用它，帶著信用卡是預防萬一，緊急情況時再用。你也可以用信用卡來預定飯店房間和租車。

傑克 好主意。

莎拉 把你的帳戶資料告訴你父母，這樣的話，如果你的錢用完了，他們可以匯一些錢到你的帳戶。

傑克 我了解了，真是太謝謝妳了。嘿，我有個好主意。

莎拉 什麼好主意？

傑克 讓我請妳喝咖啡吧，在妳休息時，我帶妳去喝咖啡，好

答謝妳對我的幫忙。

莎拉　這是個好主意，讓我拿一下外套。

Answers

D　1) 莎拉的好主意有哪些？

C　2) 傑克為什麼要帶莎拉去喝咖啡？

B　3) 他們什麼時候要去喝咖啡？

D　4) 誰需要加拿大的貨幣？

Unit 2

Who Knows?

誰知道會怎樣？

Jack goes to the bank to get some money.

Sarah	Good morning, Jack. It's nice to see you.
Jack	Thank you, Sarah. How are you today?
Sarah	I'm good. I'm seeing you all of the time. What brings you to the bank today?
Jack	I just need to take some money. I like to see you more than the banking machine.
	The bank machine is not as friendly as you are.
Sarah	What a nice thing to say. Thank you, Jack.
Jack	You're welcome.
Sarah	So, just a withdrawal today?
Jack	Yes, please. Here is my withdrawal slip.
Sarah	It will take just a minute.
Jack	Thank you.
Sarah	Do you have any interesting news?
Jack	Billy and I are still saving for our trip.
Sarah	That's good.
Jack	My parents want to move to a bigger house.
Sarah	That's interesting.
Jack	My mother got a better job. She's making more

money. They can afford a nicer house.

Sarah How will they pay for a new house?

Jack They will need a mortgage. They can make a down payment but they cannot pay the entire cost of a new house.

Sarah wants to help Jack's parents get a mortgage.

Sarah Please tell your parents to come see me. I can give them good information about mortgages.

Jack What if they don't use this bank?

Sarah The information that I'll share with them is good information. It doesn't matter which bank they go to. It will help them.

Jack You are so helpful. I hope that this bank is paying you well.

Sarah Thank you. I like helping people. Here is your money, Jack.

Jack Thanks. I should go now.

Sarah Where are you off to next?

Jack Who knows? Maybe I'll find my friends Jean and Billy.

Sarah Is your friend Jean going to Newfoundland with you?

Jack I don't think so. She's only fourteen. I don't think that her parents will let her travel outside of the province.

Sarah Who knows? Maybe her parents will let her go with you.

Jack	I would be happy is she could go with us. She's fun.
Sarah	That's nice.
Jack	While I'm here, how do I apply for a credit card?
Sarah	We can do that right now, if you like.
Jack	No, thank you. I don't want to use up my free day with any more banking. I want to go have fun. I was just asking because I'm already here.
Sarah	Here is a credit card application form. I'll give it to you to take home. Fill out the application form. Bring it back to me.
	I'll process your application. It won't take long.
Jack	Thanks Sarah. I'll fill this out and bring it back to you soon.
Sarah	Thank you for banking with us today, Jack.
Jack	See you soon.
Sarah	Bye now.

Questions

1) Who will need a mortgage?

   A) Jack
   B) Sarah
   C) Jack's parents
   D) Jean and Billy

2) Why does Jack take an application form home?

   A) He is applying for a credit card.

B) He is applying for a job.

C) He is applying for a mortgage.

D) He is applying for a withdrawal.

3) How old is Jean?

A) Fourteen

B) Forty

C) Four

D) Four Hundred

4) How much money did Jack deposit?

A) Fourteen dollars

B) Forty dollars

C) Four dollars

D) Jack did not deposit anything.

Vocabulary 字彙

| afford | v. | 買得起 |

會話中譯

傑克到銀行領錢。

莎拉 早安，傑克。很高興見到你。

傑克 謝謝妳，莎拉。妳今天好嗎？

莎拉 我很好。我常常看見你來銀行。今天又是什麼風把你吹來了啊？

傑克 我只是需要領錢，我比較喜歡見到妳，而不是提款機。

櫃員機沒有妳這麼友善。

| 莎拉 | 你的嘴真甜。謝謝你，傑克。 |

| 傑克 | 不客氣。 |

| 莎拉 | 那今天只要提款囉？ |

| 傑克 | 是的，麻煩妳了。這是我的提款單。 |

| 莎拉 | 等一下子就好了。 |

| 傑克 | 謝謝妳。 |

| 莎拉 | 有什麼有趣的事可以說來聽聽？ |

| 傑克 | 比利和我還是在存旅費。 |

| 莎拉 | 那很好啊。 |

| 傑克 | 我爸媽想搬到大一點的房子。 |

| 莎拉 | 有意思。 |

| 傑克 | 我媽媽找到一個較好的工作，現在賺的錢較多，所以負擔得起一間較好的房子。 |

| 莎拉 | 他們要怎麼支付新房子的款項呢？ |

| 傑克 | 他們需要房屋貸款，他們能夠付得出頭期款，但沒法支付新房子所有款項。 |

莎拉想幫傑克的爸媽申請房屋貸款。

| 莎拉 | 請告知你的爸媽，過來找我吧，我可以提供他們不錯的房貸資料。 |

| 傑克 | 萬一他們沒有使用這家銀行的服務呢？ |

| 莎拉 | 我要給他們看的資料，還蠻不錯的，這跟他們使用哪家銀行的服務沒有關係，這份資料可以幫助他們。 |

| 傑克 | 妳真是熱心助人，我希望這家銀行付妳很好的薪資。 |

| 莎拉 | 謝謝你，我喜歡幫助別人。這是你提領的款項，傑克。 |

| 傑克 | 謝啦。我該走了。 |

莎拉	你下面要去哪裡？
傑克	誰知道？也許我會去找我的朋友珍和比利吧。
莎拉	你朋友珍也要和你們去紐芬蘭嗎？
傑克	我想應該不可能，她只有十四歲，我想她爸媽不會讓她去其它省份旅行。
莎拉	誰知道？也許她的爸媽會讓她跟你一起去呢。
傑克	如果她可以一起去的話，我會很開心。她很風趣。
莎拉	那很好啊。
傑克	趁我還在這裡，我想請問一下，要怎麼申請信用卡？
莎拉	如果你願意的話，我們現在就可以開始申請手續。
傑克	不，謝謝妳。我不想把閒暇時間都用在處理金融業務上。我想去逛逛，我問這個問題，只因為我人還在這裡。
莎拉	這裡是一份信用卡申請表格，我讓你把表格帶回家，填好再交給我。
	我會幫你處理申請事宜，不會花很久時間的。
傑克	謝啦，莎拉，我會填好這份表格，然後儘快交給妳。
莎拉	謝謝你今天到行裡來進行銀行金融交易，傑克。
傑克	下次見。
莎拉	再見。

Answers

C   1) 誰需要抵押契約？

A   2) 傑克為什麼要把申請表格帶回家？

A   3) 珍幾歲？

D   4) 傑克存了多少錢？

Unit 3

Interacting

互動

MP3-46

Sarah goes to the bookstore to get a book.

Billy	Hello, Sarah.
Sarah	Hello, Billy. This is the second time that we have met outside of the bank.
Billy	Yes. You haven't been in this book store before, have you?
Sarah	No, I haven't. It's a lovely store. There are many books to choose from.
Billy	Yes. I think that it is a good book store too. I've been in many stores because I like books but this is my favorite.
	Can I help you find anything?
Sarah	I'm looking for a book on Newfoundland. Do you have any?
Billy	Why? Are you going to Newfoundland too?
Sarah	No. I would like to go there some day. For now, I'll just read about it. I cannot afford to go. I have a daughter to look after.
Billy	How old is your daughter?
Sarah	She's fifteen. Her name is Patti.
Billy	I would like to meet her some time.
Sarah	That's a good idea.

Billy   Maybe she could go bowling with Jean, Jack and I.

Sarah   I'll ask her. I think that she would enjoy making new friends.

Billy   Good. Here is a very good book on Newfoundland. There are more but this one sells the most.

Sarah   Thank you, Billy. I'll take this one.

Billy learns how to use the debit machine.

Billy   How would you like to pay for that?

Sarah   Do you take Interac?

Billy   I don't know. I haven't been here very long. Let me find someone to ask.

Sarah   You don't need to go and find someone to ask. I work in a bank. I can see your Interac machine right beside the cash register.

Billy   They use that for credit cards.

Sarah   You can use it for bankcards also. It's called paying with Interac.

Billy   Don't you have to get money out from the ATM machine with your bank card?

Sarah   Didn't you know that you could use your bankcard to pay for things in stores?

Billy   No, I didn't.

Sarah   Your bank card is what you use to do your banking. You can use it with a teller like me. You can use it in the bank machine. You can also use it in almost all stores to buy things with and to pay for things.

You can use it in restaurants and even at the movies. Almost all places in Canada will take your bank card. It's called Interac. You slide the bankcard through the same machine that's used for credit cards.

Billy   I didn't know that.

Sarah   I'll show you. Take my card. Slide the card through the slot on the little machine. Do it just like you would with a credit card. See on the little screen? It will tell you what to do next. That's all.

Billy   That was easy.

Sarah   See? You don't have to be in school to learn new things.

Billy   And I don't have to be in a bank to learn bank things. Thank you for shopping in our store.

Sarah   Bye, Billy.

Questions

1) What does Sarah buy?

   A) A bankcard
   B) Interac
   C) A book
   D) Newfoundland

2) How does Sarah pay?

   A) Check
   B) Interac

C) Bank card

D) Both (B) and (C)

3) **Why does Sarah help Billy when she pays?**

A) He does not know what to do.

B) She knows what to do.

C) She works in a bank.

D) All of the above.

4) **What is Sarah's daughter's name?**

A) Billy

B) Patti

C) Jean

D) All of the above

Vocabulary 字彙

afford	*v.*	負擔
Interac		扣款卡
slide	*v.*	刷（卡）

會話中譯

莎拉到書店去買書。

比利 哈囉，莎拉。

莎拉 哈囉，比利。這是我們第二次在銀行以外的地方相遇了。

比利 是啊，妳還沒來過書店，對吧？

莎拉 對啊，這間書店真溫馨。有好多書可以選擇。

比利 是的，我也認為這是一間好書店。因為我喜歡書，所以

去過很多家書店。而這一家是我的最愛。

我能幫妳尋找妳要的書嗎？

莎拉 我在找一本關於紐芬蘭的書，你們這裡有這類的書籍嗎？

比利 為什麼妳想找這類的書籍？妳也要去紐芬蘭嗎？

莎拉 不是的，將來總有一天我會想去那裡旅行，但目前我只想閱讀相關書籍。我負擔不起去紐芬蘭的費用，而且還要照顧我的女兒。

比利 妳的女兒幾歲了？

莎拉 她十五歲，叫做派蒂。

比利 我希望能有機會見見她。

莎拉 這是個不錯的主意。

比利 也許她可以和我、還有珍和傑克一起去打保齡球。

莎拉 我會問她的，我想她也會喜歡結交新朋友。

比利 好的。這是一本關於紐芬蘭的好書，還有很多其它的書籍，但這一本賣的最好。

莎拉 謝謝你，比利。那我就買這一本書。

比利學習如何使用扣款機。

比利 妳要什麼方式付款？

莎拉 你們接受 Interac 扣款卡嗎？

比利 我不知道，我在這裡工作的時間不長。我找人問問看好了。

莎拉 你不需要去問別人，我在銀行工作，我已經看到收銀機旁邊有一台 Interac 扣款機。

比利 他們用那個機器來刷信用卡。

莎拉 你也可以用它來刷金融卡。這叫做「Interac 扣款支付」。

比利	妳不先用金融卡去 ATM 領錢嗎？

莎拉	你不知道你可以用銀行金融卡在商店付款嗎？

比利	我不知道。

莎拉	你的銀行金融卡是用來進行金融交易，在你和我一樣的銀行櫃員面談時，便使用金融卡，也可以在櫃員機使用金融卡，還可在大部分的商店，用金融卡買東西和付款。
	你在餐廳用餐、甚至是看電影時，都可以使用金融卡。幾乎所有加拿大境內的商店都接受金融卡，它叫做「Interac 扣款卡」，你就用刷信用卡的機器，來刷這張金融卡就可以了。

比利	我以前不曉得有這回事。

莎拉	我教你。你拿我的卡，從那台小機器的插槽刷過去，就像刷信用卡一樣。看到那個小螢幕了嗎？它會告訴你接下來該怎麼做，就這樣囉。

比利	真是容易。

莎拉	懂了吧？你不用身處學校，也能學到新事物。

比利	而且我也不用身處銀行，就能學到銀行金融方面的事。謝謝妳今天來我們的書店購物。

莎拉	再見，比利。

Answers

C 1) 莎拉買了什麼？

D 2) 莎拉怎麼付款？

D 3) 為什麼莎拉在付款時，要幫比利？

B 4) 莎拉的女兒叫什麼名字？

Chapter 8

All About Options

關於選項的一切

MP3-47

Unit 1

A Lot of Names
好多名稱

Jean is working at the bookstore when Sarah comes in to buy a book.

Jean Good morning.

Sarah Good morning.

Jean Can I help you?

Sarah Yes. I'm looking for a book on Newfoundland.

Jean I'll show you where they are.

Sarah Thank you.

Jean This is the area where we keep the travel books. Here are the Canadian travel books. Here is a very good book on Newfoundland.

Sarah There are a lot of books on Newfoundland. I already have that one. I would like something else.

Jean This one sells a lot too.

Sarah I'll take it.

Jean Is there anything else that I can help you find today?

Sarah No, thank you.

Jean Two friends of mine are going to Newfoundland. They hope to go when they graduate from high school at the end of this year.

Sarah	Are you talking about Billy and Jack?
Jean	Yes, I am. How did you know?
Sarah	I know them both. They bank where I work.
Jean	Do you work at the bank down the street?
Sarah	Yes.
Jean	I bank there, too. My name is Jean.

Sarah remembers Jean from a few weeks ago.

Sarah	Hello, Jean. I think that you just opened a new account not too long ago.
Jean	Yes.
Sarah	I helped you. My name is Sarah.
Jean	Hello, Sarah. Are you going to Newfoundland?
Sarah	No. I like reading about new places. Are you?
Jean	I would like to go with the boys but my parents won't let me. They think that I'm too young to go without an adult.
Sarah	Yes.
Jean	How would you like to pay? We accept check, MasterCard, cash, and debit.
Sarah	I'll pay with my Interac card.
Jean	Sure. Just type your PIN number on the machine.
Sarah	All done.
Jean	Great! the transaction went through. Thanks for shopping with us. Bye.

Questions

1) Why isn't Jean going on the trip?

A) She is too young.
B) She is too young to go without an adult.
C) Her parents think that she is too young to go without an adult.
D) She doesn't want to.

2) How many books on Newfoundland does Sarah now own?

A) Two
B) One
C) Three
D) None

3) Where is Newfoundland?

A) In America
B) In Canada
C) On the book shelf
D) In the book store

4) What are some other names for a bank code or bank password?

A) PIK
B) PIK number
C) PID
D) None of the above

Vocabulary 字彙

accept	v.	接受

會話中譯

莎拉進來書店買書時，珍正好在書店上班。

珍	早安。
莎拉	早安。
珍	我能幫妳什麼忙嗎？
莎拉	是的，我想找一本關於紐芬蘭的書。
珍	我告訴您那些書放在哪裡。
莎拉	謝謝妳。
珍	我們旅遊方面的書都放在這一區，這些是加拿大的旅遊書籍，而這本關於紐芬蘭的書很好。
莎拉	有好多關於紐芬蘭的書。我已經有這一本了，我想再買其它的書。
珍	這一本也賣的很好。
莎拉	那我就買這一本吧。
珍	您今天還需要我幫您找其它的書嗎？
莎拉	不用了，謝謝妳。
珍	我有兩個朋友要去紐芬蘭，他們希望在高中畢業後，今年年底時，去紐芬蘭玩。
莎拉	妳說的是比利和傑克嗎？
珍	是啊，妳怎麼知道？
莎拉	我認識他們兩位。他們都到我工作的銀行進行銀行金融交易。
珍	妳在下一條街的那間銀行上班嗎？
莎拉	是的。
珍	我也在那裡進行銀行金融交易。我的名字叫珍。

莎拉想起來她幾星期前曾見過珍。

| **莎拉** | 哈囉，珍。我想妳不久前才開了一個新帳戶。 |

| 珍 | 是的。 |

| **莎拉** | 我曾經幫過妳開戶。我的名字叫莎拉。 |

| 珍 | 哈囉，莎拉。妳要去紐芬蘭嗎？ |

| **莎拉** | 不是，我喜歡閱讀關於新地方的書。妳要去紐芬蘭嗎？ |

| 珍 | 我想和他們一起去，但我爸媽不讓我去。他們覺得我還太小，沒有大人的陪同，不能單獨旅遊。 |

| **莎拉** | 沒錯。 |

| 珍 | 妳想要用什麼方式付款呢？我們接受支票、萬事達卡、現金和扣款卡。 |

| **莎拉** | 我用 Interac 扣款卡付款好了。 |

| 珍 | 沒問題。請在機器這裡鍵入妳的 PIN 碼。 |

| **莎拉** | 好了。 |

| 珍 | 太好了，交易完成。謝謝妳來我們書店購物，再見。 |

Answers

C　1) 珍為什麼不去旅行？

A　2) 莎拉現在擁有幾本關於紐芬蘭的書？

B　3) 紐芬蘭在哪裡？

D　4) 銀行密碼除了 bank code 和 bank password 之外的其它名稱為何？

Unit 2

Just a Thought
只是一個想法而已

MP3-48

Jack goes to the bank to get some cash.

Sarah	Well, hello, Jack. What brings you to the bank today?
Jack	Hi, Sarah. I need to take out some money, please.
Sarah	No problem.
Jack	Here is my withdrawal slip.
Sarah	Thank you. What is new with you?
Jack	Nothing. Nothing is new. What about you?
Sarah	Well, I had an idea.
Jack	What is it?
Sarah	It's just a thought.
Jack	What is your thought?
Sarah	I was thinking. I have a daughter that's Jean's age. Her name is Patti. I would like Patti to meet you and your friends.
Jack	Sure. Why don't you have her come down for lunch? I'll meet the two of you at the restaurant on my lunch break.
Sarah	Okay.
Jack	If she likes me and I like her, she can meet the rest of my friends.

Sarah	Good.
Jack	It will be fun. I'll see you at lunch.
Sarah	Don't go yet, Jack. You need to sign my receipt.
Jack	Okay.
Sarah	Here is your receipt and your cash.

Sarah has some big ideas.

Sarah	I also want to tell you something else.
Jack	What?
Sarah	My daughter Patti has been reading the books that I've bought about Newfoundland. She would like to go there. Maybe she could go with you.
Jack	Maybe. It's important that we meet first.
Sarah	Of course. One more thing.
Jack	Yes?
Sarah	It's just a thought.
Jack	What is your thought?
Sarah	Maybe I could go with you. You would have an adult going with you.
	Jean might be able to go if there is an adult going on this trip. Her parents might let her go.
Jack	That's a great idea. Let's start with Patti. I'll meet her at lunch today. I hope that we have fun. I hope that we like each other.
Sarah	I hope so too. I think that you will. Patti is nice and you are nice. Billy is a good person and so is Jean.
	I think that Patti will be a good friend to all of

you.

Jack   We will see. I'll see you at the restaurant soon.

Sarah   Okay, Jack.

Jack   I'm hungry now. I can't wait for it to be lunch. I hope that they have cream of mushroom soup. I love cream of mushroom soup.

Sarah   Who knows what they will have for soup. It changes every day.

Jack   Well, it was just a thought.

Questions

1) Why did Jack go to the bank?

    A)   He wanted to make a withdrawal.
    B)   He wanted to talk to Sarah.
    C)   He wanted to ask Sarah about her daughter Patti.
    D)   He wanted to ask Sarah out for lunch.

2) When will Jack meet Sarah's daughter?

    A) Jack is meeting her at dinner today.
    B) Jack is meeting her at supper tonight.
    C) Jack is meeting her at lunch today.
    D) Jack is meeting her for a snack tonight.

3) What does Jack want for lunch?

    A) He wants an apple.
    B) He wants a bag of chips.
    C) He wants some soup.
    D) He wants some lunch.

4) Where is Jack meeting Sarah's daughter?

A) He is meeting her at the restaurant.
B) He is meeting her in Newfoundland.
C) He is meeting her at the bank.
D) He is not meeting her.

會話中譯

傑克去銀行提領一點現金。

莎拉	哈囉，傑克，今天來銀行要辦什麼事？
傑克	嗨，莎拉，我需要提領一點現金，麻煩妳了。
莎拉	沒問題。
傑克	這是我的提款單。
莎拉	謝謝你。最近有什麼新鮮事嗎？
傑克	沒有，沒什麼事發生。妳呢？
莎拉	嗯，我有過一個想法。
傑克	什麼主意？
莎拉	只是一個想法而已。
傑克	什麼想法？
莎拉	我是在想，我有個和珍同年齡的女兒，她的名字叫派蒂，我想讓派蒂見見你和你的朋友們。
傑克	好啊，妳讓她來和我們一起午餐吧？我中午休息時，可以和妳們兩個在餐館碰頭。
莎拉	好啊。
傑克	如果她喜歡我，我也喜歡她的話，就可以見見我其他的朋友。
莎拉	很好。

傑克	一定會很有趣的，那午餐時見囉。
莎拉	先別走，傑克。你必須在我的明細表上簽名。
傑克	好的。
莎拉	這是你的明細表和現金。

莎拉想到一些很棒的主意。

莎拉	我還想跟你說其它的事。
傑克	什麼事？
莎拉	我女兒一直在閱讀我買的關於紐芬蘭的書。她很想去那裡，也許她可以和你們一起去。
傑克	也許。重要的是我們必須先見過面。
莎拉	那當然。還有一件事。
傑克	什麼事呢？
莎拉	只是一個想法而已。
傑克	什麼想法？
莎拉	也許我可以和你一起去，這樣的話，就有大人和你們同行。
	珍也許會因為有大人陪同的關係，就可以和我們一起去紐芬蘭，她的父母也許會讓她去。
傑克	這個主意很棒，讓我先見見派蒂吧。今天午餐時，我就會見到她了，希望我們到時候玩得愉快，也希望我們喜歡對方。
莎拉	我也是這麼希望。我想你們會合得來的，派蒂人很好，而你也是，比利是個好人，珍也是。

我想派蒂會和你們大家成為好朋友。

傑克	我們再看看囉。待會就在餐館碰頭了。

莎拉	好的。傑克。
傑克	我現在肚子餓，快撐不到午餐時間了。希望他們有奶油蘑菇湯，我好喜歡奶油蘑菇湯。
莎拉	誰知道他們會有什麼樣的湯，他們每天都換不一樣的湯呢。
傑克	只是想想而已嘛。

Answers

A　1) 傑克為什麼去銀行？

C　2) 傑克什麼時候會和莎拉的女兒見面？

C　3) 傑克想吃什麼午餐？

A　4) 傑克要在哪裡見莎拉的女兒？

Unit 3

Getting Along

相處甚歡

MP3-49

Billy sees Jack on the street.

Billy	Jack! Wait up!
Jack	Hi, Billy. What are you up to?
Billy	I have to do some shopping. I need a new shirt and some new pants.
	I'm going to the clothing store that is beside the bookstore. Are you on your way to work?
Jack	Yes.
Billy	Do you have plans for lunch today? We should go for lunch.
Jack	I do have plans for lunch. I'm meeting Sarah for lunch. She's bringing her daughter, Patti.
Billy	Good. I think Sarah is nice. If Patti is like her mom, she will be nice too.
Jack	Sarah said that if we all get along, Patti might be able to go to Newfoundland with us.
Billy	That would be fun. I hope we all get along.
Jack	Sarah also said that if we all get along, she might come with Patti and the rest of us on this trip.
Billy	That's a great idea. It would be a good idea to have an adult go on this trip with us.
Jack	I'll meet Patti and I'll call you after. I'll tell you

how our meeting went. If it goes well, we can take Patti bowling. Then she can meet all of us.

If we all get along when we go bowling, we can talk about the trip.

Billy Okay.

Jack I have to get to work now. If I don't hurry, I might be late.

Billy Oh, no. I have a problem.

Billy realizes he doesn't have his bankcard.

Jack What?

Billy I have no money.

Jack Go to the bank and take some out.

Billy I don't know where my bankcard is.

Jack Did you leave it at home?

Billy I thought that I put it in my back pocket. Now I can't get money from the ATM and I can't pay by Interac.

Jack Do you have a credit card?

Billy No.

Jack Do you have checks? Maybe you can pay by checks.

Billy I do have a checking account. I don't have a check on me. I don't like to carry checks. People steal them. It's easy to use them if you are a thief.

Jack Most stores don't take checks any more. They prefer to take Interac.

Billy What am I going to do? I have no way to pay for the clothes I want.

Jack You must find your bankcard. That's very important. Go home and see if you left it there.

If it isn't there, look for it. If you can't find it, someone might have stolen it out of your pocket.

Billy What if someone did steal it?

Jack You will have to report the card as stolen.

Billy I'm going home right now.

Questions

1) Where was Billy going?

    A) To the bank
    B) To the clothing store
    C) To the book store
    D) To the restaurant

2) What happened to Billy?

    A) He does not know where his bankcard is.
    B) He bought a new shirt and some new pants.
    C) He went to the clothing store.
    D) He met Sarah's daughter Patti.

3) What did Jack tell Billy to do about his problem?

    A) Forget about it.
    B) Go get help.
    C) Call the police.
    D) Go home and look for it.

4) Why is Billy worried?

A) His card might be stolen.
B) He wants to buy some clothes.
C) Patti might come with them on the trip.
D) Sarah might come with Patti on the trip.

Vocabulary 字彙

go well		順利
get along		和睦相處
thief	*n.*	小偷
steal	*v.*	偷
report	*v.*	報告

會話中譯

比利在街上看見傑克。

比利	傑克！等一下！
傑克	嗨，比利，你在這裡做什麼？
比利	我必須買點東西。我需要一件新的 T 恤和長褲。
	我正要去書店隔壁那家服飾店。你要去上班了嗎？
傑克	沒錯。
比利	你今天中午有事嗎？我們應該一起吃午餐。
傑克	我中午的確有事，我要和莎拉一起吃午餐，她還會帶她女兒派蒂過來。
比利	很好啊，我覺得莎拉人很好，如果派蒂跟她媽媽很像的話，她也會是個好人。
傑克	莎拉說如果我們大家都處得來的話，派蒂也許能夠和我

們一起去紐芬蘭。

| 比利 | 那一定會很有趣，我希望大家能相處甚歡。 |

| 傑克 | 莎拉還說如果我們大家都處得來的話，她也許會和派蒂、還有我們一起去旅行。 |

| 比利 | 這個主意太棒了。有大人陪同我們一起去旅行，這是個很好的主意。 |

| 傑克 | 我先去和派蒂見面，然後再打電話給你。我會跟你說見面的結果如何，如果順利的話，我們可以帶派蒂去打保齡球，然後她可以和大家見個面。 |

| | 如果去打保齡球時，我們都處得來的話，就可以討論旅行的事。 |

| 比利 | 好的。 |

| 傑克 | 我現在該去上班了。不快一點的話，就要遲到了。 |

| 比利 | 喔，不。我有麻煩了。 |

比利發現他並沒有帶金融卡。

| 傑克 | 什麼事？ |

| 比利 | 我身上沒錢。 |

| 傑克 | 去銀行領點錢啊。 |

| 比利 | 我不知道我的銀行金融卡在哪裡。 |

| 傑克 | 你放在家裡了嗎？ |

| 比利 | 我以為我放在褲子後面的口袋裡。我現在沒辦法從 ATM 提款，也沒辦法用 Interac 扣款卡付款了。 |

| 傑克 | 你有信用卡嗎？ |

| 比利 | 沒有。 |

| 傑克 | 那你有支票本嗎？也許你可以用支票付款。 |

| 比利 | 我是有一個支票帳戶，但是我沒有帶支票出來，我不喜 |

歡帶著支票，有人會偷支票。小偷如果想使用偷來的支票的話，那是很容易的。

傑克 大部分的商店都不接受支票了，他們比較喜歡 Interac 扣款的付賬方式。

比利 我該怎麼辦？我沒辦法買想要的衣服了。

傑克 你一定要找到銀行金融卡，這是很重要的。回家看看是不是放在家裡。

如果家裡沒有的話，趕緊找一找。

如果找不到，可能已經有人從你口袋裡偷走金融卡。

比利 萬一真有人偷走我的卡，要怎麼辦呢？

傑克 你必須呈報卡片遭竊。

比利 我現在就回家了。

Answers

B   1) 比利要去哪裡？

A   2) 比利怎麼了？

D   3) 傑克怎麼跟比利建議處理他的麻煩？

A   4) 比利為什麼擔心？

Chapter 9

All Sorts of Problems
各式各樣的問題

Unit 1

What a Relief

終於可以放心了

MP3-50

Billy goes to the bank to get a new bankcard.

Billy   Sarah, I have lost my bankcard. I think that someone might have stolen it!

Sarah   Oh, dear. That's not good. Do you have your last monthly bank statement?

Billy   Yes, I do. Here it is.

Sarah   We will put a stop on that card right now. We will cancel it right away.

When did you see that it was missing?

Billy   About an hour ago. I saw Jack. He said that he had seen you. I was on my way to the clothing store.

I wanted to buy a shirt and some pants. I looked in my pocket for my bankcard. I needed to get out some money from the bank machine. I couldn't find my card.

Sarah   What did you do?

Billy   Jack told me to go home and look for it. It wasn't there. I looked for it in the street where I had walked. I didn't find it. I came here next.

Sarah   It's good that it has only been an hour. Let me take a look at your account.

Sarah looks at Billy's account.

Sarah	I can see your account information. There have been no transactions on your account since yesterday. Yesterday there was a withdrawal for forty dollars.
Billy	Yes. That was me. I took out forty dollars. I bought a Christmas present for my sister with it.
Sarah	That's good news. No one has made any transactions on your account. Now we will cancel that card.
	There. That card can no longer be used. Your money is safe. I'll give you a new card.
Billy	What a relief. I was so worried.
Sarah	You did the right thing by coming here so fast. If you had taken more time, there might have been money taken out of your account.
Billy	What a relief. I'm so happy.
Sarah	Here is a new bankcard. I need to see your ID please.
Billy	Here is all of my identification.
Sarah	Thank you. Okay. I need you to sign here, please.
Sarah	Great. Do you feel better?
Billy	Yes, I do. I'm glad that's all over.

Questions

1) When did Billy go to the bank?

A) One day after his card went missing
B) One week after his card went missing
C) One hour after he couldn't find his card
D) One day after he couldn't find his card

2) Why did Billy go to the bank?

A) He thought his card might be stolen.
B) He thought that Sarah might be stolen.
C) He thought that the bank might be stolen.
D) He needed to withdraw forty dollars for a present.

3) Who did Billy buy a present for?

A) Sarah
B) His sister
C) Sarah's sister
D) Sarah's daughter Patti

4) When did Billy buy the present?

A) He has not bought it yet.
B) He bought it a long time ago.
C) He will buy it tonight.
D) He bought it yesterday.

會話中譯

比利到銀行申請新的金融卡。

比利 莎拉，我的銀行金融卡不見了。我想可能有人偷走了我的卡。

莎拉 喔，親愛的，這可不是件好事。你有帶上個月的銀行結算單嗎？

比利 有的，在這裡。

莎拉 我們現在要中止你的金融卡,並馬上註銷這張卡。你什麼時候發現卡遺失的?

比利 大約一個小時前。我遇到傑克,他説他要和妳碰面,而我正要去服飾店。

因為我想買一件 T 恤和長褲。我在口袋裡找金融卡,因為得先到櫃員機領錢,但是我找不到我的卡片。

莎拉 那你怎麼處理呢?

比利 傑克告訴我先回家找找看,但金融卡沒有在家裡。我就到走過的街道找,還是找不到,於是我就來銀行了。

莎拉 還好只過了一小時而已。我幫你查看帳戶一下。

莎拉查看比利的帳戶。

莎拉 我現在看到你的帳戶資料,從昨天開始就沒有任何交易紀錄,而昨天有一筆四十元的提款交易。

比利 是的,那是我。我領出四十元,然後幫我姐買了聖誕節禮物。

莎拉 那是個好消息,沒有人用你的帳戶進行任何交易。我們現在要註銷這張卡。

你看,這張卡已經不能再使用了,你的存款很安全,我再給你一張新的金融卡。

比利 終於可以放心了,我本來很擔心。

莎拉 你很快的來這裡處理問題,這是正確的舉動。如果你隔久一點才過來,錢就很有可能被有心人士提走。

比利 終於可以放心了,我好開心。

莎拉 這是一張新的銀行金融卡。我需要看一下你的身分證件,麻煩你。

比利 這是我所有的身分證件。

莎拉 謝謝你。好的,我需要你在這裡簽名,麻煩你。

莎拉 好啦。你覺得好一點了嗎？

比利 沒錯。我很高興一切都結束了。

Answers

C　1) 比利什麼時候去銀行？

A　2) 比利為什麼去銀行？

B　3) 比利幫誰買禮物？

D　4) 比利什麼時候去買禮物的？

Unit 2

What about You?
那你呢？

MP3-51

Jack comes into work at the bookstore.

Jack　Hi, Jean.　Isn't it a beautiful day?

Jean　If you like fall, then, yes, it's a beautiful day.　I don't like fall, Jack.

I have a problem with fall.　It makes me sad.　All of the leaves are off of the trees.　It gets dark sooner.　It's colder.

I like summer better.　I miss summer, Jack.

Jack　Autumn is not that bad.　It's better than winter.

Jean　Yes.　It is but fall just tells you that winter will be here quickly.

Jack　It seems like you and I have worked together here at the bookstore for such a long time.　How long have you been working here now?

Jean　I've been here for over a month now.　What about you?　How long have you been here?

Jack　I've been working here for a little more than four months.　Do you still like it?

Jean　Yes.　I've made new friends here.　I like the work.　It is quiet and the people who come in are nice.　What about you?　Do you still like your job?

Jack　Yes.　It's good.　Have you learned how to use

the cash register? Do you know how to use the credit card machine?

Jean I've learned how to use the cash register. I know how to use the credit card machine. Isn't it called the debit card machine?

Jack Some people call it the credit card machine. Others call it the debit card machine. It's used for both. That's why people use both of those names.

Jean That makes sense.

Jack and Jean chat at their coffee break.

Jack Did you hear about Billy? He lost his bankcard.

Jean Oh, no.

Jack It's okay. Everything worked out. He had the card cancelled. No one used it. All of his money was still in his bank account.

Jean How do you cancel a bankcard?

Jack He went to Sarah at the bank. She did it.

Jean I think Sarah is smart. She knows everything. I like her. What about you? Do you like Sarah?

Jack I like Sarah and I also like her daughter. Did you know that she has a daughter named Patti?

Jean Yes. When did you meet her?

Jack I met her last week. Sarah brought Patti to the restaurant. The three of us had lunch together.

Jean What did you have for lunch?

Jack I had cream of mushroom soup. I love mushroom soup. What about you?

Jean	I like it too. I think everybody likes cream of mushroom soup. When will I get to meet Patti?
Jack	I thought that we could all go bowling tonight. What about you? What do you think?
Jean	I think that's a good plan. I'll call Billy when I get home from work.
Jack	Okay. I'll call Patti when I get home.

Questions

1) What time of year is it?

    A) It is winter.
    B) It is almost spring time.
    C) It is fall.
    D) Both (B) and (C) are right.

2) How long has Jean been at the bookstore?

    A) Jean has been at the bookstore for over a month.
    B) Jean does not know.
    C) Jean has been at the bookstore for a little over four months.
    D) Jean has not been at the bookstore for very long.

3) How did Jack get along with Patti?

    A) Patti did not like Jack.
    B) Jack did not like Patti.
    C) Patti and Jack got along well.
    D) Patti has never met Jack.

4) What did Jack have for lunch?

A) Cream of mushroom soup
B) Cream of tomato soup
C) A sandwich
D) All of the above

Vocabulary 字彙

cash register		收銀機
chat	*v.*	聊天;閒談
coffee break		休息時間

會話中譯

傑克到書店上班。

傑克 嗨,珍,今天天氣真好,不是嗎?

珍 如果你喜歡秋天的話,那麼今天天氣是很好,沒錯。但我不喜歡秋天,傑克。

秋天會困擾我,讓我感到悲傷。所有的樹葉都從樹上落下,天色很快就變暗,又比較冷。

我還是比較喜歡夏天,我真想念夏天,傑克。

傑克 秋天也沒那麼不好吧,總比冬天好。

珍 沒錯,是比冬天好。但是秋天的到來,就告訴你冬天很快就要來了。

傑克 妳和我好像已經在書店上班很久了。妳在這裡工作多久了?

珍 我在這裡工作已經超過一個月了。你呢?在這裡工作多久了?

傑克 我在這裡工作已四個多月了。妳仍喜歡這份工作嗎?

| 珍 | 喜歡。我在這裡結交了新朋友，我喜歡這份工作。這裡很安靜，進來書店的人都很好。那你呢？你也還喜歡這份工作嗎？ |

| 傑克 | 是的，這是一份好工作。妳已經學會怎麼使用收銀機了嗎？妳知道怎麼使用信用卡刷卡機嗎？ |

| 珍 | 我已經學會怎麼使用收銀機，也知道怎麼使用信用卡刷卡機。它不是叫作扣款卡刷卡機嗎 |

| 傑克 | 有人叫它信用卡刷卡機，其他人則叫它扣款卡刷卡機，這台機器具有以上兩種功能，因此大家也用這兩種名稱來稱呼它。 |

| 珍 | 蠻有道理的。 |

傑克和珍在休息時間聊天。

| 傑克 | 妳聽説比利的事了嗎？他的銀行金融卡不見了。 |

| 珍 | 喔，不會吧。 |

| 傑克 | 沒關係，所有事情都迎刃而解了。他去把金融卡註銷，沒有人可以使用這張卡了。他所有的存款都還在他的銀行帳戶裡。 |

| 珍 | 要怎麼註銷銀行金融卡？ |

| 傑克 | 他去莎拉上班的那間銀行，是她幫比利註銷的。 |

| 珍 | 我覺得莎拉很聰明。她總是知道所有的事，我喜歡她。那你呢？你喜歡莎拉嗎？ |

| 傑克 | 我喜歡莎拉，也喜歡她的女兒。妳知道她有個女兒，名叫派蒂嗎？ |

| 珍 | 我知道，你什麼時候見到她的？ |

| 傑克 | 我上禮拜見過她，莎拉帶派蒂去餐館吃飯，我們三個人一起吃了午餐。 |

| 珍 | 你們午餐吃了些什麼？ |

傑克　我喝了奶油蘑菇湯，我很喜歡蘑菇湯。那妳呢？

珍　　我也喜歡蘑菇湯，我想每一個人都喜歡奶油蘑菇湯吧。我什麼時候有機會見到派蒂呢？

傑克　我想今天晚上我們可以一起去打保齡球。妳覺得如何？

珍　　這是個好計畫。我下班回家後，再打電話跟比利說這件事。

傑克　好的，我回家時，再打電話給派蒂。

Answers

C　1) 對話中的季節為何？

A　2) 珍在書店工作多久了？

C　3) 傑克和派蒂相處的如何？

A　4) 傑克午餐時吃了些什麼？

Unit 3

The More, the Better

越多越好

MP3-52

Sarah goes to the bookstore looking for a book.

Jack　What kind of book are you looking for?

Sarah　I'll read almost anything.

Jack　How about something from the top ten?

Sarah　Sure, I will take the top seller.

Jack　We sell lots of this book everyday.

Sarah　I'll take it. If you say that it is good, I know that it is good.

Jack　Did Patti have a good time the other night?

Sarah　Yes. When she came home from bowling with you and your friends, she was very happy. She said that she had a good time.

Jack　We did have a good time. She will be a good friend to all of us. Are you going to let her go to Newfoundland with us?

Sarah　She can go if I go.

Jack　I think that you should meet my mom and dad.

Sarah　Yes.

Jack　I think that you should meet Billy's parents and Jean's parents.

Sarah Yes.

Jack If everyone likes this idea, you will take all of us to Newfoundland. Patti will be able to come with you. Jean might be allowed to go too.

Sarah I'll be glad to meet your parents. I'll be glad to meet everyone's parents.

Jack When you meet everyone, you can help them with any banking questions that they have. You can help them just like you have helped all of us.

Sarah I know that Jean's parents are looking to buy a house.

Jack Yes. And my parents still want to buy a bigger house. You can talk to them about mortgages.

Sarah I'll also talk to all of the parents about the money for you to travel. If there is an emergency, they need to know how to transfer money.

Jack I'm glad that you are coming on this trip.

Questions

1) Why is Billy glad that Sarah is going on the trip?

   A) Sarah tells funny jokes.
   B) Sarah knows a lot about money.
   C) Sarah is a good cook.
   D) All of the above

2) How will the parents know how to transfer money?

   A) Sarah will teach them.

B) Jack will teach them.
C) Another teller will teach them.
D) They do not need to know that.

3) What else do the parents need to know?

A) They need to know about life.
B) They need to know about soup.
C) They need to know about love.
D) They need to know about mortgages.

4) Why did Sarah come to the bookstore?

A) To talk to Jack
B) To buy a book
C) To talk to Jean
D) To buy a book store

Vocabulary 字彙

| top ten | | 排行前十名 |
| seller | *n.* | 銷售品 |

會話中譯

莎拉到書店去找書。

傑克	妳想找什麼書？
莎拉	我幾乎什麼書都看。
傑克	排行前十名的書怎麼樣？
莎拉	好啊，我就買最暢銷的那一本。
傑克	這本書我們每天都賣出很多。

莎拉	我就買這本吧。如果你說它是本好書，我知道它一定就很好。
傑克	派蒂幾天前玩得愉快嗎？
莎拉	是的。她和你，還有你的朋友們打完保齡球回到家後，顯得非常快樂。她說玩得很開心。
傑克	我們的確玩得很開心。她會成為我們大家的好朋友。妳會讓她和我們一起去紐芬蘭嗎？
莎拉	我去的話，她就可以去。
傑克	我想妳應該和我爸媽見個面。
莎拉	沒錯。
傑克	我想你也應該和比利的爸媽、還有珍的爸媽見面。
莎拉	是的。
傑克	如果每個人都喜歡這個主意的話，妳就可以帶我們大家去紐芬蘭，派蒂也可以和妳一起去，而珍的爸媽可能也會允許她一起去。
莎拉	我很高興能見見你的爸媽，也會很高興見到其他人的爸媽。
傑克	當妳見到大家的時候，可以幫他們解決銀行方面的問題。妳可以像幫助我們一樣的幫助他們。
莎拉	我知道珍的爸媽在找房子。
傑克	是的，而我爸媽仍想買一間較大的房子，妳可以和他們討論抵押契約的事。
莎拉	我還會和所有的爸媽們討論你們的旅費，如果發生任何緊急事件的話，他們必須知道怎麼匯款。
傑克	我好高興妳能和我們一起去旅行。

Answers

B　1) 比利為什麼對莎拉可以一起去旅行感到高興？

A　2) 爸媽們要怎麼知道如何匯款？

D　3) 爸媽們還需要知道什麼事？

B　4) 莎拉為什麼去書店？

Chapter 10

Time to Go

該出發了

Unit 1

Helping Out
幫忙

Jean is surprised to see Billy come into work on a Saturday.

Jean	Hi, Billy. What are you doing here? It's Saturday. You don't work on weekends.
Billy	I know, Jean. Jack is sick today. He phoned the manager.
	She phoned me and asked if I could come in to help. I told her that I would be happy to come in.
	I could use the money. I'm still saving money for my trip.
Jean	Wasn't it fun the other night when we went bowling? I had fun.
Billy	I had fun too. I liked Patti.
Jean	So did I.
Billy	I liked Patti so much that I asked her to go to a movie with me.
Jean	Is she going to go to the movie with you?
Billy	Yes. We are going to a movie tonight. It's a scary movie. I can't wait. I love scary movies. Has Sarah met with your parents yet?
Jean	No. She's meeting them tonight. I hope that my parents like her. Maybe then I can go to

Newfoundland with you.

Billy　That would be good.　Is she going to talk to your parents about getting a mortgage?

Jean　Yes, actually, they use the same bank Sarah works at.　Maybe they have already met and don't know it.　They have been banking there for fifteen years.

Billy　Sarah has worked there for more than ten years.

Jean starts to have second thoughts about going to Newfoundland.

Jean　Even if they let me, maybe I shouldn't go on this trip.

Billy　Why?

Jean　My parents are trying to buy a house.　They cannot afford to send me on a trip.　I don't have any money saved because I didn't think I would be going.

Billy　That's why a line of credit is good.　It's like getting a loan from the bank.　The interest rates are low.

It's as useful as a credit card but with less interest.　They can pay it back a little bit each month.

Jean　Maybe I could pay it back with them.　Maybe I could help with each monthly payment.　I would feel better if I gave some money.

Billy　That's a good plan.

Questions

1) How long have Jean's parents been with their bank?

A) Fifty years
B) Five years
C) Fifteen years
D) None of the above

2) Why can't Jean's parents send her on the trip?

A) They are trying to buy a house.
B) They cannot afford it.
C) Jean has not saved any money.
D) All of the above

3) Who is going to a movie?

A) Patti and Billy
B) Patti and Jean
C) Jean and Billy
D) All of the above

4) Who had fun bowling?

A) Sarah
B) Jean's parents
C) Billy's parents
D) None of the above

會話中譯

珍對於比利星期六還來上班，感到很驚訝。

珍　嗨，比利，你在這裡做什麼？今天是星期六，你週末不用上班啊。

比利　我知道，珍。今天傑克生病了，他打電話給經理。然後經理打給我，問我是否可以過來幫忙，我跟她說我很樂意來上班。

　　我需要今天加班的薪水，因為我還在存旅費。

珍　我們前幾天去打保齡球，是不是很好玩？我玩得很開心呢。

比利　我也玩的很開心。我喜歡派蒂。

珍　我也是。

比利　我好喜歡派蒂，所以約了她去看電影。

珍　她要和你去看電影嗎？

比利　是的，我們今天晚上要去看電影。是一部恐怖片，我等不及了，我好愛看恐怖片。莎拉和妳的爸媽見過面了嗎？

珍　還沒，她今天晚上會和他們見面。我希望我爸媽會喜歡她，這樣的話，也許我就可以和你們一起去紐芬蘭了。

比利　那將會很棒。她會跟妳爸媽討論抵押契約的事嗎？

珍　會的。其實我爸媽用的銀行服務，和莎拉上班的那間銀行是同一家，他們可能早就見過面，彼此卻不知道吧。他們在那家銀行進行金融交易，已經十五年了。

比利　而莎拉在那家銀行工作超過十年了。

珍對於要去紐芬蘭旅行的事，開始感到遲疑。

珍　就算他們讓我去，也許我還是不應該去旅行。

比利　為什麼？

珍　我爸媽想買房子，沒辦法負擔我的旅費，而我也沒有存錢，因為我以為我不會和你們一起去。

比利 這就是為什麼信貸很好用啊。就像和銀行貸款一樣，但是利率很低。

它和信用卡一樣好用，但有較低的利息，妳爸媽可以每個月償還一點點款項。

珍 也許我可以用這個方法，和他們一起償還款項，也許我可以付每個月的款項，如果我可以支付一點金額的話，會覺得好多了。

比利 那是個好計畫。

Answers

C 1) 珍的爸媽已經使用銀行服務多久了？

D 2) 為什麼珍的父母沒辦法讓她去旅行？

A 3) 誰要去看電影？

D 4) 誰打保齡球時玩得很開心？

Unit 2

Boys and Girls
男孩和女孩

MP3-54

Jack runs into Billy on the way to Patti's house.

Jack	Hey, Billy. How are you?
Billy	Hi, Jack. I'm good. What are you doing?
Jack	I'm on my way to Sarah's house. I'm going to see Patti.
Billy	Really? Does she know that you are coming?
Jack	Of course, she does. I phoned her and she said to come over.
Billy	Oh.
Jack	What did you do last night?
Billy	I went to a movie.
Jack	Who did you go with?
Billy	I went with Patti.
Jack	Really? Did you run into her there?
Billy	No. I went to her house and then we went to the movie together.
Jack	Oh.
Billy	I think we might have a problem.
Jack	Maybe.
Billy	I think that you like Patti.

Jack	I think that you like Patti.
Billy	I do.
Jack	So do I. You are right. We do have a problem.

Jack and Billy decide their friendship is too important to let a girl get between them.

Billy	Well? What are we going to do?
Jack	I'll tell you what we are going to do. You are going to come over to Patti's house with me.
Billy	Three friends are better than two. I'll come with you to Patti's house. We can all be friends.
Jack	That's what is best. I don't want a girl to come between you and I.
Billy	I don't want that either. I won't ask Patti out on a date if you don't ask Patti out on a date.
Jack	It's a deal.
Billy	Did you hear the good news?
Jack	What?
Billy	Jean's parents met with Sarah. They recognized her as soon as they saw her. They all got along great. Jean is allowed to come on the trip.
Jack	That's great news.
Billy	Four friends are better than three.
Jack	That's right.

Questions

1) How did things go with Sarah and Jean's parents?

   A) Things went poorly.
   B) Things went okay.
   C) Things went very well.
   D) Things went to the movie.

2) What have the boys decided about Patti?

   A) They will not date her.
   B) They will just be friends with her.
   C) All of the above
   D) None of the above

3) When well Sarah see Billy's parents?

   A) She is not going to see Billy's parents.
   B) She is going to see Billy's parents tonight.
   C) She will see Billy's parents on the trip.
   D) She saw Billy's parents last night.

4) How do the boys feel about Jean going on the trip?

   A) It is bad news.
   B) It is not important.
   C) It does not matter.
   D) It is good news.

Vocabulary 字彙

ask sb. out on a date　　跟某人約會

recognize	v.	認出

會話中譯

傑克在前往派蒂家的路上,遇見比利。

傑克	嗨,比利,你好嗎?
比利	嗨,傑克,我很好。你在這裡做什麼?
傑克	我正要去莎拉家,要去找派蒂。
比利	真的嗎?她知道你要過去嗎?
傑克	她當然知道。我打電話給她,她叫我過去。
比利	喔。
傑克	你昨天晚上做了什麼?
比利	我去看電影。
傑克	你和誰一起去?
比利	我和派蒂一起去的。
傑克	真的嗎?你在電影院碰到她的嗎?
比利	不是,我先去她家,然後一起去看電影。
傑克	喔。
比利	我想我們之間可能有個問題。
傑克	也許吧。
比利	我覺得你喜歡派蒂。
傑克	我覺得你喜歡派蒂。
比利	我是喜歡她。
傑克	我也是。你說得沒錯,我們之間的確有個問題。

傑克和比利覺得他們的友情十分重要，不該受到一個女孩的影響。

比利	那麼…？我們該怎麼辦？
傑克	我告訴你我們該怎麼辦吧。你和我一起去派蒂家。
比利	三個朋友聚在一起，總比兩個好。我和你一起去派蒂家，大家都可以成為朋友。
傑克	這樣做最好了。我不想讓一個女孩卡在我們兩個中間。
比利	我也不想這樣。如果你沒有約派蒂出去的話，我也不會約派蒂出去。
傑克	就這麼說定了。
比利	你聽說了好消息了嗎？
傑克	什麼好消息？
比利	珍的爸媽和莎拉見過面了，他們一見到莎拉，就馬上認出是她。他們大家都相處甚歡，珍也可以和我們一起去旅行了。
傑克	這消息真的很棒。
比利	四個朋友聚在一起總比三個好。
傑克	沒錯。

Answers

C　1) 莎拉和珍的父母相處得如何？

C　2) 男孩們打算怎麼處理關於派蒂的事？

A　3) 莎拉什麼時候要和比利的爸媽見面？

D　4) 男孩們對於珍要和他們一起去旅行感到如何？

Unit 3

Happy Endings
快樂的結局

Sarah finds Jack at the local restaurant.

Jack   Hello, Sarah. What are you doing here? Did you come to have lunch with me?

Sarah   I came to find you, Jack. I thought that you would be here.

Jack   I'm on my lunch break. Would you like to join me?

Sarah   Sure.

Jack   Pull up a chair. Sit down.

Sarah   Thank you.

Jack   Do you want some of my mushroom soup?

Sarah   No, thank you. I don't like it.

Jack   Do you want a bite of my roast beef and cheese sandwich?

Sarah   Sure. I love roast beef.

Jack   They have very nice roast beef here.

Sarah   You are right. It's very good.

Jack   Have a sip of my juice.

Sarah   Thank you. Where's Jean? I had hoped to speak to both of you.

Jack   She said she was meeting a friend for lunch.

They went to the restaurant two blocks from here. Where is Patti?

Sarah	She said that she was meeting a friend for lunch. She said that she would be at the restaurant that's two blocks from here.
Jack	Isn't that funny? They have gone for lunch together.
Sarah	I'm so glad they are getting along. All four of you get along so well.

Sarah talks turkey with Jack.

Jack	What did you need to talk to me about?
Sarah	Everything is perfect. Jean is allowed to go on the trip. You and Billy are going on the trip. Patti and I are coming with you.
Jack	Yes, that's good but we knew all of that already.
Sarah	There is more.
Jack	What is it?
Sarah	I got along so well with both your parents and Billy's parents. I know all of them already. They bank with my bank.
Jack	Well, I'm glad that you got along with everybody. But I knew that you would.
Sarah	There's more.
Jack	What is it?
Sarah	Both your parents and Billy's parents are going on the trip too.
Jack	That's great. I didn't think that my parents could get time off from their jobs.

Sarah	I've more good news. You won't believe it.
Jack	What is it?
Sarah	Jean's parents are coming also. All parents can get time off from their jobs. All parents get along. All of you kids get along.
	We will all vacation in Newfoundland together.
Jack	This is amazing. All of the parents and all of the kids. Everybody gets along and everybody has someone to have fun with.
	This is the best news ever. Here we go! Off on an adventure!

Questions

1) What did Jack have for lunch?

    A)   He had chicken and French fries for lunch.

    B)   He had chicken noodle soup and a bun for lunch.

    C)   He had a roast chicken sandwich with cream of chicken soup for lunch.

    D)   He had mushroom soup, a roast beef sandwich, and some juice for lunch.

2) Where is Jean?

    A)   She is at a different restaurant.

    B)   She is having lunch.

    C)   She is with Patti.

    D)   All of the above

3) What is the good news that Sarah shares with Jack?

A) All of the parents and all of the kids are going on the trip together.
B) She does not have any good news.
C) All of the parents and all of the kids are getting new jobs.
D) She does not like anybody.

4) How does Jack feel about Sarah's news?

A) He is not pleased
B) He is very pleased.
C) He does not care.
D) He does not believe it.

Vocabulary 字彙

talks turkey		說話坦率
vacation	v.	度假

會話中譯

莎拉在餐館裡發現傑克。

傑克 哈囉，莎拉，妳在這裡做什麼？要來和我一起吃午餐嗎？

莎拉 我來找你的，傑克。我想你應該會在這裡。

傑克 現在是我的午餐休息時間，妳想和我一起吃午餐嗎？

莎拉 好啊。

傑克 拿張椅子過來坐吧。

莎拉 謝謝你。

傑克 妳要喝一點我的蘑菇湯嗎？

莎拉	不了，謝謝你，我不喜歡蘑菇湯。
傑克	妳想吃一點我的烤牛肉起司三明治嗎？
莎拉	好啊，我很喜歡烤牛肉。
傑克	他們這裡的烤牛肉很好吃。
莎拉	你說的沒錯，真的很好吃。
傑克	試試我的果汁吧。
莎拉	謝謝你。珍在哪裡？我本來想和你們兩個人講話的。
傑克	她說和一個朋友吃午餐。她們要去兩條街外的餐館吃飯，派蒂人呢？
莎拉	她也說要和一個朋友吃午餐。她說餐館的地點離這裡有兩條街的距離。
傑克	這不是很有趣嗎？她們兩個一起去吃午餐了。
莎拉	我很高興她們能處得來。你們四個人都很合得來。

莎拉很坦率地和傑克討論。

傑克	妳要和我討論什麼事？
莎拉	每一件事都很完美。珍可以去旅行，你和比利也要去旅行，而派蒂和我要和大家一起去。
傑克	是啊，這樣很好，但我們都已經知道這些了啊。
莎拉	還有別的事。
傑克	什麼事？
莎拉	我和你、還有比利的爸媽都相處甚歡，我早就認識他們了，他們都在我工作的那間銀行進行金融交易業務。
傑克	我很高興妳和每一個人都處得很好，但我早就知道妳會和他們處得融洽了啊。
莎拉	還有別的事。

傑克 什麼事？

莎拉 比利和你的爸媽也要一起去旅行。

傑克 太好了，我本來以為我爸媽不可能請假。

莎拉 我還有更多的好消息，你絕對不會相信的。

傑克 什麼好消息？

莎拉 珍的爸媽也要一起去。所有的爸媽都能向公司請假，所有爸媽都相處甚歡，而你們這些孩子也是。所以我們大家要一起去紐芬蘭度假。

傑克 這真是太好了，所有的爸媽和所有的小孩，每一個人都處得來，而且每個人都有可以一起玩的對象。這是最棒的消息了。我們走吧！一起去探險！

Answers

D　1) 捷克午餐吃什麼？

D　2) 珍在哪裡？

A　3) 莎拉和捷克分享什麼好消息？

B　4) 捷克隊莎拉的消息感到如何？

國家圖書館出版品預行編目資料

銀行金融英語看這本就夠了/克力斯.安森.張瑪麗 合著
. – 增訂1版. -- 新北市：哈福企業有限公司, 2024.01

　　面；　公分. -- (英語系列；85)
ISBN 978-626-98088-3-0 (平裝)
1.CST: 英語 2.CST: 銀行業 3.CST: 讀本
805.18　　　　　　　　　　　　112020076

免費下載QR Code音檔
行動學習，即刷即聽

銀行金融英語　看這本就夠了
(附QR碼線上音檔)

. . . .

作者／克力斯 . 安森 . 張瑪麗
責任編輯／ Charles Wang
封面設計／李秀英
內文排版／林樂娟
出版者／哈福企業有限公司
地址／新北市淡水區民族路 110 巷 38 弄 7 號
電話／(02) 2808-4587
傳真／(02) 2808-6545
郵政劃撥／ 31598840
戶名／哈福企業有限公司
出版日期／ 2024 年 1 月
台幣定價／ 450 元 (附線上 MP3)
港幣定價／ 150 元 (附線上 MP3)
封面內文圖 / 取材自 Shutterstock

. . . .

全球華文國際市場總代理／采舍國際有限公司
地址／新北市中和區中山路 2 段 366 巷 10 號 3 樓
電話／(02) 8245-8786 傳真／(02) 8245-8718
網址／ www.silkbook.com 新絲路華文網

. . . .

香港澳門總經銷／和平圖書有限公司
地址／香港柴灣嘉業街 12 號百樂門大廈 17 樓
電話／(852) 2804-6687
傳真／(852) 2804-6409

. . . .

email ／ welike8686@Gmail.com
facebook ／ Haa-net 哈福網路商城

電子書格式：PDF